Panic in Paris

Panic in Paris

by
Jules Lermina

translated, annotated and introduced by
Brian Stableford

A Black Coat Press Book

ISBN 978-1-934543-83-2. First Printing May 2009. Published by Black Coat Press, an imprint of Hollywood Com-
ics.com, LLC, P.O. Box 17270, Encino, CA 91416. All rights
reserved. Except for review purposes, no part of this book may
be reproduced or transmitted in any form or by any means,
electronic or mechanical, including photocopying, recording,
or by any information storage and retrieval system, without
permission in writing from the publisher. The stories and characters depicted in this novel are entirely fictional. Printed in
the United States of America.

Introduction

L'Effrayante aventure, here translated as *Panic in Paris* (because a literal translation of the title would be a trifle anodyne), was first published in book form by Tallandier in 1913. Pierre Versins' *Encyclopedie de l'utopie et de la science-fiction* gives its date of original publication as "vers 1910," presumably referring to a serial version. It was, at any rate, the last scientific romance that Jules Lermina penned, more than 50 years after he had first embarked on a career as a journalist and fiction-writer.

The second story included here, "L'Elixir de vie," translated as "The Elixir of Life," was issued as a booklet in 1890 under the imprint of G. Carré; its publication had been arranged by "Papus," who signed its preface. The preface implies that the story might have been written by Lermina from an outline or draft by Papus, but it is arguably more typical of Lermina's fantastic fiction than *L'Effrayante aventure*, and provides an interesting example of work done at the interface of scientific romance and occult romance during the heyday of the late 19th century Occult Revival.

The juxtaposition of the two stories brackets the full range of Lermina's scientific romance, illustrating its comic, melodramatic and occult aspects, and thus provides a useful introduction to his work in this vein, of which I hope to produce a further exemplary sample in due course.

Jules Hippolyte Lermina was born in 1839 and was still a child when the revolution of 1848 was followed by Louis Napoléon's *coup d'état*, which launched in the

Second Empire in 1851. He grew up to be a dedicated opponent of that Empire, working from a radical socialist viewpoint. Having married at eighteen, with a baby daughter to support, he tried his hand at various clerical jobs, but either could not settle into them or—perhaps more likely—could not hold on to them because of his political opinions and turned his hand to freelance journalism instead. His radicalism was just as hazardous in that vocation as any other employment, by virtue of the relentless vigilance and oppressive policies of Napoléon III's censors, and he soon attracted their attention. He founded a political periodical of his own, *Le Corsaire*, in 1867, which led to his being imprisoned. He was soon released in response to protest—from Victor Hugo, among others—but promptly repeated his crime, founding a new journal called *Satan*, and was imprisoned again.

By this time, the Second Empire was on its last legs, and it finally collapsed in 1870 following the disastrous French defeat by the Prussian army in the Battle of Sedan. Lermina was released from prison as soon as the new Government of National Defense took office, and promptly enlisted, either by virtue of a surge of patriotic fervor or because it was a condition of his release. He was only in uniform for a matter of months, but must have had a terrible time. He was far from being a natural soldier—he was short, thin, pale, puny and of a somewhat nervous disposition even when not fresh out of prison—and his regiment, which engaged the enemy on at least two occasions, had no chance whatsoever of stemming the Prussian tide.

Military discipline did not shut Lermina up. He prepared campaign literature with which to stand for elections to the new National Assembly, before the promised elections were cancelled, and wrote an angry open letter of protest to the government when the chief protagonists of Communist agitation were imprisoned. Had he not been busy fighting the Prussians, however, he would almost certainly have taken a hand in the subsequent insurrection, and might well have been transported along with its leaders when the Commune fell. As things were, the whole experience seems to have been rather traumatic, and he took a new direction in life thereafter. One source suggests that he became involved in a project to form the communist colony of Aiglemont in the Ardennes, but if so his participation was brief; he was soon back in Paris, where—perhaps taking some inspiration from the oft-imprisoned activist and prolific *feuilletoniste* Louis Ulbach—he launched a new phase of his career, concentrating on the writing of popular fiction.

Although Lermina's left-wing views did not change, he seems to have contented himself for the next decade with simply making a living, and his subsequent political journalism was more reflective in kind. He was still writing regularly for *Le Radical* in the 1890s, though, and his most significant work in that vein, the anarchist *L'ABC du Libertaire* [The ABC of Libertarianism] did not appear until 1906. His political beliefs are manifest in some of his fiction, including his more extravagant adventure stories—in *To-Ho le tueur d'or* (1905; tr. as *To-Ho the Goldslayer*), a noble savage who is one of Tarzan's more significant literary precursors declares war on the symbolic foundation of capitalism—but the great bulk of his fiction consisted of crowd-pleasing entertainment in the great tradition of the French *roman feuilleton*. He consciously set out to be a loyal disciple of Eugène Sue and Alexandre Dumas; he wrote a Suesque *Mystères de New York* under the pseudonym William Cobb and produced two sequels to *Le Comte de Monte Cristo*, as well as many other works in the same vein, almost all of which are nowadays long-forgotten.

Jules Clarétie, who wrote an introduction to Lermina's first collection of fantastic tales, *Histoires incroyables* [Incredible Stories] (1885), records that he and his friend had both been strongly influenced in their early days by E. T. A. Hoffmann and Edgar Allan Poe, the presiding geniuses of the 19th century French *fantastique*, and that they had both attempted work of that sort when they launched their careers in 1859. Almost all the work that Lermina published in the first phase of his journalistic career and his first decade as a *feuilletoniste* was, however, naturalistic, in accordance with the prevailing priorities of the marketplaces in which he worked. The first scientific romance that Versins credits to him is a horror story based on a popular urban myth about the persistence of consciousness in decapitated heads, "La peine de mort" [The Pain of Death / The Death Penalty] (1868), but the next is dated 1884—although Versins appears to have overlooked "L'Arbre anthropophage" [The Man-Eating Tree] (1878; reprinted in *Nouvelles histoires incroyables*, 1888, as "Titane"). Lermina also published a Poesque tale of psychological disturbance before his second term of imprisonment, "Les fous" [The Madmen] (*Le Gaulois*, 1869; reprinted in *Histoires incroyables*), which was set in America and signed "William Cobb," and some of the other stories in the two collections of *histoires incroyables* might have seen first publication at similarly early dates. "Les fous" had the distinction of attracting praise from Isidore Ducasse, *alias* Lautréamont, who mentioned it in his *Poésies* (1870)

Although the items in *Histoires incroyables* and *Nouvelles histoires incroyables* are mostly offbeat horror stories, some are frankly parodic and most of them are liberally spiced with ironic wit. Although this aspect of his work was clearly influenced by Poe, as emphasized by the frequent use of American settings and an Anglo-Saxon pseudonym, Lermina's fantasies tended to exploit the humorous aspects of the grotesque and arabesque to a greater extent than the earnestly horrific, and he seems to have been strongly infected by what Poe called "the imp of the perverse". His interested in the *incroyable* did, however, increase markedly in the mid-1880s, when he became temporarily involved with the burgeoning occult revival. Jules Clarétie, who shared that involvement, became earnestly fascinated with spiritualism, eventually becoming a regular at Camille Flammarion's *salons* and *séances*, but Lermina's initial involvement seems to have been entirely accidental.

Shortly after 1880, when she was in her early twenties, Lermina's daughter Marie-Pauline met, fell in love with and married one of the *bouquinistes* who kept stalls on the banks of the Seine, Henri Chacornac (1855-1907); their eldest son, Paul, was born in 1884. Lermina presumably provided the financial backing for Chacornac to move up-market; he opened a shop at 11 Quai Saint-Michel in 1884 under the title Librairie Générale des Science Occultes, that being his specialty as a second-hand book-dealer. The shop and its associated publishing enterprises were just in time to cash in on a remarkable explosion of interest in the occult, and they became very successful. Indeed, its descendent shops and publishing imprints—Paul Chacornac and his brothers continued trading after their father's death as Chacornac Frères—remained the central pillar of that kind of French specialty publishing long into the twentieth century; Paul did not die until 1964. The shop's clientèle included many literary men as well as would-be scholars and esoteric lifestyle fantasists, especially those associated with the nascent Decadent Movement; Henri Chacornac's publishing enterprises included some literary work—including poetry by Paul Verlaine—as well as non-fiction. Lermina inevitably jumped on to the bandwagon, publishing *Le comtesse Mercadet* (1884), the first of several stories about "animal magnetism", before assembling and filling out the two collections of *histoires incroyables*.

Two of Chacornac's most avid customers were medical students at the University of Paris who had been entranced by the works of the pioneering lifestyle fantasist Eliphas Lévi (Alphonse-Louis Constant) and had been initiated into the esoteric discipline of "Martinism," founded by the 18th century mystic Martinez de Pasqually (1727-1774): Gérard-Anaclet-Vincent Encausse (1864-1916) and Augustin Chaboseau (1868-1946). Encausse, the Spanish-born son of a chemist, who used the signature Papus (allegedly meaning "Physician" and borrowed from a document called the "Nuctemeron of Apollonius of Tyana," faked by Eliphas Lévi) went on to become one of the central figures of the Parisian occult revival, seemingly collecting Lermina along the way as he collected other potential publicists.

Encausse joined the French branch of the Theosophical Society shortly after its formation in 1884 but left within a year, dissatisfied with Madame Blavatsky's particular brand of mysticism. He then got together with two of Chacornac's other clients, Joséphin Péladan and

Stanislaus de Guaita, who were to become his chief rivals as flamboyant lifestyle fantasists, to form the Kabbalistique Ordre de la Rose-Croix. Their triple alliance did not last long, because Péladan split to form his own neo-Rosicrucian Order—which went on to enjoy tremendous success, completely eclipsing its forerunner—while Encausse, Guaita and Chaboseau decided to concentrate a revamped version of Martinism. Although he eventually completed his medical training in 1894, Encausse was frequently distracted from his studies; in particular, he took a leading role in a meeting held on 20 April 1889 by 80 delegates of some 34 occult groups and societies to organize a massive "Spiritist Congress" that was held in Paris on September 9-15 of that year. He persuaded Lermina to accept the honorary presence of the first session and give the opening address. Thomas Everitt, who attended the conference on behalf of the London Spiritualist Society, reported in the journal *Light* that Lermina, though not a Spiritualist, was a "cultured and liberal-minded person."

Encausse went on to join the Parisian branch of the Order of the Golden Dawn and numerous other organizations, gaining sufficient reputation as a modern magician to be entertained by Tsar Nicholas II on several visits to Russia (during which, he insisted, he had warned Nicholas in vain about the evil influence of Rasputin), but was always outshone by Joséphin Péladan, partly because the latter integrated a prolific and moderately successful career as a novelist into his career as a lifestyle fantasist. Eliphas Lévi had only turned to lifestyle fantasy when his own career as a *littérateur* had failed to take off, so it is hardly surprising that Encausse had literary ambitions too. He and Lucien Chamuel founded a publishing enterprise called the Librairie du Merveilleux in 1888, spearheaded by a *Revue* called *L'Initiation*, thus going into open competition with Chacornac, but Chacornac eventually bought Chamuel out in 1901. In the meantime, however, *L'Initiation* paid considerable attention to the literary aspects of the occult revival, publishing work by such Decadent heroes as Villiers de l'Isle-Adam and Catulle Mendès, as well as work by Lermina. Encausse was a great admirer of Charles Nodier, and an enthusiastic student of occult undercurrents in the work of other heroes of French literature, including Alfred de Mussest and Honoré de Balzac.

Exactly how much "Papus" contributed to the two Lermina stories whose separate publication he arranged, and for which he wrote prefaces, is unclear, but it seems probable that *A brûler, conte astral* [For Burning; an Astral Tale] (1889) and *L'Elixir de vie* ought to be regarded as collaborations. Papus went on to found many other periodicals, including *Le Voile d'Isis* [The Veil of Isis] (so-called in mocking reference to Madame Blavatsky's *Isis Unveiled*), whose editorship was taken over by Henri Charcornac himself. In 1892, he was invited to serve as guest editor of a special issue of the popular literary periodical *La Plume*, whose proprietor was the pseudonymous Willy—subsequently notorious as the exploitative husband of Colette.

Although his signature appeared on *La Science occulte* (1890), which was probably another collaboration with Papus, Lermina's involvement with the occult revival was more social than philosophical, and occult romances were always a minor component of his output. Versins opines that after 1890, "*il semble que Jules Lermina ait trouvé trop entêtant le parfum de sciences occultes dont il avait jusqu'alors innondé son oeuvre*" [it seems that Jules Lermina had found the perfume of occult science that had previously flooded his work too intoxicating], and contends, approvingly, that his *histoires incroyables* then began to take on more of the attributes of popular scientific romance—in such stories as "L'Héritage des Zippélius" (1893), an account of a new invention, and the future war story "La Bataille de Strasbourg" (1895)—but this is not entirely fair, and Lermina did produce "La Magicienne" (1892) and "La Deux fois morte" (1895) in parallel with the tales of which Versins approved.

Although he had sold stories to the first series of the Vernian *Journal des Voyages*, launched in 1877, Lermina became a much more frequent presence in its second series, launched in 1896. Most of his contributions were straightforward adventures stories of a melodramatic stripe, similar to those he had earlier contributed to the less adventurous *Terre Illustrée*, but he also provided such lively and interesting serial scientific romances as *To-Ho le tueur d'or* and *Mystère-Ville* [Mysteryville] (1904 as by William Cobb; to be translated in a future Black Coat Press volume); the latter describes a technologically-advanced breakaway civilization founded in the Far East by French protestant refugees.

It was this final phase of his career that eventually produced *L'Effrayante aventure*, which appeared amid a glut of French scientific romances inspired by the example of the British writer H. G. Wells; Lermina would probably have done more in the same vein had he been able to do so, but was then reaching the end of his career and his life; he died in 1915.

L'Effrayante aventure takes its particular inspiration not from Wells but from an older British novel that had—perhaps significantly—combined the long-established tradition of utopian fiction with both the scientific advances of the 19th century and the pseudos-cientific trappings of the occult revival: Edward Bulwer-Lytton's *The Coming Race* (1871). Bulwer had, of course, played a significant part in the inspiration of the occult revival with his highly successful Rosicrucian fantasy *Zanoni* (1842), and his Romantic account of the opportunities and dangers of magical initiation *A Strange Story* (1861), and Lermina would have been familiar with those works. Perhaps more remarkably, however, *L'Effrayante aventure* also features some intriguing anticipations of two key works by another successful British writer of scientific romance, Arthur Conan Doyle; elements of its plot prefigure both of the first two Professor Challenger stories, *The Lost World* (1912) and *The Poison Belt* (1913).

As with almost all of the *feuilleton* fiction produced in France under the influence of British scientific romance, Lermina's narrative is much closer in style and attitude to American pulp fiction—an essential frivolity greatly encouraged, in his case, by his irrepressible humor. In the extrapolation of this tendency to rampant melodrama, the climax of *L'Effrayante aventure* anticipates the Japanese monster movies of the 1950s, although it maintains a diplomatic regard for the ultimate preservation of the status quo that was typical of its time, and is not entirely to its advantage as a precursor of that tradition. It is less diplomatic in its satirical account of the methods and consequences of "yellow journalism," and is also of some interest as a tongue-in-cheek study of the tabloidization of news. Seen as a whole, the novel is, admittedly, a rather slapdash work, obviously made up as the author went along, and it overdoes the incessant repetition that serial fiction inevitably employed as a means of reminding readers of what had gone before and allowing belated starters to catch up, but it is a fascinating historical specimen, and its climax is admirably flamboyant.

"L'Elixir de vie" is not admitted by Versins to the canon of Lermina's proto-science fiction stories, but that exclusion is a trifle unreasonable. Although the story would nowadays be considered an occult romance by virtue of its employment of animal magnetism, the whole point of the narrative is to challenge the justice of the decision that had been taken by the French Académie de Médecine to rule that Mesmerism was pure charlatanry and had no place in the canon of scientific medicine.

The story's hero, presumably modeled on Encausse—although it is the villain of the piece, Monsieur Vincent, who shares one of Encause's own forenames—takes a strictly scientific approach to the enigma that confronts him, which is why he takes so long to accept what is blindingly obvious to the reader. That is not, however, the most interesting aspect of the tale as an example of proto-science fiction; by contrast with many other 19th century tales of "psychic vampirism"—here, too, Lermina anticipates Arthur Conan Doyle, who published *The Parasite* in 1895—"L'Elixir de vie" is by no means a straightforward horror story, and it comes remarkably close to endorsing the monster's excuses by virtue of an explicitly Darwinian argument that was to be reiterated incessantly in the revisionist vampire stories that became fashionable in the last quarter of the 20th century.

Its quasi-pornographic description of the vampiric process also anticipates fiction of that sort, making it a much more interesting, and less shocking, story than it must have seemed to its contemporary readers.

Both of the following translations have been made from electronic versions of the stories recently made available by ebooksgratuits.com, which have been re-set from the original texts and might therefore, include a few additional typographical errors, although they might well have corrected a few by way of compensation. I have corrected a few obvious mistakes, mostly relating to the names of actual individuals, footnoting the more significant changes. I have made no substantial alterations to the text except for eliminating some of Lermina's footnotes, which offer French translations of English phrases or explanations that are unnecessary for English readers. I have tolerated the frequent repetition of information, presumably carried over from the serial versions of the stories, on the grounds that it inherent to the narrative style.

Brian Stableford

PANIC IN PARIS

PART ONE:
IS COXWARD COXWARD?

I. The Obelisk Murder

One morning at the beginning of April—April 2, to be precise—at about 11 a.m., beneath a gentle spring Sun, howls suddenly burst forth in the Rue Montmartre, in the proximity of the boulevard. A crowd of rather inelegant individuals raced rapidly from the corner of the Rue de Croissant, some towards the crossroads, others in the direction of Les Halles, but all emitting incoherent high-pitched yelps, within which a keen ear was able to perceive sinister fragmentary phrases:

"Obelisk murder…"

"Get the *Nouvelliste*—special edition!"

"Horrible details."

After some hesitation—how many times, after all, have we been cheated by the deceits of news-vendors?— a few people bought the paper, scanned it, then stopped dead, as if petrified, and began to read, suddenly surrounded by a group of increasingly anxious faces.

"Yes, yes… a crime!"

"A murder!"

"Whose?"

"No one knows!"

"Has the murderer been arrested?"

"Who cares?"

This was the short but sensational article that generated this emotion:

This morning, at 4:30 a.m., an hour when deserted Paris belongs to the road-sweepers and the only traffic consists of water-carts, a laborer, Monsieur H***, was on his way to work. Coming from Grenelle and heading for the yards of the Madeleine with his tools on his shoulder, he was crossing the Place de la Concorde when, suddenly, from the sidewalk of the Tuileries, which he was just turning, it seemed to him that there was something out of place at the foot of the Obelisk, somewhat above ground level.

He was passing by regardless, without taking any further notice, when—having looked back one last time "to take stock"—he began to suspect that the "something" was human in form. He decided then to cross over, and walked straight towards the monument—and imagine his surprise when, from no more than a few steps away, he recognized the object that had attracted his attention as a human body, suspended at an angle from the railings, whose feet were not touching the ground.

Alarmed, and afraid of getting mixed up in some nasty business, the workman had turned on his heels and was drawing away when he chanced to meet two policemen. The latter, noticing the anxiety in his face, questioned him. Bewildered, and having difficulty finding words, he told them about his strange discovery, and all three of them went back to the Obelisk.

He was not mistaken. It was definitely the body of a man, hanging down from the spikes of the railings, with his head inside the enclosure. At first, it was thought that it was a hanging, probably a suicide, but when the policemen tried to lift the man up in order to find the rope and cut it, they perceived that their supposition was unfounded. The body was suspended from two bronze spikes, which had penetrated the chest so profoundly that, despite their efforts, the three men could not succeeded in raising the cadaver up sufficiently to release it.

One of the two policemen leapt over the railings on to the granite pedestal, but in vain. He could see the man's head, covered in coagulated blood, which formed a red mask over the face, but it was impossible for him to detach the torso from the transpiercing points.

As if by a miracle, passers-by had emerged from every direction and formed a crowd around the dead man. The policemen blew their whistles several times and two others soon arrived, pushing through the crowd. When they had been apprised of the facts, one of them went off to alert the commissariat. A quarter of an hour went by. Eventually, Monsieur Richaud, the popular Police Commissioner of that neighborhood, arrived, accompanied by yet another policeman and gendarmes from the guard-post. Joining forces, they finally succeeded in lifting of the body, which they laid down on the sidewalk.

Ii was apparent at first glance that it was not the body of a Frenchman. The cut of his clothing was undoubtedly English. The face, rapidly washed to get rid of the clotted blood that was hiding it, was broad and hairless, with a pre-eminent jaw that was certainly Anglo-Saxon in character. The frontal part of the skull bore a

19

frightful wound, evidently caused by a blunt instrument. Pieces of brain-tissue were spurting from that wound.

The body has been transported to the commissariat and the authorities have been alerted. Monsieur Davaine, the head of the Sûreté, has arrived to carry out a preliminary enquiry. Monsieur Lépine, the Prefect of Police, is also expected imminently.

It is not for us to add fuel to the rumors that are spreading; our well-known discretion places a duty upon us not to anticipate the findings of justice. However, in consequence of the examination of the cadaver and a few clues already gathered, this is what seems to have been established thus far: the dead man belonged to the world of sport. Probably as a result of some quarrel, he must have been struck down with a hammer, or perhaps a monkey-wrench. His murderer, aided by several accomplices, must have transported their victim to the Place de la Concorde and attempted to throw the body into the Obelisk enclosure, but its weight must have retained it on the spikes of the railings, where it was abandoned.

Important information has been received, which will apparently put the police on the track of the guilty party or parties immediately. In our 5 p.m. edition we shall give the details of this horrible affair, which seems bound to produce a profound sensation in the public and will very probably lead to unexpected revelations.

The emotion that ran through Paris at the news of this mysterious crime is easily imaginable—but who could have suspected the astonishing and incredible consequences that the event would unleash?

II. In which we make the acquaintance of "Monsieur Bobby"

We are easily put off by empty promises. When we have learned that a police inquiry has been opened, we release a sigh of relief and already begin to experience a feeling of security. The police benefit greatly from the inventions of novelists, from Voltaire's Zadig to Edgar Poe's Dupin and the incomparable Sherlock Holmes; we gladly suppose that all these characters have been more-or-less attached to the service of the Sûreté and are on the payroll at the Quai des Orfèvres—and it is always surprising when, one after another, we are obliged to classify the most sensational crimes as insoluble mysteries. It is rather disturbing to think about the number of unknown murderers running around, with whom we are liable to rub elbows every day.

Would the Obelisk murder, as the present affair had been dubbed, swell the number of permanently unclosed files? People were beginning to ask whether it was really possible that such a crime could be committed in the middle of Paris, at the central point of the most luxurious quarters, without the police being able to discover the slightest clue.

All the surrounding bars had been searched, all the sportsmen of high and low rank interrogated, and the English ambassador questioned—for the sole established fact was that the victim was English—but no missing person had been reported, either by the hotels or business establishments. Briefly, it was thought that the police were on the track—boxing professionals had declared that the unknown man must be accustomed to bouts of that sort, by virtue of certain characteristic and invariably similar traces left by fists on certain parts of the body, notably a deformation of the jaws—but nothing came of it.

The head of the Sûreté, Monsieur Davaine, who had been put in rather awkward position by several recent failures, rebuked his agents roundly. At the Morgue, where the body had been taken, informers mingled with the crowd, interrogating the visitors' faces and provoking their confidences, in vain; the end-result of the enquiries was always the same: not known!

A rather singular rumor began to circulate. An autopsy had been carried out, it was said, and the illustrious medical examiner who had undertaken the operation had declared that the individual in question had not died from the wound on his skull, nor from the horrible injuries inflicted by that sort of impalement on the spikes of the railings, but that he had been dead already—which would seem to indicate that he had been murdered elsewhere and had been transported to the Place de la Concorde as a corpse. That was not the practitioner's conclusion, however; according to him, the unknown man had died of suffocation. The state of the lungs left no doubt in that regard—but the neck bore no trace of violence, no marks of strangulation. All that was established—at least according to a reporter from the *Nouvelliste*—was that the death could not be attributed in any fashion to the wounds to the head or torso, which had only been inflicted after death.

On the other hand, the place where the cadaver had been found, which was in the middle of an enormous empty space, made it difficult to accept the theory that the malefactors had chosen such an open spot to deposit the corpse of their victim. Even at the dead of night— given that the Moon was full and the sky clear—it was contrary to all credibility that they could have made such a long journey without being seen.

"And yet," cried Monsieur Lavaur, the deputy head of the Sûreté, in private conference with his superior, "the fellow can't have fallen out of the sky..."

"Be that as it may, Monsieur Lépine is furious, and I've just been subjected to a torrent of the most unpleasant reprimands... We must work harder, search, find..."

"Between the two of us," said the deputy head, "we know perfectly well that if chance doesn't throw something up, we'll flounder about in the dark without discovering anything..."

At that precise moment—as in fairy tales, when certain spoken words evoke the anticipated character or event—the office door opened and an inspector poked his head around it.

"Are you available, boss?"

"That depends... If it's not some time-waster..."

"It's an Englishman, who says he's a detective attached to the Prefecture over there, and who's asking to speak to you..."

The chief and his subordinate exchanged a rapid glance. An English detective—was chance, in fact, about to come to their aid?

"What's his name?"

"He gave me this card."

"Let's see it." Monsieur Davaine took the visiting-card at read it. "Bobby! That's not a name—it's a nickname! Show him in anyway." Addressing himself to Monsieur Lavaur, he added: "That doesn't commit us to anything."

"Should I leave?"

"No, no, stay."

The door opened again and the inspector reappeared, preceding the person he had announced. The latter came forward, bowler hat in hand. He was a man of about thirty, short, slim and spare, very correctly dressed, all in black, with a white collar that made a border above his tie. His face was clean-shaven, his short copper-colored hair neatly brushed. His face was thin and rather pale, his eyes small but very clear. His gloves and shoes were good quality. All in all, he looked like a protestant vicar.

"Monsieur Davaine?" he said, bowing at the question mark.

"That's me. This gentleman is my deputy, Monsieur Lavaur. You can talk with complete confidence. One thing, first: your card bears the single word *Bobby*. I know enough English to know that that's the popular nickname of all policemen... Will you please tell me your real name?"

"Monsieur," said the man, with a strong British accent, "here is my official commission, signed by the Director of Scotland Yard. It is issued in the name of Bobby, which is my own... One can't help one's name..."

"That's true," said Monsieur Davaine, reading the piece of paper that had been handed to him. "In that case, Monsieur Bobby..."

"I will add, if you please, that the name has a certain—how do you say it in French?—celebrity in London, by virtue of certain important services that I have rendered... I'm the one who arrested the Greenwich forgers...."

"Ah!" said the French official, who had never heard of that affair.

"I'm the one who tracked down and arrested Lewis Bird, the parricide... who was hanged..."

"Ah!"

"I'm the one who…"

"Forgive me," Monsieur Davaine interrupted, in a rather dry tone, "I don't suppose that it was merely to list your exploits that you asked to see me…"

The Englishman stood up straight, with a slightly offended dignity. "I thought it best, before anything else, to make myself known…everyone has his own value…"

"Quite right! So, Monsieur Bobby, I hold you in the esteem you deserve. What do you want with me?"

"Permit me to take things in order. Let us first stipulate the principle that, as a member of the police force of His Majesty the King of England and Emperor of India, I am not bound by any obligation, of any nature whatsoever, to the police force of the French Republic."

Very solemn, was Monsieur Bobby.

"That's stipulated," said Monsieur Davaine. "And?"

"Moreover," Bobby went on, "the very particular situation in which I presently find myself militates absolutely against the step that I am taking at this moment… I am presently on leave and am not supposed to occupy myself with any event, even if it were in the interests of my own country…"

The head of the Sûreté, who was no more patient than he needed to be, felt an intense desire to throw this loquacious and inconvenient individual out of his office—but Monsieur Lavaur addressed a slight gesture to him. The man was an eccentric, but that did not prove that he could not be of service. This might be the chance—the fortunate chance!

"Continue, then, my dear Monsieur," said Davaine, with his most gracious smile. "Anything that you care to communicate to me is of the greatest interest, and bodes well for the aftermath of your discourse. We are ready to give you our utmost attention…"

This academically formal speech pleased Bobby no end. He was finally being treated with the consideration he merited. With a gesture of his hand, Monsieur Davaine had invited him to sit down—but Monsieur Bobby preferred to remain standing so as not to sacrifice any of his height.

"I had to make you understand, Monsieur le Chef de la Sûreté, that if I introduced myself to you, it was by my own free will, without being constrained by any professional obligation. I'm simply a tourist, who has come to visit Paris, a truly beautiful city"—this interpolation was added in a condescending tone—"and whom an entirely spontaneous impulse of generosity has led to render you a small favor…"

"Too generous, in truth—but would you be so good as to render me this… small favor… as soon as possible… I have so much on my plate at present that I'm rather busy…"

A shadow passed over Monsieur Bobby's face. "If you would prefer," he said, coldly, "I could come back at another time."

"Oh, no! Of course not!" exclaimed Monsieur Davaine. "Monsieur Bobby, I can see that you're a perfect gentleman… but quite honestly, I could not be more impatient to know the true reason for your visit… and if you could, in a few words, calm that impatience…" Privately, the policeman was beginning to ask himself quite seriously whether he ought not to throw the imbecile down the stairs.

As for Monsieur Bobby, he shrugged his shoulders slightly. The French—always the same! Light and frivolous! Then, as if a catch had been released, he pro-

26

nounced these brief words: "You don't know who the dead man at the Obelisk is?"

Lavaur started.

"No," said the head of the Sûreté.

"I know him…"

"Well, tell us, quickly."

"A stroll took me to the Morgue. I saw…"

"And you recognized…?"

"A vulgar individual…"

"Whose name is?"

"Coxward, the pugilist—the boxer. There!"

III. Mercantile Rivalry

Two hours later, the following details appeared in the *Nouvelliste*:

Coxward (John) was a professional boxer, not one of those athletes who claim the title of world champion, but someone on the circuit of circus booths, undertaking bouts for a few shillings, winning or losing, without doing any substantial damage to his adversaries or himself, not unknown to the gambling fraternity but crafty enough, at the end of the day, to earn a living. He was also an inveterate drunkard, disrespectful of the wealth of others, already initiated into the delights of prison and the treadmill.

In sum, not a very interesting person.

Monsieur Bobby, the celebrated English detective, supposed that the individual in question had taken it into his head to seek his fortune in Paris, where boxing matches, at the present time, were attracting a crowd that was as elegant as it was savage to one of its most notorious music halls, whose clientèle discussed the "swings" and "knock-outs" of the corpulent competitors in these bull-fights in the manner of "aficionados."

Would Coxward have done well in these top-flight "fights?" It is hardly probable, but illusion is an ardent adviser, hard to resist—without mentioning the attraction that Paris can exert upon such a person.

As for knowing the sequence of events that had led the slain Coxward to be found at the foot of the Obelisk, interest was, in sum, rather slight. The public would soon have forgotten him, had a very particular circumstance not cropped up, which gave the affair a further boost of publicity.

Everyone knows that, although the *Nouvelliste* holds the lead in the field of informative journalism, it is closely followed by a competitor, the *Reporter*, which is becoming more fashionable every day. The *Nouvelliste*, disdainful of its rival, loses no opportunity to assert its superiority, in terms often ungenerous to the *Reporter*, which, for its own part, seeks by any means whatsoever to find fault with its adversary. There is a cut-throat war between the two newspapers, which amuses the gallery, but in which the two exasperated combatants gladly exchange arguments whose courtesy leaves much to be desired.

Now, it happened that in the affair of the Obelisk, the *Nouvelliste* had got in first, both in the story of the discovery and the results of the investigation. The *Reporter*, for its part, was following a trail among French sportsmen when the *Nouvelliste*, directly informed by the Prefecture, had demolished its entire framework of deductions by revealing Monsieur Bobby's deposition. And it had followed this publication with this bittersweet observation:

We keenly regret that the simple truth reduces to nothing the very ingenious hypotheses in which certain of our colleagues have become embroiled. Once again, the Nouvelliste *has proved the reliability of its information, which has nothing in common with the fantastic imagination of a press unscrupulous enough to invent fallacious items of information wholesale.*

This was a derisive dig at the *Reporter*, accused of carelessness and almost of mendacity, and the other newspapers did not fail to notice the blow. In the offices of the *Reporter*, moreover, there was great annoyance;

the editor fulminated and sacked two of his reporters, while riposting by means of a patriotic note:

The Reporter *admits that it is only staffed by Frenchmen and does not obtain information from foreign collaborators. In any case, we regret that the event underlines in such a disagreeable fashion the superiority of the English police to ours. And besides, we do not accept with closed eyes the affirmations that the Prefecture seems to us to have welcomed much too easily.*

And it added:

This Coxward—if it is Coxward—did not arrive in Paris by balloon. He must have entered into communication with people of his own world and specialty. This man has been murdered by someone or other. The Reporter *is launching an inquiry that will shed light on the matter. And who knows? Perhaps he who laughs last will laugh longest.*

All in all, this challenge looked remarkably like a bluff, but the public was amused by it, and as, at that particular moment, there was no question of the government falling or of any foreign earthquake, the contest, as discourteous as ever, captivated the general curiosity.

Now, it is necessary to recognize that, despite the collaboration of the English detective, the affair had not advanced by a single step. Every day, the *Nouvelliste*, drawing its documentation from reliable sources, reported the evidence of various witnesses that the Investigating Magistrate, Monsieur Mallet du Saule, summoned to his office, and which, unfortunately, always concluded with the concise but scarcely satisfactory formula: "Monsieur Coxward is entirely unknown to us."

The *Reporter* remained silent, contenting itself with sly insinuations, in which Monsieur Bobby was hardly spared.

One day, the *Nouvelliste* thought it had won. An English girl had been discovered in the lowest depths of Ménilmontant who had recognized Coxward's photograph—except that she declared that she had seen him in Dieppe, two years before, when he had spent 24 hours in France on a pleasure trip. The girl had been arrested and grilled in the usual fashion, but she had not changed her story. She had not seen the aforementioned Coxward, nor heard mention of him, for two years.

Other depositions contributed to the complication of the puzzle. Some attributed the name of Coxward to individuals from the sporting world who were very much alive, under the names—which were their own—Coxwell or Coxburn. The business had become increasingly confused for a fortnight, when the *Reporter* suddenly appeared with a headline in enormous type, which read:

HE LAUGHS LONGEST WHO LAUGHS LAST

This is the article that followed it:

Our readers will not have failed to notice the discretion that we have shown in our reportage of the Coxward affair. They know, too, that it is our custom only to say what we know and not to accept information that might have reached us without passing through the sieve of criticism. If we occasionally permit ourselves to hazard a few hypotheses, that is the label we give them, and yet, we have been charged, in bad faith, with being careless of the truth. If the cap fits, wear it!

That said, we affirm—this time without hesitation or ambiguity—that the deposition of Monsieur Bobby, the celebrated English detective, which has so strongly excited opinion, slightly irritated by the intervention of a foreigner in our domestic affairs; that this deposition, we repeat, before which everyone has been so hasty to bow down, as if it were and could not be other than the gospel truth; that this deposition is ERRONEOUS AND INEXACT IN EVERY RESPECT!

Those who have accepted it so hastily will doubtless be very grieved to learn that they have been victims OF AN ERROR OR AN IMPOSTURE.

THE DEAD MAN OF THE OBELISK IS NOT COXWARD!

And, as a guarantee of our affirmation, we are putting up a stake of ONE HUNDRED THOUSAND FRANCS against anyone who wishes to match it. We have deposited that sum today, in full and in current coinage, with Maître Falloux, Notary.

Time and space are lacking to explain more clearly. The confirmation of our statement will be found at length in our 5 p.m. edition.

"Go find Monsieur Bobby for me!" cried the head of the Sûreté, on reading this impertinent announcement.

The English detective arrived in a rather bad mood. He was in Paris solely for pleasure, and he had been interrupted just as he was about to board a Thomas Cook coach for Versailles.

Without paying any heed to his rather sulky expression, Monsieur Davaine held the newspaper out to him. "Have you read this?"

"Yes, Monsieur."

"What do you have to say about it?"

"Pure humbug," Bobby declared. "I have a question to ask you on the same subject. These 100,000 francs are there for the taking. What do I have to do to make sure they're paid to me?"

"Write a very explicit letter to the *Reporter*—but a word, in my turn: be careful, Monsieur Bobby. You've put me in a very delicate situation. I've accepted your declaration as emanating from a man in the profession who knows what his responsibilities are, and a gentleman incapable of playing games with someone else's confidence. Today, in the presence of these denials, are you sure of yourself? After all, one might be misled by a resemblance... you're obviously not unaware of the story of Lesurques and his double Dubosc.[1] Are you absolutely certain that you weren't mistaken?"

Monsieur Bobby, whose complexion was ordinarily rather pale, had suddenly turned crimson, and there was a tremor in his jaw that boded ill. "I'm neither a child nor a madman, Monsieur," he replied, in a strangled voice. "I am in the service of His Britannic Majesty, and it is purely by condescension, I remind you, that I am consenting to reply to you, despite the profound slur you have just cast on my dignity as an English citizen. I swear that the murdered man really is John Coxward—and I shall do more; I shall match the stake with 4000 pounds..."

"And if you were to lose? The *Reporter* would not have dared to mount that challenge if it were not in possession of serious documentary evidence."

"Monsieur, I have said what I have said. Journalists are notorious liars, and if I have to, I shall stuff their impostures down their throats."

He bowed, turned on his heels, and left.

---

[1] The execution of Joseph Lesurques for the murder of a Lyons courier in 1796 became the most famous French instance of a miscarriage of justice when it was discovered that he had been mistaken by witnesses for the actual highwayman, Dubosc. The case became the basis for one of Sir Henry Irving's most famous stage roles, in which he played both men in a melodrama called *The Lyons Mail*.

The man seems sincere, thought Monsieur Davaine. *The information regarding him furnished by the English ambassador is of the highest order—and yet, I have to admit that I have a bad feeling about this.*

Indeed, he could not deny that this error, if it were proven, would cover with ridicule not only the English detective—which was of scant importance—but the French police, which was infinitely more serious, especially for Monsieur Davaine, whose position was already under threat. Thus, one can imagine how impatiently the head of the Sûreté awaited the next edition of the *Reporter*. He had tried his utmost to find a means of obtaining an advance proof of the promised article, but the printing-works was well-guarded and all his attempts had been fruitless.

Furthermore, all the idlers and curiosity-seekers in Paris were on the alert. The fight between the two rival newspapers was interesting, without there being any marked sympathy for one over the other. It is amusing to see people exchanging blows, without bothering to pre-judge which of them will emerge the victor. Thus, there was a crowd on the boulevard by 4:45 p.m.; the weather was mild and the terraces of the cafés were full. The news-vendors were displaying posters advertising *The truth of the Coxward Affair*, which certain naïve individuals bought, thinking that they might find the key to the puzzle therein—but they were only advertisements for a new boot-polish.

Finally, the first of the *Reporter*'s vendors came out of the printing-works on the Rue de Croissant and ran through the crowd, shouting advertisements for the expected edition. The sheets, still damp, were snatched from the hands of these individuals, who had trouble getting hold of the price. By way of compensation, however, some of them received large-denomination coins for which they did not have the leisure to give change.

The headline was sensational:

COXWARD IS ALIVE!

It was short, but decisive.

Then, lower down:

Monsieur Bobby has lost 100,000 francs!

And under these resounding headings, this was read:

We have received from Monsieur Bobby, the illustrious and impeccable English detective, a letter in which he declares his acceptance of the wager of 100,000 francs that we have offered. It is to our great regret, in view of the entente cordiale, *that we have to notify Monsieur Bobby that he will have to disperse the sum in question to the poor of Paris—which is to say, to put it into the hands of Monsieur Mesureur, the eminent director of Public Assistance, for which a receipt will be given to him.*

For, two facts will be now established. The first, which cannot be contested, is that the cadaver of the unknown victim was found at the foot of the Obelisk on the April 2 at 5 a.m. The second, of which the proofs are indisputable, is that the aforementioned Coxward, professional boxer, was to be found on April 1, between midnight and 1 a.m.—that is to say, on the night of April 1 to April 2—in a tavern by the name of The Shadow's Bar located on Liverpool Road, in Islington.

Islington is, as everyone knows, one of the suburbs of London.

If, therefore, Coxward was in Liverpool Road at 1 a.m. on April 2, to admit that he could be suspended from the railings of the Obelisk at 5 a.m. on that same morning, it would be necessary to establish that one can travel from London to Paris in four hours, without counting the time necessary for the assassination, and that there is a train at that hour, North or West,[2] capable of operating at that vertiginous rapidity—facts that the railway companies will surely not jealously keep secret.

How can we establish that Coxward was in London on the night of April 1 to April 2? In the simplest possible fashion, and without having any need to inquire in high places. Let us say, in passing, that it is all too easy to be content with received information without taking the least trouble to check its accuracy. We confess to being more skeptical, preferring as often as possible to make our own investigations. It was not in Paris but in London that we had to make our investigations, and that is what we did.

Now, what no telegraph line—no matter how direct it might be—to the capital of England was able to tell us, is that on the morning of April 2, the name of Coxward the boxer featured in a paragraph in very small print among the unimportant news items in a small local newspaper appearing in Islington, where we read the following:

"Last night, a commotion broke out in one of the ill-famed taverns scattered profusely in Liverpool Road. A boxer named Coxward, whose exploits have already indemnified the judiciary purse several times over, had

---

[2] At that time there were several possible routes that a traveler might follow in going as rapidly as possible from London to Paris, depending on where he elected to cross the Channel; in every case, however, he would have to complete the journey by arriving either at the Gare du Nord or the Gare Saint-Lazare, which were operated by different companies, here represented by the directions they served with respect to Paris.

been engaged to take part in a boxing match at The Sha-dow's Bar, owned by a certain Pat O'Kearn, Irishman.

"The audience comprised people of the poorest class, and bets were laid in pence rather than pounds, or even shillings. The performance was worth no more, and the bout provoked more boos than plaudits. The afore-mentioned Coxward was, moreover, very drunk and could hardly hold himself upright, with the result that he was knocked down several times, to the jeers of the pub-lic. At about 1 a.m., it became obvious that he was in-capable of standing up, and he declared that he had had enough and was going—which everyone acknowledged with mocking applause.

"Coxward, who was exhausted by fatigue and drunkenness, went into the room next to the parlor in order to put his clothes back on. One of his adversaries, who knew him to be an untrustworthy individual, sud-denly conceived a suspicion, went into the room where Coxward was and surprised him just as the wretch, hav-ing finished dressing and gone through the pockets of the other clothes, had taken possession of a gold watch and was making his exit through a ground-floor window.

"The man threw himself forward to stop him, but Coxward got away from him and ran away outside. In response to cries of 'Thief!' the clients of The Shadow's Bar launched themselves in pursuit, and a veritable man-hunt began. Coxward had a rather long start, and also knew the neighborhood well, which is cut through by numerous winding lanes. He had run in the direction of Highbury, and finally succeeded in throwing off his pursuers and disappearing. A complaint has been laid against Coxward, who will not be long delayed in falling into the hands of justice again."

This was a rather banal occurrence, but one which takes on a singular importance, given the circumstances. Did Coxward, stealing a watch at 1 a.m. at The Shadow's Bar, in a distant quarter of London, enjoy the gift of ubiquity to such a degree that he was able to be in Paris at the same time, in the vicinity of the Place de la Concorde?

It only remained to verify: 1, whether the facts reported in the local newspaper in question were true; 2, whether the day and the date mentioned were accurate; and 3, whether there was any doubt as to the identity of the aforementioned Coxward.

Our colleague Labergère, to whom we entrusted this inquiry, immediately made contact with one of the most renowned solicitors in London, Edwin Battleworth, Esq., of Temple Street, Lincoln's Inn Fields, who proceeded to gather reliable information and collect indispensable witness statements, with all the guarantees of sincerity that the law confers. The following witnesses have been heard under oath:

Mr. Pat O'Kearn, Irishman, tenant of The Shadow's Bar tavern.

Mrs. O'Kearn, née O'Keefe.

Mr. Gailbraith, pugilist.

Mr. Bloxham, butcher.

Plus seven other regulars at the tavern in question, belonging to the working class.

And all of them declared:

That Coxward was, without any doubt, the individual who had boxed at The Shadow's Bar, had stolen a watch, and had been pursued;

That they had all known him for a long time, and that no mistake was possible, or even imaginable;

That the incident reported by the newspaper was true in every detail;

And finally, that the scene had definitely taken place between 11 p.m. on April 1 and 1 a.m. on April 2.

These documents—whose authenticity cannot be put in doubt—are pinned up in our dispatch-room; the Parisian public can therefore judge how well-founded certain discourteous criticisms are that certain spiteful competitors have thought it appropriate to heap upon us. This retribution of truth against bluff is sufficient for us.

But we were right:

THE OBELISK CADAVER IS NOT THAT OF COXWARD THE BOXER

Undoubtedly, our ineffable head of the Sûreté, Monsieur Davaine, and his illustrious colleague, the ridiculous Mr. Bobby, have nothing in common with the legendary Sherlock Holmes. We remind the celebrated Mr. Bobby that the coffers of the Public Assistance are situated in the Avenue Victoria, a few steps away from the Hôtel de Ville.

There was an immense outburst of laughter throughout the city

No one was any longer concerned with the crime that really had been committed—neither the murderer nor his victim. The moment that he was not named Coxward, it seemed that the dead man was no longer interesting. Something survived, though, and that was the name of Bobby—the illustrious Bobby, the admirable detective—and in the following morning's newspapers there was a deluge of jokes, ferocious in tone. Caricatures flayed him, with representations of varying degrees of insanity. People were selling Bobby postcards, Bobby this and Bobby that. He had become the hero of the day, and groups of people gathered in front of the hotel in which he was staying, shouting at the tops of their voices:

"Down with Bobby!"

"Off to Charenton [3] with him, right away!"

What put the cap on this general excitement was that Mrs. Bobby had herself taken by carriage to the offices of the *Reporter*, went past the office-boys like a gust of wind, climbed the staircase and, opening at door at hazard, fell into the editorial office—and without any warning, that tall, thin and dried-up woman, of the old English type with long teeth, threw herself upon the editors, with her umbrella at battle stations, and distributed blows to her right and left, carving and lunging, at the serious risk of putting her adversaries' eyes out.

It was no small matter to master this fury, who claimed to be avenging her husband's honor. They finally succeeded in getting hold of her and putting her into the hands of the police, who had to tie her up to render her powerless—not without receiving some vigorous blows. She was carried to the guard-post, where the agents had still to defend themselves against her combative eccentricities. On orders from the Prefecture, she was not put in the cells, but was immediately taken to Monsieur Lépine's office.

Fortunately, she had calmed down somewhat and deigned not to respond by doing any injury to our chief magistrate. Still quivering, she explained that Mr. Bobby, an English citizen, and Mrs. Bobby, a Scotswoman, would not tolerate the outrages that the French newspapers were heaping upon them; that it was infamous to accuse Mr. Bobby of being mistaken or lying; that he had never been mistaken in his life; and that she swore

---

[3] The then-location of Paris' lunatic asylum.

by Mary Stuart's head on the block that the dead man of the Obelisk was Coxward.

"But do you know this Coxward yourself Madame?"

"What do you take me for? Do I keep company with people of that sort?"

"Then how do you know that he's the one who...?"

"Mr. Bobby told me."

"Very good, very good!" said a clear voice—that of Mr. Bobby, who had just been introduced. "That reply is in conformity with the instruction of reason. A wife ought to believe all of her husband's assertions..."

"Ah, here you are, Monsieur Bobby!" said the Prefect, in a rather dry tone. "You're an English citizen, so you know what the words *to keep the peace* signify. Now, if I don't dispute your opinions, I consider that you have no right to raise a scandal to affirm them, and before making a decision in your regard that I might regret, I must ask you whether you and Mrs. Bobby will promise to keep the peace—which is to say, not to commit any disturbance. Answer me, please..."

Mr. Bobby stood up straight, with an imposing dignity. "Which is to say that you wish to impose upon me, a free citizen of England, the opinion, contrary to the truth, that Coxward is not Coxward."

"I don't intend to impose anything at all upon you—except that you remain calm and don't assault people here, as the honorable Madame Bobby was wrong to do."

"Mrs. Bobby, acting according to her conscience, is not to blame..."

"At least give me your word that you will not recommence..."

"I refuse."

"And you, Madame Bobby."

"I refuse."

"Then I am constrained to employ the rights that the law confers upon me. You, Monsieur Bobby, will return to your hotel and make your preparations for departure. The train for Calais leaves at 8 p.m. You will find Madame Bobby at the Gare du Nord, and, notification having been made to you of an expulsion order, you will embark immediately for England."

"That's all right," said Mr. Bobby, nobly. "That doesn't mean that Coxward isn't Coxward."

And Bobby and his irascible spouse left Paris that same evening.

Was the affair ended and the file to be closed?

People would have been very surprised—and, above all, fearful—if they had been able to foresee the frightful events that would follow in the wake of the Obelisk murder.

PART TWO:
THE CHEMIST, THE DETECTIVE
AND THE REPORTER

I. Mr. Bobby's Notebook

This is taking place in London.

Mr. Bobby is alone in the little parlor of his cottage in which he has been living for 20 years, at the corner of Islington Gardens. Mrs. Bobby is not there. He has opened a drawer in his little writing-desk, left to him by his father, which is locked by means of a steel key.

This is the journal of his life, kept up to date since childhood—the age of seven—in accordance with the poetic principle of *nulla dies sine lines*, without a day ever having passed without his having written at least one line.

Mr. Bobby is melancholy, but his pursed lips and set jaw testify to a will that nothing can bend. He has put the notebook on the table-top and activated the catch. He thumbs through it, opens it, and begins to read it back to himself.

I, an English citizen, born in the city of London, a pure-blooded Cockney, having heard the bells of Bow Church mingle their grave intonation with my first wails, have been expelled from France, and was unable to resist. Forgive me, my ancestors of Agincourt, but Providence—which no one can resist—had decided that its faithful servant would not drain the cup of bitterness by virtue of that insult.

The day after my return to my fireside, a summons, whose dry tone was not a good omen, called me to Scotland Yard, where I was received by Mr. Sewingthrow, my immediate superior. Encouraged by Susan's—i.e., Mrs. Bobby's—firmness I presented myself as a man sure of the righteousness of his cause. But what are the confirmed merits of a man worth, in the face of calumny and what I dare to call unintelligence?

He reproached me for getting mixed up, in a friendly country, in details that were not my concern, of having attracted to myself and to England the malevolent attention of crowds, and—a consideration more painful to me than any other—of having made the British police ridiculous and suspect of incoherence.

I explained myself in vain. I exposed the principles that had been my guides—love of truth, the desire to be useful—and recalled in vain the moral and religious instruction that I had forced myself to put into practice. Evidently, I was condemned in advance. None of my arguments produced the effect that I had the right to expect. Eventually, I was informed that I was suspended from duty until further orders. Nothing remained for me but to bow down to inevitability.

In a few words, with which I have reason to be satisfied, and which were not without eloquence. I protested respectfully against the measure taken against me. "Mr. Sewingthrow," I said, by way of conclusion, "the blood of martyrs, falling upon the ground, has brought forth a harvest of truth; without it being appropriate, in my humility, to compare myself with those precursory saints, permit me to affirm that the error of which I am the unfortunate victim will perhaps have regrettable repercussions on public morality."

My superior, disconcerted, replied with a statement that I catalogue under the heading of unmerited outrages. "You're an imbecile," he said. "Calm down and await developments."

And I came home, happy to pour out into the bosom of my companion the bitterness with which my heart was swollen.

"Mr. Bobby," my remarkable wife said to me, "the insult of which you are the object rebounds upon me. I expect you to rehabilitate both of us."

These words dictated my duty. It was necessary for me, henceforth, to devote my life to the search for that truth: to find out how Coxward, murdered in Paris on April 2, had contrived to be in London only four hours earlier.

For here, I must make a confession. I have taken cognizance of the newspaper in which his presence between 11 p.m. on April 1 and 1 a.m. on April 2 was related, and I have too much respect for the press of my country to have entertained a moment's doubt as to that affirmation—which, emanating from French journalism, appeared to me to be more than suspect. And I was not surprised when, the following day, having remade on my own account the inquiries previously made by my critics, I acquired the certainty that the witnesses had told the truth. They had witnessed the boxing-match in which Coxward had been disqualified. It was in response to an uppercut to the chin that he had tottered, at first attempting a clinch, but finally being felled by a left hook that had knocked him down. The promptness with which he proclaimed himself defeated had been considered cowardly. All things considered, however, it appeared to me that Coxward had a particular plan, which was to conserve his strength for the misdeed that he had in mind—which is to say the theft of which, a moment later, he had rendered himself guilty.

My precisions were established in the clearest possible manner

It was exactly 12:55 p.m. when Coxward, very much alive and perfectly alert, had leapt out of the window on the ground floor of The Shadow's Bar and had fled, pursued by the furious mob of his adversaries.

That Coxward was a thief was no surprise to me; his character had long been established. Nothing in that adventure was contrary to plausibility. The witnesses could not have been mistaken as to his identity, for he had been known to them for a long time, as he was to me, who had set the hand of the law upon him on several occasions.

Now, since the moment that Coxward, pursued, had disappeared, some distance from Highbury Crescent, had he reappeared? No. No one had heard mention of him. The numerous taverns that he normally frequented had not had the honor of his company, and I ought to add that, in breach of all my usual delicacy, I had lowered myself so far as to seek out a certain Bessie Bell, a woman of dubious reputation, with whom he entertained an unspecifiable relationship, and that, having found her, and despite the repulsion that these creatures inspire in me—especially when I am not acting under orders—I interrogated her and learned from her that she too had not had a visit from him...a circumstance about which she was not unduly troubled, as she cynically informed me.

Thus, the fact was established. For whatever reason, it seemed that Coxward had left London, or was perhaps dead. I had established that he had remained invisible in all the haunts associated with his base

sport—which, God knows, are numerous. The hypothesis
of sudden death was the most plausible—for someone
other than me, of course; even so, I acted as if it were
possible. A dead man leaves traces; he is buried, thrown
in the water or burned, as among the Hindus.

There was not the slightest vestige of a cadaver.

Therefore, and I believed that I had established the
fact in support of my own conviction, Coxward was
alive, because nothing proved the contrary, and yet I
had seen him, in the Morgue in Paris. Which raised this
question: what had happened to Coxward between 1
a.m., the moment when he had been lost to view in the
vicinity of Highbury Crescent, and 5 a.m., the time when
he had been found—him, and no other—hooked on the
railings of the Obelisk?

Seek and thou shalt find, saith the Lord. I shall
seek.

Mr. Bobby's notebook carefully related the twists
and turns of the minute inquiry to which he had devoted
himself, beginning with the point that, according to information carefully gathered, Coxward had been prodi-
giously drunk at the time of the match and the theft—
and, in consequence, was not capable of covering a very
long distance.

Mr. Bobby had, therefore, methodically studied,
one by one, all the streets, side-streets and lanes in the
vicinity of Highbury Crescent, even introducing himself
into the homes of the local inhabitants under more-or-
less specious pretexts, suffering rebuffs philosophically,
but remaining impassive and unyielding. The circle of
his search tightening inexorably, he had eventually noticed a peculiar house in Corsica Street—a new tho-
roughfare traced across the fields, where the buildings
were sparser. It was a detached building whose windows

and shutters were always hermetically closed. A rather high wall surrounded the property, which, at first glance, seemed to be unoccupied.

Naturally, Mr. Bobby had not neglected an attempt to be introduced into this rather mysterious house, whose appearance was bound to provoke curiosity. Let us read, over his shoulder, the information in his notebook.

Anyone else but me would have given up in face of the difficulty of the task that I had set myself. No trace of Coxward. I am certain—certain, I say—that he had not gone into any of the houses in the neighborhood of Highbury Crescent; I have visited all of them, except one.

I have, of course, presented myself at the door of this last dwelling and, ringing and knocking, employed all the means available to obtain an introduction. Wasted effort. My calls went unanswered; the occupant or occupants of the house presumably refuse, on principle, to greet any visitor.

I asked around in the neighborhood, but there too my curiosity remained unsatisfied—or, at least, what I was able to learn merely excited it further,

The house belongs to a certain Sir Athel Random— a descendant, it appears, of one of the oldest families in London. This individual bought the property in question for a rather high price, immediately settling up, as they say, "cash on the nail." He devotes himself to research in chemistry and mechanics. At least, that is what is supposed, according to the indications offered by enormous boxes brought by haulers since he moved in. He lives alone, without servants, and—surprisingly—no supplier has ever been seen to bring him provisions of food.

He very rarely goes out, in an automobile of a rather bizarre sort, of such small dimensions that no one can figure out where its engine might be lodged. This vehicle moves with exceptional speed—but on that subject, I could obtain very few details. A rumor has gone around that he used to live in Kilburn, near Brondesbury Station. One night, the house blew up, and Sir Athel was obliged to pay a considerable indemnity to the landlord and the neighbors. I have verified this allegation, which is true. Some say that he is a madman, others a magician.

During the early days of his sojourn in Highbury, he was accused of complicity with anarchists, or at least propagandists. There was also mention, but in an even vaguer fashion, of a proposed marriage between Sir Athel Random and Mary Redmore, the daughter of a rich landowner of the neighborhood—but the engagement was abruptly broken off, for some unknown reason. This is only supported by the prattling of domestic servants—what is usually known as idle gossip. It seems that there is not, and cannot be, any connection between the existence of this mysterious individual and the disappearance of Coxward; it is, however, necessary to leave no stone unturned...

Ten days later.

Perhaps there is a glimmer of light in the darkness. In view of the difficulties I have encountered in getting into Sir Athel Random's house, I have turned my artillery in another direction.

It was not very difficult for me to discover the residence of Jedediah Redmore, who is in possession of a large fortune and has set himself up in a veritable mansion near Newington Park. The millions he has amassed have been acquired by the manufacture of chemical products. The Redmore company—successors of Blackwith—is still one of the most considerable in the city. He is a widower and has a daughter, Mary, of whom he is passionately fond.

Information obtained from his staff has confirmed the vague rumors I had heard. Sir Athel, who had made the acquaintance of Mr. Redmore as a purchaser of chemical products, had indeed become a regular visitor at the house, and a sterling sympathy had gradually developed between him and the young lady. The quality of his birth, education and fortune being most satisfactory, Mr. Redmore had not raised any objection to his daughter's choice, and the marriage had been fixed for the following summer, in June or July. Suddenly, and without anyone even being able to guess the reason for the turnabout, it had all been broken off. I have only succeeded in determining that Sir Athel ran to Mr. Redmore's house one morning, pale and exhausted, with the appearance of a madman, that he had been admitted to Miss Mary's presence, that a rather long conversation had taken place, punctuated by the outbursts of a desperate voice that was Sir Athel's, and that he had eventually gone away again, with his face covered in tears and his features distraught, and had never been seen at the mansion again.

Miss Mary, despite the discretion imposed on young ladies, had not been able to hide the profound grief that had overwhelmed her, and has worn mourning-dress ever since.

For myself, to whom sentimentality is utterly foreign, and being preoccupied with matters much more important than an amorous adventure, I would only have been able to devote an exceedingly superficial attention to these facts had not one detail struck me forcibly. From Mr. Redmore's chauffeur, with whom I had a long chat at the King's Arms public house—whose whisky is highly recommended—I learned... that the visit made by Sir Athel at which the rupture had occurred had taken place ON APRIL 2 LAST, AT 9 A.M...

And is that not a glimmer of light in the darkness?

II. In which the light increases

With an aplomb that testified to his skill as a detective—honorary, for the time being—Mr. Bobby presented himself at the Redmore mansion, asking straightforwardly whether he might see Miss Redmore. To his great surprise, he was immediately admitted and taken to a sort of library where he was invited to wait.

A rather long time went by, but Mr. Bobby had made patience his rule of conduct, and never lost respect for it when his plans hit any kind of snag. Finally, a door opened and someone came in: a sort of giant, with enormous shoulders, red hair and a beard, wearing gold-rimmed spectacles. He had a paunch, long legs, and the feet of a king, if not an emperor. Mr. Bobby had not hesitated for a second before recognizing him as Mr. Jedediah Redmore. The millionaire's stature could not deceive him.

And, indeed, it was Mr. Redmore—who, in a slightly coarse voice softened by courtesy, asked the intruder to what he owed the honor of his visit.

Despite his strength of character, Mr. Bobby hesitated momentarily before replying; he would have preferred to find himself facing a young woman, who would have been more easily overwhelmed by his lofty intelligence. The anxiety was brief, however. "Mr. Redmore," he said, "I work on the principle that frankness is still the only means of achieving one's goal. I have no plausible or palpable reason for presenting myself to you."

"What?" said Mr. Redmore, in a less cordial tone.

"Since I have come, however, I evidently have reasons—which I shall categorize as subtle and delicate—

and I beg you to give me a few minutes of attention." In response to an impatient gesture of acquiescence, Bobby went on: "A few questions first. If they seem inappropriate to you, I implore you from the outset to forgive me, for I am only acting with excellent intentions…"

"My dear sir," Mr. Redmore cut in, "if you haven't explained why you've come here in five minutes, I'll take hold of your tie and throw you out of the window!"

Bobby put on an exquisite smile. "Five minutes will suffice," he said. "Would you do me the extreme courtesy of telling me whether you are acquainted with a certain Sir Athel Random of Corsica Street, Highbury?"

Red as he was, Redmore became even redder. "Oh, you've come on behalf of that wretch, have you?" he exclaimed. "Well, sir, you're wasting your time. Head for the door, so that I can kick you out."

"The five minutes have not yet elapsed, and I trust in your word as a gentleman. The name is evidently known to you, since it annoys you. I shall continue. Did a certain scene take place here on the morning of the April 2, which put an end to a relationship that had been amicable until then?"

"Yes, sir, on April 2. I've no reason to hide it—but, in God's name what has it got to do with you?"

"Believe me, I am not asking out of mere curiosity; I have no wish to involve myself in your private affairs. On that same date, however, another incident occurred, which, some instinct tells me, is not unconnected with what happened here."

"An incident? What incident? Where?"

"In Paris," Mr. Bobby replied, graciously.

Mr. Redmore was making a visible effort to contain himself, but at the mention of the word Paris his composure abandoned him. Convinced that he was being mocked in the most outrageous fashion, he deluged the gentle Mr. Bobby with epithets that were scarcely cordial, and finally ordered him to leave. Bobby, however, seeing that the game was lost in that respect, risked everything and cried out at the top of his voice: "If Miss Mary Redmore will deign to hear me out, we might be able to save Sir Athel Random!"

The idea was ingenious, for the door opened immediately and Miss Mary appeared: a delightful child, twenty years old, plump, with a charming shock of blonde hair that formed an aureole around her. "What's the matter, father?" she asked, excitedly. "Who pronounced the name of..." She blushed deeply, finally perceiving the presence of Bobby—who, being a gentleman to the toes of his boots, bowed in order to signify his respect for beauty.

"It was this imbecile," Redmore replied, "who's been spouting God knows what nonsense... he's talking about the morning of April 2—a date that we can never forget..."

Miss Mary, with a very delicate gesture, had put her hand on her heart, as if that date had struck her there. "Papa," she said, "painful as any allusion to that unfortunate day might be, remember that I have the greatest possible interest"—she emphasized these words—"in knowing what happened in the home of the person in question, and thus discovering the reasons for a rather horrible adventure. With your permission, I should like to interrogate Mr...?"

"Bobby," our man supplied, in response to the inquiry.

Mr. Redmore keenly regretted not having thrown the intruder out of the window sooner, but his daughter's voice was so soft and tugged at his paternal heartstrings so delightfully, that he did not have the strength to refuse her anything. He turned on his heels abruptly, and left.

Round one to Bobby.

"Speak, sir," Miss Mary said to him, forcefully. "What do you know about Sir Athel?"

"Nothing, alas, at present, Miss—but as I had the honor of telling your respectable father, I am a man of intuition, with a good nose, and I'm convinced that, with a little help, I shall be able to solve a redoubtable mystery—which, perhaps, will interest you as much as it does me."

"Your meaning is rather obscure. Do you know Sir Athel?"

"I have done everything possible to get to him—but I have not succeeded."

"But what connection is there between you and him?"

"None, at present. Please, Miss, listen to me for a few moments, I beg you. On the morning of April 2, did not Sir Athel present himself to you, pale and in disorder, with the appearance of a madman, and did he not say things to you that both surprised you and left you desolate?"

"That's true."

"Dare I ask you, Miss, what he said—or, at least, everything therein that you will consent to repeat to me?"

The young woman hesitated momentarily. She looked at Bobby, and formed the impression that he was an honest man.

"Sir Athel," she said, "whom I had seen two days before, friendly, benevolent and confident in the future that—I say it without shame—I was to share with him, presented himself here on April 2, at 9 a.m., haggard and drawn, unrecognizable. Then, when I pressed him with questions, he told me that he was dishonored... that he had committed a horrible crime—him! so honest!—and that he could no longer demand from me the accomplishment of the promise that we had exchanged... that I could not and must not bind my life to that of a criminal! What else can I say? His jerky speech, and the sobs that punctuated it, frightened me... I begged him to explain more clearly, assuring him that even if he had committed some imprudence, I would forgive him... that I would help him make reparation. Suddenly, he fled... and since then, he has not come back....=" She melted into tears, hiding her head in her hands.

Bobby had listened attentively. "Had you ever noticed any signs of mental disturbance in Sir Athel?"

"Never! To be sure, he was often preoccupied. I knew that he was devoting his entire life, and all his intelligence, to the realization of a new invention that he sometimes tried to explain to me... despite the attention I paid to his words, though, my ignorance of scientific matters did not permit me to follow his reasoning..."

"To what field of endeavor were his researches directed?"

"He told me once that if he succeeded fully in his efforts, dirigible balloons and airplanes would be no more than children's toys, and that he would be able to go from London to New York in two hours."

Mr. Bobby started and, obedient to a force superior to his will, danced a little jig, while singing the chorus of an old minstrel song: "*Buffalo gals won't you come out tonight...*"

"Are you going mad yourself, sir?" cried Miss Mary, a trifle anxiously.

Mr. Bobby recovered his composure, shouldering arms. "Excuse me, Miss. I'm not mad and had no intention of offending you—but what you have just told me... if you only knew! A thousand leagues in two hours! In that case, London to Paris—350 kilometers—is nothing! Ten minutes, perhaps. Then Coxward... yes, evidently... The connection exists! It's real!"

"I don't understand."

"Neither do I!" Bobby relied. "But my intuition's working, my nose is doing its job!" He stopped abruptly; then, his voice becoming formal again, he said: "Miss Mary Redmore, it's absolutely necessary that I see Sir Athel. I assure you, on my word as an English citizen, a pure London cockney, that throughout this business I have had none but perfectly honorable intentions. I will add that, touched by your personal situation—I'm married, Miss, and I know what affection a woman has for the man she has chosen—I am entirely ready to help you to repair, if possible, the consequences of the morning of the second of April. Help me to see Sir Athel, and I shall bring him back to your feet..."

"Oh, if you could accomplish that miracle..."

"Well, Miss, looking at you, it does not appear to me that the miracle is unrealizable. I'm certain that it isn't with a glad heart that Sir Athel has renounced the happiness of being your spouse. Some catastrophe must have occurred in his life, which I sense and divine, but cannot define... and whose effects I might perhaps succeed in palliating..."

"How happy I am to hear you say that! I had lost all hope, alas, and I don't know why... but I have confidence in you..."

"Then reply to my question. Is it possible for you to obtain an interview with Sir Athel for me?"

"I don't know what to tell you. Already, casting all self-respect aside, I've written to him... he hasn't replied..."

"But your letters have reached him?"

"I'm sure of it. It was my governess herself who put them through his letter-box."

"And who will be able to deliver a new one!"

"Yes."

Mr. Bobby struck himself on the forehead. "Write, Miss, write! Tell Sir Athel that you implore him to receive a gentleman who will present himself this very day, at 5 p.m..." He paused; then with a decisive gesture, he said: "Come on! He who risks nothing, has nothing." Resuming his dictation, he continued: "...And who desires to converse with you on the subject of the individual whose photograph is enclosed..."

He took a photograph from his pocket, and Miss Mary obediently put it into the envelope. It was Coxward's.

III. Two Visitors Instead of One

At 4:45 p.m. exactly, someone rang Sir Athel Random's doorbell.

The door immediately turned on its hinges. A man of rather tall stature, young and very pale, representative of the modern English type, his black hair neatly divided by an impeccable parting, his moustache drooping to either side of his lips in the Celtic style, appeared within the oaken frame. On seeing a stranger before him, Sir Athel Random said in a slightly strained voice: "I've received Miss Mary Redmore's letter. You're welcome, sir. Come in..."

The visitor accepted the invitation addressed to him without hesitation. Sir Athel preceded him across a little courtyard, at the rear of which stood a single-story building that had the appearance of a studio. He opened a second door in the left-hand part of the building, stood aside, and invited the other to go in with a courteous gesture.

It was a sort of study, brightly illuminated by its windows, with a long table in the middle, which was loaded with scientific instruments, ranging from a graduated barometer to a double-stemmed retort, as well as numerous papers and graphic designs.

Sir Athel pointed to a chair and the newcomer sat down.

The young Englishman—who was not far from giving rise to a suspicion of madness—was a handsome young man of about 25. Beneath a broad and elevated forehead, his eyes—slightly sunk into their orbits—shone with intelligence, and perhaps also with an internal fever, combated by will-power. His mouth was firm, fleshy and vigorous. The whole ensemble betrayed an energetic and courageous spirit.

The newcomer was of sturdy build, his rather thin face barred by a cosmetically-pointed moustache. He was about fifty years old, his grey hair neatly groomed. His bearing was correct, his hat—which he had removed—had been slightly tilted to one side when he arrived. His hand, solid and hairy, held a walking-stick that that would almost have passed for a cudgel.

As Sir Athel considered him briefly before speaking, the other—who was not Mr. Bobby—took a wallet from his pocket, and a visiting card from the wallet, which he held out.

Sir Athel took it, and read: *Arthur de Labergère*. In the lower left-hand corner, a word had been crossed out, above which, written in pen, this annotation was readable: *Le Nouvelliste, Paris.*

Sir Athel did not flinch.

"I am a journalist, Monsieur," said Labergère. "Chief reporter of the Paris *Nouvelliste*, formerly attached to the *Reporter*, which I left in the wake of incidents of no interest to you, and I have come to ask you for a few minutes of conversation…"

"You're the person whose visit I was told to expect by Miss Redmore?"

Labergère bowed, mutely—which was not compromising.

"And you've come to talk to me about the man whose photograph has been sent to me, in the same letter that advised me of your visit…?"

Self-possessed as the chief reporter of the *Nouvelliste* was—he had formerly been on the editorial staff of the *Reporter* and had only quit the latter newspaper to go over to its competitor as a result of simple circumstances about which we shall say a few words in due course—Labergère gave a slight start of surprise. He had left Paris that same morning, and was totally unaware that a young woman whose name was quite unknown to him had advertised his visit. As for the photograph of which mention had been made, he knew nothing about that, either. "Monsieur," he said, "I am certain that it will only require a few words to demonstrate to you the interest of my request, for you and for me. Let me tell you, first, that the newspaper I represent has a million readers, which will indicate to you the notoriety that it enjoys, in France and abroad…"

"I never read newspapers," said Sir Athel, softly.

"I am sorry to hear that, Monsieur, for the press is the great educator of the world. Let's pass on! Would you be good enough to answer me one question: are you Sir Athel Random, of Highbury, London?"

"That is, indeed, my name—but before you continue your interrogation, permit me to ask you a question in my turn. Are you the man I was told to expect by Miss Mary Redmore, yes or no?"

"But I assure you…"

"Have you any information to give me regarding the man whose photograph has been sent to me? This one."

Very coldly, entirely master of himself, Sir Athel handed Labergère the photograph that the young woman had slipped into the letter whose tenor had been dictated by Bobby.

Let us recall that Labergère was attached to the *Reporter* during the Coxward/Bobby incident in Paris; his inquiries in London, with the aid of the solicitor Edwin Battleworth, had concluded with the establishment of the presence of Coxward in London on the night of April 2. Thanks to the proofs that he had gathered, the *Reporter*'s victory over its rival the *Nouvelliste* had been complete and humiliating. It was then that, although very well remunerated by the *Reporter*, Labergère—who always put business before sentiment—had gone in search of the editor of the *Nouvelliste* and had offered, for a higher salary than he could aspire to at the *Reporter*, to employ all his talents as a newshound to inflict on the aforementioned *Reporter* a revenge whose inconveniences the latter would suffer in its turn. The delicacy of the move was debatable, but it is necessary to accept the mores of certain milieux in order to evaluate them, and not to climb on the much-too-high horse of simple probity.

Now, Labergère—whose ability was undeniable and universally recognized—specialized in keeping up to date with the smallest and apparently-insignificant details of an incident, and drawing unexpected consequences therefrom. He was, besides, a man of tireless energy and well-tried courage, ready to do anything, even something generous, the moment his interests were involved.

Sir Athel presented the photograph in question to his eyes without any vestige of suspicion. Miss Mary had not told him the name of the expected visitor, so why should he not be called Labergère?

The latter looked at the portrait. Now, it is necessary to remember that he had only seen the person briefly, in the condition of a horribly-mutilated cadaver, with his eyes convulsed and his jaw broken, bearing no strong resemblance to this photograph of a living man with a brutal and bellicose physiognomy. Involuntarily, obedient to a sentiment of sincerity—regrettable in a man of his profession—he replied: "I don't know him."

"In that case, sir," said Sir Athel, getting to his feet, "I have no wish to enter into communication with you, and I beg you..."

The sentence was cut short by the loud ringing of a bell coming from inside.

Sir Athel seized Labergère by the wrist—and the seemingly-frail Englishman was, in fact, uncommonly strong. The pressure he exerted forced Labergère to get up, pushed him towards the door of the room, then outside, and compelled him to cross the courtyard. He opened the outer door, and was about to throw him out, when two cries rang out simultaneously:

"Monsieur Bobby!"

"The man from the *Reporter*!"

Bobby had recognized at the first glance the newspaperman who had mocked him so ferociously. Fists forward, he was about to throw a choice punch at him when, seeing Sir Athel, he recovered his composure. Reverting to formality, he bowed and said to the latter: "On behalf of Miss Redmore..."

Surprised by the intervention of this third party, who pronounced the "Open Sesame!" for which he was waiting, Sir Athel had released Labergère—who, rather discomfited by the adventure, propped himself up on the door-frame. He too had recognized Bobby, and felt deeply embarrassed by his unexpected appearance.

Bobby stepped in front of him with unconcealed arrogance. "Did you recognize the photograph?" he asked Sir Athel.

"Then it's you I was expecting..."

"Yes, sir! As for this fellow, I can't help wondering why I find him on your doorstep—in any case, I know that he's a villain and a traitor, and I suggest that you throw him out..."

"What's that you say!" cried Labergère. "Do you know that you're beginning to make my ears burn?"

"Monsieur," said Sir Athel, coldly, "I beg you to keep quiet. I don't know you and I have no wish to know you. You have sought to introduce yourself into my house fraudulently—I have no idea why—and I invite you to remove yourself."

"So be it!" said Labergère, who had replaced his hat on his head, nutcracker-fashion. "You have presented me with a photograph that I did not recognize; for my part, I present this to you, and hope that you will recognize it..."

He had abruptly unbuttoned his jacket, and had extracted a half-open piece of paper from the pocket of his wallet on which a commercial heading and a few lines of writing were visible.

Sir Athel looked at it, and exclaimed: "Certainly! It's a fragment of a letter..."

"Which is addressed to you, which bears your name, and which, so far as I understand it, relates to an order for chemical products...."

"That's absolutely right," said Athel, whose voice was trembling, "but how does this letter come to be in your hands? Where did you find it?"

"I shall explain it to you, Monsieur, when your courtesy has obtained the upper hand over whatever whim it was that almost led me to doubt your sanity."

Sir Athel reflected momentarily. "You're right," he said, "and I beg you to accept my excuses. Mr. Bobby, would you go into my study. As for you, Monsieur Labergère, I beg you to grant me half an hour, perhaps an hour... if you wish, you may wait in my laboratory..."

A true reporter has to set self-respect aside and never stand on formality. What did Labergère want? To talk to Sir Athel. What did an hour more or less matter?

"I am at your disposal," he said, bowing, almost politely.

Bobby—who, on due reflection, did not want to start a quarrel—went into Sir Athel's study.

The latter led the reporter to a small building situated in the middle of the garden and, ushering him into it, showed him shelves covered with a variety of flasks, bowls and jars. "In your own interests," he said, "I advise you not to touch any of these products; some are very dangerous, even including explosives, and I would be desolate were I to be the cause of another accident." He pronounced the penultimate word through clenched teeth.

"Don't worry," said Labergère, laughing heartily. "I hold my skin too precious to ignore the advice. An hour, you say? I strongly recommend that you don't abuse my patience…"

"I'll do everything possible to cut that interval short," said Sir Athel.

The two men bowed once again, and the Englishman went out.

IV. Mr. Bobby's Triumph

In the meantime, Mr. Bobby was chewing his knuckles. By what fatality did he find one of his deadly enemies on his track—a wretch who had insulted and humiliated him—at the very moment when he felt, thanks to an intuition of genius, that the Coxward affair was about to take on an entirely new form?

"Come on, Bobby!" he murmured. "Set personal rancor aside. You have a mission to fulfill; you have to rehabilitate the name that you have given to your worthy spouse. Be a man and deploy all the resources of your remarkable intelligence. Your vengeance will come later—a dish best served cold, as the poet says!"

Sir Athel came back in. Bobby bowed in a military fashion.

"Sir," the young Englishman said to him, "you present yourself under the auspices of a young woman who is dearer to me than life itself, and from whom a dreadfully tragic circumstance has constrained me to distance myself. There was a photograph enclosed with her letter..."

"Do you know that man?" incapable of keeping his impatience in check any longer.

"Can I say that I know him? Alas, I only saw him for a few seconds... and in such terrible and atrocious circumstances that it is a miracle that his features are engraved in my memory..."

"You have no idea who he is?"

"Absolutely none."

"And when did you see him?"

"Oh, that date will never be erased from my mind. It was…"

"Let me finish: the night of April 1—during the early hours of April 2."

"Oh! But how did you know that?"

Bobby made a little gesture with his head, which his swords accentuated: "What can I say? A little divination… intuition, Sir Athel, intuition! That date is exactly accurate, then?"

"Absolutely."

"And it was between 1 a.m. and 2 a.m."

"At 1:35 a.m. Yes, that was the moment that, under the impact of some frightful fatality, my entire life was smashed… that dolor, despair and remorse entered into my heart and took possession of it, never to leave again… never… never!"

The young man let his head fall into his hands.

"One moment!" said Bobby, with an authoritative gesture. "I don't know yet what has happened, but if it is for the sake of that person that you are in this state, for John Coxward—it appears that you don't know his name…"

"It's the first time I've heard it pronounced."

"For John Coxward, I say, is—or rather, was—the most worthless good-for-nothing that has ever dragged his hob-nailed boots through the London underworld…"

"Was, you say? What! So it's true that he's…"

"Dead! Utterly dead. For which it's only necessary to be moderately sorry, the incident having allowed him to escape the scaffold that was waiting for him in very short order…"

"What does that matter? He was a man, and I had no right to take his life—but tell me, how do you know that he's dead?"

"By virtue of simple observation. I recognized his corpse."

"Ah! They've found his body. Where was it?"

"At this point, sir, I beg you to summon up all your strength, for this is the heart of the matter, the crest of the mysterious slope that I am attempting to climb. The cadaver of John Coxward was found in the middle of a public square, on that same night of April 2, at 5 a.m., in Paris."

"In Paris!" cried Sir Athel, straightening himself up.

"Yes, sir—which is to say, 250 miles from here, as the crow flies. Now, from 1:35 a.m. to 5 a.m. gives us exactly three hours and 25 minutes, from which it is necessary to deduct the ten minutes that Paris is in advance of us,[4] thus three hours 15. Now, is it possible that a man, voluntarily or otherwise, could make that journey in such a short time?"

"Yes, it is possible!" Sir Athel declared. "More than that—that interval is three or four times as long as it would need to be. 250 miles, sir, is a matter of 3/4 of an hour at the most!"

It is understandable that Bobby did not interrupt. For him, the light of which he had earlier seen a faint glimmer, had grown and expanded to be blinding. "Nothing is impossible," he said, "but you must admit

---

[4] Although the modern time-zones—which set Paris time an hour in advance of London time—had been agreed as early as the International Meridian Conference of 1884, they were not universally instituted for some time thereafter, individual cities often sticking stubbornly to their own local calculations, despite the mess it made of railway timetables. The Eiffel Tower began transmitting signals determining Paris time in 1910.

that it is difficult to believe that the aforementioned John Coxward, a virtual vagabond, without a penny to his name, was in possession of such a rapid means of locomotion. Despite all the confidence you merit, you will permit me a slight doubt. In your opinion, given what you say, from 1:35 a.m., a man could not be 100 leagues from here at 5 a.m.!"

Sir Athel made an angry gesture. "But if I tell you that he could be in Paris at 2:30 a.m. at the latest..." And he added, in a softer voice: "Yes, I remember, the vriliogire [5] was orientated towards the east..."

"Vrilio...what?" cried Bobby, in an interrogative tone.

"Ah! You don't understand... you can't understand... you don't know... that the worthless creature I am is in possession of a prodigious force, with which no miracle is impossible... and that when the catastrophe in question happened, I only had a few more miserable details to set in order for that formidable energy, of which I was the master, to be revealed to the stupefied world."

"What catastrophe?" cried Bobby. Seeing the excitement that had taken possession of the young Englishman, he went on, softly: "Sir Athel, my name is Bobby, a member of His Britannic Majesty's police force. Because of the misfortune suffered by this wretch Coxward, I am in the process of being hounded out of my job—which is to say, dishonored before the entirety

---

[5] The French *vrille* signifies something spiralling or spinning, like a drill, while *giration* can be directly transcribed as gyration, so the suggestiveness of this invented word to a French reader is obvious, although Sir Athel will eventually admit to having derived the first half of the portmanteau term from a different source.

of England—and, which is even more painful for me, in the eyes of Mrs. Bobby, my worthy spouse. I have a calm and precise mind, which seeks out facts, nothing but facts... I implore you, tell when, where and how you saw the aforementioned Coxward and how he was able to accomplish the prodigy of being alive here and dead in Paris three hours later."

Sir Athel passed his hand over his brow. "You're right. In any case, my secret is choking me—and since it's already half-revealed, it would be a definite relief for me to surrender the whole of it." He began pacing up and down his study at a feverish pace. "Know, then, that by the study of rare earths..."

"What?" said Bobby, involuntarily.

"Oh, that's true—you're entirely ignorant of science. Iridium, gallium, thallium and polonium are barbarous words to you, presenting no precise meaning...."[6]

"I've heard mention of radium," said Bobby, timidly.

"Let's leave that aside... in brief, I discovered a means of condensing an astonishing, colossal amount of radiographic force into a volume of incomparable smallness and lightness." He took an object that resembled a watch from his waistcoat pocket. "Wait... look at this. I

---

[6] The term "rare earths" is nowadays narrowly applied to yttrium, scandium and the 15 lanthanides, so none of the elements named here is a rare earth in modern terms. Lermina may simply be using the phrase more loosely, but fact that the subsequent lists he gives (one of which includes yttrium) do not overlap with this one suggests that he is deliberately misusing it as a throwaway term, quite consciously and careless of the misrepresentation

would only have to make a single gesture, the push of a finger, to blast you apart instantaneously…"

Mr. Bobby recoiled slightly. He thought about Mrs. Bobby.

"Have no fear," Sir Athel went on, in a voice that was suddenly much calmer. "I'll continue. I've constructed an apparatus of aviation—that is to say, one that is heavier than air, requiring nothing from the air itself as a means of sustaining itself, acting by virtue of its own force without any external assistance, unaffected by either wind or tempest, but moving forward in the fashion of a cannonball departing its artillery piece, with the power of its innate propulsive force—which is, moreover, inexhaustible."

"That's marvelous," hazarded Bobby—who, seeing the excessive brightness of his interlocutor's eyes, wondered whether he might really be confronted by a veritable madman, whose acquaintance might perhaps become dangerous.

"It's simply beautiful," Sir Athel corrected. "So, this apparatus, still incomplete, but having almost attained perfection, was out there in the little courtyard. It comprised a simple hull of metal and wood, capable of resisting the most violent shocks. I had personally tuned up the motor—which is to say, the active part, the center, both the brain and the solar plexus of the apparatus—on the morning of the first of April. I had also set in place the vriliogire's exceedingly comfortable pilot's seat.

"I had charged the motor, installing a sufficient quantity of the generative material in the interior pockets of the hull, as well as provisions of food for several weeks—all that only took up a trivial amount of space. I had decided to depart at sunrise on April 2. To go where? I wanted to go straight up, across the sky, through space, to intoxicate myself with immensity—and, above all, to savor the inexpressible joy of having, personally and alone, definitively realized the conquest of the air...

"And then, on my return, with what pride I would have run to Miss Mary Redmore... and I would have cried out to her: 'Master of the universe, I lay myself at your feet!' Alas, Fate was lying in ambush—and the blow that it was about to deal me would, by annihilating my hopes, ruin my life forever!"

He interrupted himself and his face expressed a profound despair.

"Come, come!" said the excellent Bobby, straightforwardly. "A son of old England does not allow himself to be disheartened. Why, the man who is speaking to you, Bobby, who is not just anyone, has suffered great crises in his life—but he has always stood up straight before Fate, and he has conquered it!"

Sir Athel did not appear to have heard this heroic symphony. He continued: "I spent the day of the first of April going over certain calculations and testing certain parts of my apparatus. I had written Miss Mary a letter in which I informed her of my departure and my imminent return. Modestly, and without boasting, I informed her of the immense importance of the work that I had accomplished. And after a hasty meal—two Berthelot pills[7]—I installed myself in an armchair here, in front of

---

[7] The distinguished chemist Marcellin Berthelot published a widely-publicized prediction in *Science et Morale* (1894) that by the year 2000, organic chemists would have replaced conventional food by synthetic nutritive tablets. Lermina must have been delighted to read it, because the same idea had been

this window, gazing lovingly at the apparatus, which, in the soft moonlight, stood forth robust and elegant...

"I was slightly drowsy, lulled by my dreams of the future, when an unusual noise suddenly made me shiver. I opened my eyes and I saw the silhouette of a human form on top of the wall, beside the gate. I got up precipitately and raced outside. Alas, rapid as my movement had been, it was already too late.

"With a vigorous leap, the wildly-gesticulating man—whose face I saw clearly in the moonlight—ran towards the apparatus, whose form was reminiscent, as I should have told you, of a sedan chair. Abruptly, he opened the door and got in. 'For the sake of your life!' I cried, 'Don't move!'

"What happened? I can only form a hypothesis. Presumably the unknown man, having sat down in the seat that I had arranged in such a way that all the mechanical elements of my apparatus were within reach, set his hand at hazard on one of the levers, whose action brought fully into play the force about which I have told you...

"In brief, before I was able to intervene by any other means than warning cries of which he took no notice, I saw the superior propeller start to whir with vertiginous rapidity. The vriliogire was lifted from the ground more easily than a wisp of straw, climbed into the air with the rapidity of a mortar-shell, and disappeared into the sky, into the night, into the dark and profound immensity.

---

the central hypothesis of one his earlier scientific romances, "Maison tranquille" (in *Histoires incroyables*, 1885; tr. as "Quiet House" in the Black Coat Press anthology *The Germans on Venus*).

"It seemed to me that I had received a blow to the head. I fell down as if thunderstruck, because—understand this, Mr. Bobby!—my life, so peaceful, entirely comprised by patient study, had abruptly been turned upside-down by a double catastrophe. I had killed a man—an unknown, to be sure, but one of my human brothers..."

"Killed? Killed?" said Bobby. "He surely killed himself!"

"But wasn't it me who furnished the instrument of his death? Why had that formidable apparatus, which I alone knew how to navigate, been left in a courtyard?"

"Which could only be reached by climbing over—which is to say, by a drunkard or a madman! One does not climb over a wall, damn it—or, if you do, it's at your own risk and peril. Now, you've definitely recognized the man whose photograph I showed you..."

"Short as the time was in which I saw him, I haven't the slightest doubt... the poor fellow!"

"Rather say the wretch, the bandit! John Coxward would have been hanged, so that society might be rid of him; without meaning to, you've done him a favor, and a big one!"

"His face haunts me every night—as does the horrible scream he released when he felt himself snatched from the ground..."

"No sentimentality!" Mr. Bobby went on, in a peremptory tone. "A rogue's life, a rogue's chances! Don't waste any more pity on the fate of that villain. In your opinion, though, what happened to cause him to be found dead, hooked on the railings of a public monument in Paris—as a corpse might be found here, for instance, folded in two over the railings surrounding Nelson's column in Trafalgar Square..."[8]

"Alas, the explanation is perfectly simple. Carried off by the vriliogire, the man must have been bewildered and flabbergasted at first, not understanding what had happened. The installation having been arranged by me, and for me, I knew every detail of it and adapted myself to it without any difficulty, but the same could not be true for an intruder.

"The vertiginous speed of the flight, the noise of the propeller, perhaps the roar of the motor—which, not being controlled, must have been rotating with a frightful intensity—all in the darkness of the night, together with the natural apprehension provoked by the immense space around him, must have contributed to the panic of my victim, who tried to escape from the infernal machine..."

"And fell into the Place de la Concorde, in Paris! So Coxward really is Coxward! I have recovered my honor! Oh, Sir Athel, how grateful Mrs. Bobby will be to you! And how hard I shall come down on those stupid French journalists who have deluged me with outrages! Oh, they won't be happy, I promise you..."

Now, at this precise moment, Labergère, who had waited patiently for more than an hour—for Sir Athel's recitation had lasted rather a long time—had emerged from the room in which he had been sequestered, having decided, at whatever risk, to come in search of the man he had come to interview. He had easily found the courtyard again and spotted the door through which he had

---

[8] The foot of Nelson's column is, in fact, surrounded by the basin of a fountain, not by railings, as Mr. Bobby would surely be aware.

seen Bobby go inside, and, not to put too fine a point on it, disturbed an overly-prolonged conversation. He simply put his hand on the door-handle and opened it abruptly and opened it, at the moment when Mr. Bobby, with all the ferocious joy of anticipated revenge, was emphasizing his monologue with angry gestures.

Perceiving Labergère at this point, and finding himself once again face-to-face with one of his persecutors, Bobby rushed towards him, seized him by the cravat and began howling: "Ha, ha! Coxward wasn't Coxward! Ha! Being in London at 1 a.m., Coxward could not have been in the Place de la Concorde at 5 a.m., eh? Well, he was, Monsieur Journalist, *he was*—and I'll prove it!"

Labergère, who was rather solidly built, seized the enraged Bobby's wrists and, drawing away from him, forced him to sit down. Then, addressing himself to Sir Athel, he said: "I sincerely beg your pardon, Monsieur, but I would be grateful if the delay were not excessively prolonged. Now that you have granted an audience this imbecile, would you deign to hear me in my turn?"

Sir Athel had only been paying slight attention to this new incident. He was absorbed in thought, but had already calmed down somewhat, thanks to the information that Bobby had furnished with respect to the identity of his victim. Coxward was a bandit! The crime was transforming into an accident. "A thousand pardons, Monsieur," he said to Labergère. "But you will forgive me for having forgotten you, I suppose, by reason of the importance and the profound interest of the news that Mr. Bobby has just brought me."

And the incorrigible Bobby cried: "With regard to Coxward, you'll recall how the entire mob of French pamphleteers stamped on my toes when I maintained that the Obelisk corpse was that of Coxward. How they laughed! How they insulted the police of my country and sought to dishonor England in the humble person of her loyal citizen… Well, Monsieur, it will be necessary to recant and admit that it was you miserable scribblers who, inflicting your stupid lies on a man of good will, have committed an utterly reprehensible action, whose punishment you will bear in this world and the next…"

Labergère looked at Bobby with some astonishment. Why was the man driveling on with his story of the ubiquitous Coxward? He knew perfectly well, himself, that this simultaneity of presence as impossible, since he was the one who, as a reporter for the *Reporter*, had, on that paper's behalf, instituted and conducted the enquiry whose authenticity had been certified by the London solicitor. Now, however, as he was working for the *Nouvelliste*, he was perfectly convinced that Bobby was not mad, and that, in defiance of all plausibility, Coxward of London and the dead man in Paris really and definitely were the same man. It was permissible for him to mock the *Reporter*, his former employer, to the benefit of the *Nouvelliste*, his new employer, which still maintained a colossal rancor against it rival, and would pay dear for the right to spike its guns. He addressed himself to Sir Athel, who was seemingly indifferent to the quarrel. "It seems," he said, "that your conversation with this gentleman concerned that ridiculous Coxward affair that impassioned Paris briefly. It cannot be correct that Coxward was in Paris at 3 a.m. on April 2…"

"Alas," said Sir Athel, shivering, "it must have been considerably sooner than that…"

"So he was not in London on the evening of the first?"

"Indeed he was… I know it only too well."

"But that's impossible!"

"It might seem impossible to you," said Sir Athel, coldly, "but it's true. The unfortunate Coxward left here, from this very courtyard that you see, at 1:35 a.m…"

"Then he must have covered 350 kilometers in two hours…"[9]

"In much less than that, Monsieur."

"I don't understand!"

"It's obvious," cried Bobby, "that French ignoramuses are incapable of understanding anything. Are they familiar with the rare earths, tadium, foronium…?" The brave detective was slightly confused in his scientific nomenclature, but he continued: "And the vriliogire, Monsieur Journalist! And the electric force that will turn the world upside-down! And the journey from London to Peking in 30 minutes! Do you have he slightest inkling of any of that?"

Labergère, like all the French journalists of old, was endowed with a rapid imagination, combined with a keen facility of assimilation. "Is there an electric machine involved?" he asked Sir Athel.

"The word isn't precisely correct… a radioactive machine, in fact—but I was obliged to employ the term *electric* to be clearer…"

"And this machine," Labergère continued, "is an apparatus of aviation?"

"Indeed…"

"And it's by means of this apparatus that Coxward was able to make the journey from London to Paris? On the night of April 1 to April 2?"

"Alas, I'm only too convinced of it. That is why I have been mourning the death of a man and the destruc-

---

[9] The ebooksgratuits text has 450 kilometers in four hours, but I have altered the figures for the sake of consistency.

tion of an engine, the planning and construction of which has cost me two years of work... and which I shall probably never have the courage to reconstruct..."

"An engine..." said Labergère, who seemed violently emotional. "One more thing... approximately what form does it take?"

"That of a sentry-box or a sedan chair."

"But it's with respect to of a machine of that exact sort that I'm on a journalistic mission to London. Don't you recall that I showed you a letter, addressed to you, from a chemical company?"

"Yes! Yes!" cried Sir Athel. "Assailed by so many emotions, I'd forgotten that detail. That letter does indeed belong to me. Where did you find it, then?"

"On a waste ground in the Carrières-d'Amériques neighborhood, in Paris."

Let us explain the story attached to this new twist...

V. The Mystery of the 19th Arrondissement

The Coxward incident, amusing as it had been for the gallery of Parisian idlers—especially by reason of the epic struggle that had been joined by the two great newspapers, the *Nouvelliste* and the *Reporter*—had very quickly fallen into the dustbin of oblivion, in view of various political events that had suddenly given a new aliment to curiosity.

Blows had been exchanged in open Parliament between rather highly-placed individuals in the running for ministerial office, and scandalous rumor, always on the lookout for human weakness, had revealed that the reasons for this quarrel were less concerned with the national budget than that of a certain pleasantly plump young woman, who was playing the role of a damsel-fly with great success in a revue at the *Variétés*.

Then there had been the sensational arrest of a ministerial official who, avid for the joys of the high life, had secretly frittered away the heritages of 50 families—a rather banal affair.

Finally, let us mention a massacre on the Boulevard Ménilmontant, the marriage of an American billionairess to a penniless person with an illustrious name—and a sudden lull had descended once more on Parisian journalism, which became severely depressed. Headlines multiplied in vain, with respect to a bankruptcy or a small fire—but the public was not biting, as they say, and unsold copies piled up.

Now, the true talent of a reporter is to find an affair that is of scant importance in itself and, by methodically making a fuss about it, exaggerating its smallest details, to give it an apparent quality of strangeness that excites people. Labergère was a master of this sort of operation. Newly employed by the *Nouvelliste*, which had built him a golden bridge to tear him away from the *Reporter*, he therefore searched very actively for some event to which he might attach all the bells of publicity.

This is what he had learned:

In one of the eccentric neighborhoods on the outskirts of Paris is the Buttes-Chaumont, where, on the far side of the Place du Danube and the Hôpital Hérold, a land still empty of buildings extends to the fortifications. These fields are on top of ancient mine-workings, formerly known by the name of Carrières d'Amériques, whose exploitation has long been abandoned. Important works of filling-in and shoring-up have been undertaken at great expense, but it seems that the ground itself rests on moving foundations. From time to time, despite all the precautions taken, deep fissures open up, which are liable to cause serious accidents.[10]

A few months before, in fact, an unfortunate working girl passing through the vicinity had been surprised by one of these sudden depressions of the ground and would certainly have been engulfed if help had not reached her quickly. Even so, her salvation had only been effected at the cost of the greatest efforts; as chance would have it, she had been extracted safe and sound. In consequence of the accident, however, to avoid a repetition, the waste ground had been closed off by a wooden

---

[10] The Carrières d'Amériques were so-called because stone from the gypsum mines were used in he construction of the White House in Washington, D.C. Napoléon III had founded a park on the site, occupying a considerable portion of the Buttes-Chaumont, but not the whole.

fence, and, until new work was done to consolidate the ground, access to it had been officially prohibited.

As time had gone by, vagabonds, tramps and hooligans had made openings in this palisade and often elected to take shelter from any possible interference from the police in a place protected by both its isolation and a certain apprehension on the part of the nearest neighbors.

One morning, some children playing truant from school took it into their heads to go through the fence and had spread out over the open ground, all sand, stone and rubble, with the perfectly innocent intention of peacefully playing some game involving a ball and running around. Suddenly, horrible screams were heard, and the children fled into the street, some of them livid and semi-conscious, with contorted limbs, others merely trying to help them. They ran hither and yon, releasing inarticulate cries. Although the place was fairly deserted, passers-by came running, and a crowd soon gathered around them, lifting up those who had fallen down, seemingly prey to veritable convulsions. Others interrogated those who seemed most able-bodied.

The children replied, incoherently, that there was something out there in the waste ground: a beast, a monster, which had hurled itself upon them, clawed them, bitten them, half-devoured them...

There was certainly some exaggeration in these tales, since all of the children were still equipped with intact limbs; however, something had definitely occurred... and, although doubtless very courageous, the helpers remained outside the palisade without making any attempt to go in. Meanwhile, some affirmed, a sort of dull roaring sound could be heard behind the planks, which was not suggestive of anything good.

Fortunately, two uniformed policemen were spotted and summoned. They approached with the majestic slowness characteristic of their profession. They saw three children, between eight and 12 years old, now inert and motionless, lying on the ground. Their questions were again answered with incomprehensible explanations, in which the words "monster" and "wild beast" featured prominently.

Having blown their whistles to summon their comrades, the policemen—who now numbered four—divided themselves into two pairs, the first of which carried the children, still alive but seemingly plunged into a profound prostration, to the commissariat, while the second stood guard, swords in hand, on the opening made in the palisade.

"Suppose we take a little peep at what's inside!" said one.

"All right," said the other.

Valiantly, they squeezed their broad shoulders through the rather narrow gap.

The waste ground was a good 100 meters broad and 400 meters deep. It was uneven and undulating, with heaps of stone and sandy hillocks here and there, on which meager clumps of grass grew. In one of these places—the nearest to the street—there was a funnel-shaped hole abut a meter deep, and there they saw something bizarre and incongruous sticking out from a chaos of pebbles and clods of dry soil, like the top of a news-vendor's kiosk or a square advertising-hoarding.

The two *sergots*[11] examined it suspiciously; they had occasionally seen strongboxes, stolen by burglars,

---

[11] Lermina adds a footnote to define this word as a police officer with a rank immediately above that of *sergent*; the uni-

abandoned on waste ground in this manner, but that criminals might have stolen a tradesman's booth or a public urinal in order to transport it into this fenced-off enclosure seemed rather singular, if not incredible.

As if in expectation of an encounter with a wild animal—perhaps escaped from some menagerie—our two heroes had their weapons drawn. One of them, leaning over the edge of the funnel and stretching out his arm, touched the projecting object with the tip of his cabbage-cleaver. Suddenly, he cried out in pain, leapt up in the air to a height of a meter, and then slumped into his companion's arms.

"Hello! What's up with you, old chap?"

But the "old chap" did not reply; his arms and legs were shaken by quasi-convulsive moments. The worst of it was that the other experienced a malaise himself, whose nature he did not understand—a sort of prickling feeling in all his limbs. At the same time, bright sparks whirled before his eyes. Reflexively, he let go of his companion, who fell to he ground. Then he suddenly felt relieved—but an invincible lassitude gripped him, and he let himself fall to his knees, his head lolling forwards like that of a man struck on the head by a baton. He did not recover his senses until the moment when the Police Commissioner came through the gap in the fence, accompanied by his secretary and half a dozen uniformed policemen.

The crowd around the enclosure had grown and now, reassured by the presence of the authorities, followed them in. A handful of street-urchins made up an

---

formed police officers of the day retained the obsolete designation of "*sergents de ville*" [town sergeants], although they were the direct equivalent of English constables.

escort. The policemen, perceiving that their comrades were in a bad way, ran to help them. Scarcely had they touched them than they felt a few tremors themselves, which merely served to astonish them, with no unfortunate result.

"Come on, what's going on?" asked the official, "How did you get into that state?"

The second policeman, who had recovered the power of speech, said: "An infernal machine! There in the hole!"

Following the direction of his gesture, the Commissaire saw the roof of the kiosk—let us call it that, for the sake of clarity—surmounted by some sort of metal shaft, doubtless intended for a flag or some similar accessory.

"What's that?"

"If we only knew!" retorted the policeman. "My comrade here touched it with the tip of his sword and was knocked to the ground like my wife when she's clipped round the ear."

"But I was told there was a dangerous animal, a wild beast..."

"There's nothing but that instrument there—which must be some anarchist device."

The Commissaire shrugged his shoulders. Although perplexed, he refrained from touching the object and forbade his men to make contact with it. After all, the idea of anarchism might not be so crazy...

Now, however, a sort of intermittent purr could be heard from the interior of the booth, like that produced in the throat of an angry lion, or some enormous piece of clockwork or similar machinery. It was not continuous, proceeding in fits and starts, but was no more reassuring for that.

The policeman with the cabbage-cleaver had been reanimated by a large draught of kirsch, but was incapable of furnishing the slightest explanation as to the nature of his sensations—of which all that could be determined was that they had not been very pleasant.

What was to be done? Fortunately, the administration has principles that serve as a guide in any circumstances. In this case, the rule was quite simple: refer it to their superiors. The Commissaire, resolving to follow this precept, whose observation would relieve him of all responsibility, then set about gathering all the information necessary to make a formal statement: first of all, describing as exactly as possible the mysterious object that was lying there, half- or three-quarters-buried in stones and sand. Approaching the object with all the prudence compatible with his civic duty, the official dictated notes to his secretary.

The roof of the object, rounded and vaguely reminiscent of the form of a German helmet, was set on four metal columns, connected together by cross-pieces that seemed to be made of silver, or—more probably—of nickel. Its general form was square. This cage—the word was definitely more appropriate than "kiosk"—projected from the ground to an extent of about 80 centimeters, and the inferior part was buried therein. On cocking an ear, one could hear a noise in the interior that was rather difficult to define, as if a switch had been turned on that set a flywheel or something similar in motion.

The formal statement described, in the most punctilious manner, the bizarre phenomena that were produced when anyone touched the engine, which, in spite of his admitted incompetence, the Commissaire did not hesitate to describe as "electrical, or something similar."

One small incident occurred. One of the children roaming around the patch of land found a piece of metal in a corner, deeply embedded in the fence. It was narrow, quite long, with rounded ends: some sort of vane or fin. As he attempted to pull it out, the Commissaire forbade him to do so, considering that it was now the prerogative of a higher authority to carry forward the investigation that he had begun so intelligently.

Needless to say, the Commissaire interrogated the nearest neighbors, who were all in accord in saying—with rare unanimity—that they were absolutely ignorant as to what the machine in question might be and how it came to be on the waste ground.

We should add that after half an hour, the children and the *sergot* that had been so abominably shaken up by the incomprehensible commotion were entirely restored to normality.

A carpenter was requisitioned to block up the holes in the fence. One policeman was placed on sentry-duty and all the rest went blithely about their business, the formal statement making its way in a leisurely fashion to the prefecture—where perhaps, in view of the quite anodyne nature of the adventure, it would doubtless have been laid peacefully to rest in box number 7 or file number 23... but that left out of account our friend Labergère, who, as we have explained, was in search of a sensational affair. Like King Richard III of Shakespearean memory, he would gladly have given his horse, or his automobile, for a three-headed calf or a cataclysm in Nogent-sur-Marne.[12] Now, having his means of ferret-

<hr>

[12] Lermina, whose many writings included translations of Shakespeare, knew perfectly well that the luckless Richard

ing—to use his own expression—well-organized, he had been one of the first to learn about the strange affair of the Rue des Carrières-d'Amériques, and his reporter's blood soon came to the boil. It might be nothing at all, but—from the very first moment—he told himself that it might become something...

He certainly did not suspect that it was the beginning of the most terrible, stupefying and extraordinary ordeal to which the city of Paris had ever been subjected. Perhaps, had he been able to see into the future, he would have recoiled before the frightful events that he was about to unleash. But no! Professional duty above all! The *Nouvelliste* paid very well; he had to do what was necessary to earn his money.

The following day, he flaunted this headline:

A sinister phenomenon in the heart of Paris
Three children electrocuted
A policeman struck down

He recounted, in the most emotive terms, the discovery of the infernal engine and the first catastrophes it had caused, and concluded with this virulent criticism:

Twelve hours have already passed, and we regret to observe that the administration has not taken any steps to ward off the very real danger that the population is running. We are entitled to demand whether it is not in circumstances such as these that the Municipal Laboratory ought to prove its usefulness, so often contestable.

Naturally, the *Reporter*, exasperated by the defection of its senior news-editor, hastened to enter the arena:

---

had offered his kingdom *for* a horse, and would not have found any use for a three-headed calf.

Certain newspapers, short of new sensations, are making a lot of noise about a matter of no importance. We affirm that it is merely a matter of some physical apparatus, electrical machine or Leyden jar that burglars have abandoned on waste ground. A few electric sparks have been produced, causing more emotion than genuine pain...

Ah! His former employers were entering the lists! Labergère would have some fun. He was the top dog and he would prove it to them. The following issue of the *Nouvelliste* marched straight ahead:

The hoarse barking of a press that has lost its voice will not prevent us from pursuing our task. We have called attention to an unknown, mysterious danger whose effects have, until now, defied all analysis. And we are not intimidated by accusations of exaggeration.

It will be remembered that we reported the discovery yesterday of a strange engine—some sort of electrical, or perhaps radiographic, apparatus—found on waste ground on the far side of the 19th arrondissement, which almost cost the lives of innocent children and a brave defender of public order. We have received news of these victims this morning, and we have learned that their condition, although satisfactory, gives rise nevertheless to cause for alarm. The inmates at the Hôpital Hérold that we have been able to question have spoken about the details of the event. All agree in declaring that scarcely had they touched the engine in question when they experienced a violent commotion—like a whiplash in the marrow-bone, as one of the children said, or like a rabbit-punch on the neck, as the policeman put it. Sparks burst forth before their eyes, at the same time as a feeling of numbness paralyzed their limbs.

It is obvious that these are effects of an electrical nature and that we find ourselves in the presence of an unknown apparatus, giving off radiations whose effect is reminiscent of those of the most powerful batteries. We were too hasty, moreover, in criticizing the administration by reproaching it for its incuriosity. This morning, Monsieur Lépine—who never spares his activity or his fatigue—accompanied by Monsieur Loustalot, the head of the Municipal Laboratory and his assistants, went to the waste ground in the Rue des Carrières-d'Amériques. A considerable crowd was already obstructing the streets neighboring the designated spot and it was necessary to take considerable measures to restrain it.

A rumor had gone around that the engine in question—which has an approximate capacity of two cubic meters (the part embedded in the soil does not permit a more exact calculation)—was probably full of explosive materials, which might blow up at the least-expected moment and lay waste to the entire neighborhood. Already, tenants were leaving their houses, taking their furniture with them, miserable refugees—for the quarter is one of the poorest in Paris.

When the police succeeded in clearing a passage through the crowd for our courageous Prefect, everyone took off their hats respectfully. Monsieur Lépine, in a suit and bowler hat, maintained, as usual, a very calm expression, with a slightly skeptical smile on his lips. He has seen it many times before. His calm courage was already reassuring for the groups of curiosity-seekers, and it required a great deal of effort to prevent them from surging forward through the gap opened in the fence. A few of those energetic words of which our prefect has the secret were necessary to prevent a veritable invasion. Flanked by a dozen policemen, however, Mon-

sieur Lépine, Monsieur Loustalot and the employees of the Municipal Laboratory were left alone in the vast enclosure.

They immediately gathered around the engine. One of the policemen, who had been one of the first to go in and examine the mysterious engine the day before, declared that, in his opinion, it had changed its position slightly. It had, he affirmed, rotated slightly on its axis and was buried a few centimeters deeper.

The first necessity was to establish whether the electrical effects observed the previous day were still being produced. Monsieur Loustalot had insulating apparatus distributed which, it was explained, would, if necessary, fulfill the role of lightning-rods and—sustaining the electricity, as it were—if the engine really were saturated with it, would force it to discharge into the ground. These preparations lasted rather a long time. The impatience of the public was increasing by the minute. In spite of the efforts of the agents, people climbed up the planks of the fence, above which hundreds of heads appeared.

Monsieur Lépine conferred briefly with Monsieur Loustalot, who refused to admit that there was any real danger. In any case, he concluded, we were in the process of facing it. "Go on, then," said the Prefect, who is of the first rank, with his customary bravado. Monsieur Loustalot then summoned one of his assistants, who approached, armed with a long metal rod, which a rubber glove prevented from coming into contact with his skin. After making sure that the earthing apparatus was working perfectly, he brought the metal rod into contact with the roof of the engine.

At that moment, there was a terrible detonation, like that of a small caliber cannon; at the same time, a flame *several meters long whistled through the air, making a fearful din. Despite the insulating material that was protecting him, the unfortunate electrician was hurled into the air to a height of two meters and fell back on Monsieur Lépine—who, braced on his legs, fearless and unyielding, caught him in his arms and broke his fall.*

A horrified clamor had greeted this incomprehensible phenomenon, and within a second, the fence was devoid of spectators, who were fleeing in all directions releasing screams of terror. Fortunately, the electrician, who was named Dargent (Emile), was more frightened than hurt. A brief faint having followed his fall, a cordial and a few inhalations of oxygen had put an end to the malaise caused by his shake-up. In view of what had occurred, it was obvious that there would be grave dangers in carrying out an experiment in such conditions. Besides, Monsieur Loustalot—despite his indisputable competence—seemed to be at a loss, and repeated these discouraged words: "I don't understand! I don't understand! What shall we do?"

The Prefect, however, still smiling and satisfied that the event had not had more tragic consequences, quickly took the necessary measures, with his habitual initiative. "What shall we do?" he replied to Monsieur Loustalot. "It's quite simple—nothing at all! This experiment suffices to demonstrate that it would be perilous to persist any longer. We don't believe in the supernatural, do we? Thus, there's nothing diabolical in this. We have enough scientists in Paris for this petty problem to be swiftly resolved. It's merely a matter of protecting the population from its own imprudence. After that, we'll see."

Indeed, soldiers arrived an hour later and sealed up all the means of access to the waste ground in question. Monsieur Lépine went to the Ministry of the Interior and gave an account of his preliminary investigation to the minister. A commission was immediately appointed, under the presidency of Monsieur Poincaré,[13] and composed of the most eminent members of the Académie des Sciences and the Conservatoire des Arts et Métiers.

In any case, it is opportune to remind the jokers of the press that it is far from being an electrical machine or a Leyden jar (!!!) abandoned by burglars. Perhaps our colleagues, skeptical as they are, will deign to recognize that the matter, whose strangeness we were the first to point out, is worth more than a few lines of trivial buffoonery in rather bad taste.

The effect produced in Paris by this sensational article is easily imaginable. The great city delighted in the collective panic. A breath of anxiety passed through it, circulating in concierges' lodges and the drawing rooms of high society alike. People began to be afraid. One ultra-pessimistic newspaper did not hesitate to accuse the anarchists and nihilists of preparing a monstrous assault on Paris, whose annihilation had been decided a long time ago.

There was already talk of deserting the town houses, and business was disturbed. An official note appeared, with the excellent intention of putting minds to rest, but had, as always, a directly opposite effect. At the same time—by virtue of a very human contradiction—all Paris set of for the Buttes-Chaumont, the Rue Main and the Boulevard Sérurier, where the wine-shops were making a fortune. The fortifications entered into competition with the boulevards and the Bois de Boulogne.

An initial visit by the commission had taken place, but without shedding any new light on the mater—

---

[13] The eminent mathematician Henri Poincaré (1854-1912).

except that, once again, the apparatus was embedded a little more deeply in the ground, and it was observed, not without renewed anxiety, that the surrounding terrain seemed to be disintegrating progressively.

Naturally, the reporter Labergère, who had means of getting in everywhere and was always in search of ways of insinuating himself into the most private places, had mingled with the members of the commission. While those gentlemen were exercising their ministry, grouped around the electric booth, he wandered back and forth, attentively examining the various depressions in the ground, searching for some clue that might provide his initiative with a new direction. It was in this way that he found, first a second and then a third vane of the propeller, which proved beyond a doubt that they were in the presence of some kind of locomotory apparatus, presumably a new kind of automobile that an inventor had tried out in inauspicious circumstances. That required verification. But there was more wooden debris in a hollow in the sand, bearing the remains of a lock, which evidently came from some kind of strong-box. Labergère, who missed nothing, found a piece of paper nearby which, doubtless by chance, a fragment of stone had pinned to the ground. That piece of paper was a fragment of a letter, bearing the heading of Lorell and Son of London. The address of the recipient was also there: Sir Athel Random, Corsica Street, Highbury, London NW…

And it was these various circumstances that the *Nouvelliste*'s reporter now disclosed to Sir Athel in the house in Corsica Street, in the presence of Bobby, the honorary detective. The explanations did not take long.

Sir Athel did not hesitate. Yes, the mysterious apparatus in Paris was none other than the marvelous vriliogire, and its crash in waste ground in the 19th arrondissement was the natural consequence of the terrible imprudence of Coxward. As for the danger that the Parisians might be running, Sir Athel drew no firm conclusion—but it was easy to divine, from his feverish expression, that he was not as confident as he wanted to appear. "Yes, yes," he murmured, striding back and forth in his study, "there's more than 50 grams there, the propulsive force is enormous. If piston A were to come into contact with reservoir D... that would be frightful."

"Come on, come on," Labergère interrupted. "Let's talk briefly, but to the point. You admit that, because of you—or rather your inventive genius—an entire neighborhood of Paris is in peril. Your duty is clear; it's necessary to repair the harm that you've done! It's necessary to prevent any new catastrophe from occurring."

"You're right!" cried Sir Athel. "What good does it do to wonder what the effects of vrilium might be...?"

"What did you say?"

"Oh, sorry—you don't know. I said *vrilium*—that's the name I've given to the substance that I've discovered, whose power is incalculable. So, the first necessity is to leave for Paris..."

"That's what I expected. How shall we get there? Have you some new apparatus here, be it moved by fire or the Devil, that can take us there?"

"Alas, the experimental apparatus—the only one I possessed—is already over there..."

"Good! It's therefore necessary for us to use ordinary means, like mere mortals. What time is it? Quarter past one. There's a train via Boulogne at 2:20 p.m. that arrives in Paris at 9 p.m. That's perfect! Let's be off. Are you ready?"

"Yes. Just give me five minutes—time to collect certain substances whose usage is indispensable to the operations I need to carry out..." Quickly, he opened a cupboard built into the wall, seemingly armored like the hull of a battleship. He selected three metal vials, which he put in his pockets. "Oh, presumably you haven't eaten?"

"Certainly not," said Labergère. "In our business, one makes what provision what one can."

Sir Athel presented him with a little golden box reminiscent of a snuff-box. "Take one of those capsules," he said.

"What are they?"

"Berthelot pills. With one of these capsules, you'll be nourished for more than 24 hours."

"Chemical nourishment! Hmm! I suppose I'd be spared the need for a good supper when we arrive."

"I'd like a pill too," said Bobby, timidly. Since hearing Labergère's story, he felt himself to be in a state of manifest inferiority.

"Bah!" said the reporter. "You'll dine better at home, my brave detective."

"But...but I certainly intend to go with you!"

"You!" cried Sir Athel. "What good would that do?"

"What! What good?" cried Bobby, drawing himself up to his full height. "But who has the greatest interest in all this? Monsieur Labergère, have you forgotten that the name of Bobby has be dishonored, and that it was you—yes, you—who poured universal scorn on the British police and its modest representative? I wish you were dead, I don't hide that from you—however, I'm ready to extend my hand to you, honestly, if you are willing to declare yourself, no less honestly, ready to admit publicly that Coxward really was Coxward…"

"But of course, my friend!" said Labergère, in his turn, presenting his open right hand. "That's perfectly natural… and I offer you all my apologies!"

"Ah, that's most satisfactory… it's enough for me that Mrs. Bobby will finally be able to lift up her head…"

"As high as she might wish. So you want to come back to Paris, brave Bobby—as you wish! Sir Athel, give the good detective a pill and let's not lose any more time. Let's not forget that we have to cross the whole of London to get to Charing Cross."

"There's the Underground," said Bobby. "We'll arrive in time to telegraph from the station—I'll have to inform Mrs. Bobby of my departure."

"Quite right."

"Me too," said Sir Athel. "I must reassure Miss Redmore…"

"As if I didn't have to telegraph myself," added Labergère. "The *Nouvelliste* will have a headline this evening that will be anything but small, and the *Reporter* will explode with rage!"

And as soon as the house in Corsica Street was locked up, the three men launched themselves at a run towards Islington Station.

VI. The Nouvelliste's Revenge

To tell the truth, Paris did not—to use the popular expression—go overboard, because new phenomena had occurred.

On the previous night, a peculiar glow had been seen from the apparatus, which was becoming more deeply buried with every passing minute, and from which an inexhaustible source of electricity seemed to be emitting radiation continuously.

The newspapers were in a fever. Naturally, those hostile to progress were clamoring about the bankruptcy of science. What was the Commission doing, which nurtured all our academic notorieties in its bosom and was in permanent session?

In fact, it seemed that the discussions were degenerating into futile and incoherent chatter. Only the illustrious Monsieur Verloret—the king of aviation, as he had been nicknamed since his invention of the wheeled parachute—had offered an opinion sufficiently reasonable to win general support. According to him, the Ménilmontant apparatus was some sort of helicopter, based on the principle proposed to the Académie des Sciences in 1784 by Launay and Bienvenu, which Pénaud had taken up again in 1870, using a rubber band.[14] He also recalled the magnificent experiments of

---

[14] Alphonse Pénaud's model helicopter—one of several constructed in the wake of the coining of the French word *hélicoptère* by Gustave Ponton d'Amecourt in 1861—was indeed powered by a twisted rubbed band. Christophe de Launay and

Monsieur Marey with his mechanical insects.[15] Everything indicated that they were in the presence of an apparatus of that sort, the proof of the hypothesis being confirmed by the vanes of the rotor-blades that had been discovered on the waste ground.

With that first point seemingly established, Monsieur Verloret passed on to the question of the motor, whose power appeared to be enormous, and which was very probably powered by electricity.

"Right," replied Monsieur Alavoine, the brilliant regenerator of automobilism. "That's an established fact—but it doesn't need a great scholar to formulate a hypothesis that no one would dream of opposing. An electric motor, fine—but how can it be that the motor isn't yet exhausted? How can we explain its continuous action, which, at the present moment, is even affecting the ground into which the apparatus is threatening to disappear, as if some invisible mechanism were acting as an agent of perforation? Who among us knows of a battery of such power, perpetual in its effect? The honorable Monsieur Verloret's explanation is nothing but one question added to another. Electricity, agreed—but what's the source of that electricity? How can we shut it off? That's the problem we're here to solve, and we don't seem to have made any progress at all towards that solution."

---

his mechanic Bienvenu had first demonstrated the principle in the place and year indicated.

[15] Etienne-Jules Marey (1830-1904) was one of the most important pioneers of aviation; he conducted a long and intensive study of insect flight and built models to demonstrate its principles in his lecturers at the Collège de France from 1867 onwards.

With that pessimistic remark, the discussion had turned nasty, and barbed observations had liberally spiced the arguments, which quickly degenerated into personal quarrels. Two of the illustrious bald-heads even seemed ready to grab hold of what was left of one another's hair. The serious newspaper *Le Temps*, appearing at 5 p.m., could not resist the temptation, in offering a humorous account of this momentous session, to conclude its witty article with the proverbial sentence; "And that's why your daughter is dumb."[16]

Paris would have liked to make merry, but in truth, a strange anxiety reigned. A veritable malaise clutched people's breasts, and the jokes froze on their lips. To be sure, the terraces of the cafés were full, but the sterling insouciance that makes the atmosphere of our country so light and sweet was missing. Conversationalists suddenly fell silent, as if they had heard some menacing rumor coming from an unspecifiable distance. There was something in the air reminiscent of the days of the siege of Paris. The mysterious and inexplicable character of the event reawakened a sort of fearful mysticism in the depths of the soul. A sense of superstitious doubt exists in every one of us.

The *Reporter* was the next to appear, at about 6 p.m. It was prolix in giving details of the day's incidents marking the slow but inexorable labor that seemed to be

---

[16] The quoted line concludes a speech in Molière's *Le Médécin malgré lui* (1666), delivered by a woodcutter forced to pose as a physician and called upon to offer a diagnosis. The speech is pure gobbledygook, spiced with random Latin words in the hope of making it sound learned, and its climactic *non sequitur* was widely adopted in France as an insulting response to incomprehensible and allegedly-nonsensical arguments.

going on within the mysterious apparatus and the ground into which it was burrowing. The famous commission, of course, had vituperated at will. Our scientists are dressed, as they say, in cheap paper, and these virulent criticisms were not designed to reassure the public. Parisians had been much bolder in anticipating the passage of Halley's comet—which, in the end, had been no more spectacular than a magnificent *aurora borealis*. Here, the danger seemed somehow more imminent and more tangible. Everyone had an idea, always impracticable, about the means of putting an end to it. It was necessary to fetch a cannon and pulverize the apparatus, or to bring tons of material and bury it. All well and good—but who could guarantee that the impact of a shell or the crushing weight of stones or sand would not provoke a terrible explosion?

The *Reporter* had no success, and even though it had affected at the end of its article, to adopt a tone of mocking humor, there was a ripple of irritation in the crowd which manifested itself in the worst acts of violence against the innocent paper, of which a public burning was held at the Carrefour Montmartre.

As the *Nouvelliste* was slightly delayed, compact groups gathered in front of the green-painted offices that the paper had built at the corner of the Rue Drouot. There was shouting, veritable vociferations. No one knows what caprices might grip crowds; already enraged, they threw things at the glass frames to which the newspaper was ordinarily attached, and broke them with thrusts of walking-sticks. Fists were raised at the enormous window on the second floor, which usually served to display sensational news, and which remained immaculate.

Suddenly a magnesium flare illuminated the façade; it was 7:30 p.m. and the light was fading. At the same time, all the electric lamps lit up, and large black letters appeared on the white background of the display-window.

Amid frenetic acclamations, the crowd read:

SAVED!!!

The Mystery is solved!

All danger will be averted tonight.

In a quarter of an hour, THE NOUVELLISTE *will tell the whole truth!*

COXWARD WAS INDEED COXWARD!

On the boulevard, at the moment when the vendors appeared, there was a veritable riot, in which atavistic savagery emerged more than once. The papers were literally ripped from the vendors' hands; people fought over them; whole bundles were scattered on the ground, on which people descended, tearing them apart with impatient fingernails—but what did well-paid newsvendors matter to a paper that was recovering all its popularity at a stroke and delivering a knock-down blow to the *Reporter*, after which it would have difficulty getting up again? It was, moreover, to increase the force of that blow that the *Nouvelliste* had delayed its appearance, although it had been in possession of Labergère's dispatch—which he had sent from London and which featured in large print on the paper's front page—for three hours.

It was conceived thus:

I have discovered the key to the mystery. The apparatus in question is an aviation engine powered by a newly-invented battery of incredible power. The inventor, whose name is Sir Athel Random, is leaving at this very moment for Paris, where we shall arrive this even-

ing, accompanied by Monsieur Bobby, the English detective who was so roundly vilified by certain of our colleagues and who, in recognizing the dead man of the Obelisk as the boxer Coxward, told the exact truth. Coxward had traveled from London to Paris in an hour by means of Random's apparatus, to which he has given the name of vriliogire.

All explanations and proofs will be given by the inventor, who will appear before the scientific commission this evening, if it will deign to reconvene. An hour later, the apparatus will have been neutralized. There is no more cause for anxiety. Paris is in no danger.

After half a centimeter of blank space, there was a further dispatch:

Will arrive in Paris at 9:15 p.m. LABERGÈRE.

VII. The Marvels of Vrilium

Before being sent on to the newspaper, these dispatches—as is the custom in our country, where censorship has been abolished—had been sent to the Ministry of the Interior. Their contents had been communicated, also according to custom, to the Prefecture of Police and, in anticipation of a considerable influx of curiosity-seekers at the Gare du Nord to greet the arrival of the liberators of Paris, significant measures had been taken.

That was merely a precaution, however, for the train stopped at Pantin before reaching Paris and the three travelers were requested, with exquisite politeness, to get off. Labergère recognized Monsieur Lépine—as had Bobby, who had quivered from top to toe, indignantly remembering the expulsion order served upon him and Mrs. Bobby. As for Sir Athel, he was too English and too aristocratic to allow the slightest sign of astonishment to show.

The Prefect explained himself with the utmost courtesy. He had a polite word for Bobby and explained to Sir Athel that the measures taken in this regard were solely dictated by a respectful concern for public order. He briefly described to them the feverish state in which Paris found itself, and the emotion and hope that their arrival was generating.

"I appeal to Monsieur Labergère," he added. "He can tell you that in these moments of panic it is very difficult to maintain crowds in a condition of calm rationality. I therefore thought it better to shield you, at least temporarily, from the excessive enthusiasm of our populace. If you would care to, we shall go directly to the offices of the Minister of the Interior. There, you will find the scientific commission that has been appointed by reason of the anticipated angers, and he will be able to ask you to explain in all sincerity the nature of the engine that is causing us so much anxiety, the manner in which it arrived here, and, finally, the measures that must be taken to avoid any further complication."

"I am entirely at your disposal, Monsieur," said Sir Athel, "and that of the authorities. Although the damage that has been done is absolutely no fault of mine, I know that I alone can repair it. I understand too that I need to explain as clearly and briefly as possible what I have accomplished, knowing in advance that I shall encounter a certain skepticism—which, I hope, will be easily overcome."

"May I be permitted to accompany Sir Athel?" asked Labergère.

"Certainly. You will be able to furnish useful information."

"I suppose," Mr. Bobby said in his turn, "that there is no viable reason to exclude the loyal and faithful citizen of His Britannic Majesty that I am, and who, I say with some bitterness, has certain justified grievances against the French government…"

"Given that the brave Mr. Bobby's adventure is intimately linked to that of Sir Athel's engine," added Labergère, laughing.

"How?"

"In fact," said Sir Athel, "the engine is an aviation apparatus—and it was by that means that a certain Coxward was transported to Paris…"

"My Coxward!" Bobby emphasized.

"Very well, very well," said the Prefect. "I don't entirely understand, but you'll explain soon enough. It's as well that all the interested parties are heard. At least the commission will be able to come to a decision in full knowledge of the facts…"

"Just give me a few minutes to telephone my paper," Labergère said, "and I'm all yours."

"Do it as quickly as possible. The automobile is here to take us directly to the Place Beauvau."

A few minutes later, the car was traveling at top speed in the direction of Paris. Ten o'clock was sounding at the moment when it stopped in front of the ministry steps. An official was waiting, who greeted the new arrivals and immediately led them to the corridor outside the Minister's office.

"Permit me to go in first," said the Prefect. "Don't worry—you won't have to wait long."

He went in. The Minister got up and hastened to meet him. "I've been waiting for you impatiently, my dear Prefect. I hear that the agitation's increasing by the minute, and everyone knows what our brave Parisians are capable of in the grip of passion, when a little fear is added to the mix. Is your Englishman here?"

"Yes, and I admit that his appearance seems trustworthy. A man of the world, certainly, and, to judge by his physiognomy, exceptional intelligence. His eyes will strike you, as they did me."

"And he knows what this wretched mechanism is, which is giving us so much trouble?"

"Certainly, since he claims to have invented it. I've also brought the reporter Labergère…"

"An old acquaintance. With that one, one must be very economical with one's trust."

"Unless he has an interest in telling the truth—and I think that's the case here. I'll also introduce Monsieur Bobby to you."

"Who's Monsieur Bobby?"

"Does Monsieur le Ministre not remember a certain English detective who almost turned Paris upside down by affirming that the dead man at the Obelisk, found in the Place de la Concorde at 5 a.m., was someone named Coxward, who had been seen in London at one o'clock?"

"Yes, yes—he caused a scandal in support of his lie."

"Which wasn't one!"

"You mean..."

"Monsieur le Ministre will hear Sir Athel Random and understand everything. We're not immersed in the depths of mystery but those of scientific strangeness—I believe that we shall even astonish the gentlemen of the commission..."

"So be it! As long as your intelligent Englishman can deliver us from our nightmare..."

"Don't you want to talk to Sir Athel first?"

"What for? He'd have to repeat to the commission explanations he'd already given me—let's not waste time. I'll go to the commission myself and issue a reprimand before the appearance of our fellows, for the barometer's a little on the stormy side. You'll be summoned in five minutes, at the latest."

The Prefect went back to Sir Athel, who was still grave and pensive, and had not exchanged a single word with his two companions. Shortly afterwards, a door opened and an usher appeared, saying in a loud voice: "Monsieur le Préfet de Police and the persons accompanying him."

The Prefect put his hand on Sir Athel's arm and took him in to the hall where the commission was seated, in the customary ritual manner—which is to say, around a long table covered with a green cloth.

Labergère and Bobby followed close behind.

At a sign from the president, the usher showed them to the seats reserved for them. The Prefect was at one end of the table; the Minister remained at the other, mingling with the members of the commission.

The president began speaking. "Monsieur le Préfet," he said, "it's at your request that we have been urgently recalled. We would be very grateful if you would care to tell us the reasons for this convocation; be certain that we shall listen to you with the keenest interest."

"I am only here in an introductory capacity," said Monsieur Lépine. "I therefore have the honor of presenting to you Sir Athel Random, an English subject, who will furnish you with precise explanations regarding the facts that have excited Paris so violently—and also Messieurs Labergère, reporter for the *Nouvelliste* newspaper, and Bobby, employee of the British police, both of whom will corroborate the details proffered by Sir Athel."

It ought to be mentioned that Monsieur Poincaré, finding himself unable to attend at the last minute, had delegated the presidency to the doyen of the commission, the respectable Monsieur Alavoine, whose broad and ruddy face was expanded by two enormous sets of white side-whiskers, reminiscent of fins. "Monsieur Random," he said to the Englishman, "we are listening."

Sir Athel got up.

We have said that the young Englishman was rather tall and very slim with symmetrical features lit by two black eyes of a remarkable intensity. What was most striking about him, after the development of his intellectual forehead—which recalled that of Victor Hugo—was the exquisite distinction of his entire character: the delicacy of his hands, the sobriety of his gestures and, as soon as he spoke, the harmonious sonority of a voice that was both very masculine and very captivating.

It was without any embarrassment that he replied: "Gentlemen, according to what I have been told, it appears that Paris is anxious about a singular apparatus that has fallen in an uninhabited area on the outskirts of one of the suburbs, and which it has so far been impossible to approach. This apparatus, insofar as can be determined, in view of its partial burial in the ground, has a form somewhat reminiscent of one of your newspaper kiosks or a sentry-box such as I have seen at the entrances to your barracks. In addition, the debris of a metallic propeller has been found some distance away from the engine..."

"That's correct. Can you tell us what this engine is and where it came from?"

"Nothing simpler," Sir Athel said, softly. "The engine is an aircar constructed on heavier-than-air principles, which differs from airplanes in that it has neither wings nor a rudder, that it is entirely metallic and is uninfluenced by wind or atmospheric turbulence."

"A sort of helicopter," Monsieur Verloret hastened to ask, with a challenging glance at his contradictor, Alavoine.

"If you please," said Sir Athel, "I'm giving you these details in order to convince you that I know the apparatus in question, because I'm the one who built it."

"You're a mechanic?" asked Monsieur Alavoine, with a slightly disdainful expression.

"I'll introduce myself. I am Sir Athel Random, a pupil and modest colleague of William Crookes, the president of the Royal Scientific Society of London.[17] If it is of any interest to you, I can list the titles and diplomas conferred on me by the most important scientific Institutions in Great Britain. Perhaps you might even remember a certain paper on the rare earths that I had the honor of reading, and which your late colleague Monsieur Berthelot was kind enough to eulogize in terms in terms which, I confess, would have made anyone proud."

"Why yes, I remember it quite well!" said a hoarse voice. "The paper has been published in the *Journal des Savants*. It's quite remarkable."

"Thank you," said Sir Athel. "I'll return to the issue that is before us. This apparatus is, in reality, quite simple. What differentiates it from those that have been constructed hitherto is that it has two propellers, one on top and the other beneath. They are operated by a driveshaft, a simple metal rod, which is itself obedient to a motor of very small dimensions. It is steered by a system that tilts one or other of the propellers, according to the operator's wishes.

"My intention was not to make the first and definitive trial of this new kind of flying-machine until the end of the present month. I would certainly have called in on Paris, but that would only have been a stage, my well-laid plan comprising a tour of the world, going via Rus-

---

[17] I have translated this reference as it is given rather than substituting "the Royal Society;" Sir William Crookes was only elected president of the Royal Society in 1913, so this reference must have been freshly inserted into the Tallandier edition rather than being carried forward from one earlier serial version of the story.

sia, Siberia, China and Japan and returning via North America…"

He paused momentarily. The members of the commission were beginning to show unequivocal signs of impatient incredulity. The minister wondered whether he might not be the victim of some extravagant hoax or the monomania of a madman—but the Prefect, who was more accustomed to the improbable—and who, it must be said, found Sir Athel's physiognomy very reassuring—signaled that he should continue.

Sir Athel, still very cool, resumed speaking as if he were lecturing on the simplest matters in the world. "I understand, gentlemen, that my assertions might, on first hearing, appear to be tainted by exaggeration. I beg you to believe that I have not said a single word that is not the expression of the most absolute truth; I shall, besides, have the honor of giving you definitive proof…"

"Just one observation," said the illustrious Alavoine. "You mentioned a motor. What is it? And what do you use as fuel?"

"That's what I'm about to explain to you—but permit me to resume my discourse according to the plan that I've mapped out. The question that interests you most is knowing how this apparatus, which was in the courtyard of my house in Corsica Street, in the London suburb of Highbury, at 1 a.m. on April 2, ended up in a field in your capital. This is what happened…"

Very succinctly, he recounted the story with which we are familiar: the sudden appearance of an unknown man; the instantaneous departure; the theft; the disappearance.

"The unfortunate man, whose fate I regret, was carried off at vertiginous speed; he had evidently activated the motor, unknowingly, without any idea of how to moderate it or steer. He was lifted up to a height I estimate at 2000 or 3999 meters. The motor was orientated to the east. He headed straight towards France.

"I suppose—for here I am reduced to hypothesis—that once the initial bewilderment had passed, the unfortunate panicked, and tried to escape from the cage in which he had involuntarily imprisoned himself. What did he do? Which mechanism did he activate? I shall only know that myself when I've examined the apparatus carefully. I strongly suspect that he did something to the upper propeller, in which case the descent must have been abrupt. The man, losing his balance, then fell into the center of your city and his cadaver, from what I have heard, was found at the foot of one of your public monuments...

"As for the apparatus, it seems probable to me that, under the impulsion of the unstopped motor, it made a prodigious leap—but, its equilibrium being lost, it crashed in the spot where it has been found, having dug into the Earth as if to excavate a passage. I found out yesterday that the unfortunate victim of his imprudence was a man named John Coxward, whose identity was difficult to establish because of the proximity of times that rendered his near-simultaneous presence in two places distant from one another improbable. In any case, Mr. Bobby will be able to give you precise explanations, which will be supported by the testimony of Monsieur Labergère."

The members of the commission were deeply perplexed. The whole story had been related in a serious manner that seemed, despite their perplexity, to exclude any possibility of a practical joke. Scientifically, however, it did not stand up, and our illustrious scientists dreaded nothing more than being victims of a hoax that would have tarnished the reputation of the noble Académies they represented.

They listened to Bobby and Labergère. Their stories, very solemn on the part of the English detective—who dwelt for longer than was reasonable on the unmerited humiliation that the Coxward affair had inflicted upon him—and, by contrast, very free and easy on the part of the reporter, who was delighted with the adventure, troubled the commission but did not convince them. The fear of ridicule had the upper hand.

"Far be it from us, Sir Athel," said the president, after consulting his colleagues, "to doubt your word—but you will understand that very grave issues are at stake. You have told us that you are able to extract and remove, or at least neutralize, the dangerous apparatus about which the city of Paris has every right to be anxious, but before authorizing you to make an attempt that might well put your own life in peril and, at the same time, compromise the security of an entire neighborhood of Paris, it seems to us that some further information is required. You mention a motor of very small volume, whose power is capable of activating a machine for days, weeks, perhaps months…"

"You might say years," Sir Athel corrected.

"Without being recharged?"

"Exactly."

"You admit yourself that this is a circumstance so exceptional, so contrary to all that experience has so far revealed to us, that it might be described as miraculous…"

"There is no miracle involved," Sir Athel interrupted. "It seems no stranger to me than the banal occurrence that takes place in a glass jar when two invisible gases, hydrogen and oxygen, produce water under the influence of an electrical discharge."

Monsieur Alavoine coughed; this diabolical fellow had an answer for everything. "Be that as it may, you will doubtless not find it astonishing, Monsieur, that we should ask you what, in broad terms, is the nature and mechanism of your motor, and what substance fuels it."

"I fear that my explanations might seem a trifle lengthy," said Sir Athel, "given that you must be very impatient to put an end to your city's anguish; however, it is not for me to refuse your request. My motor is not fuelled by any substance, for it is the substance itself that produces movement by its own action. It has a colossal force, for a milligram would suffice to pulverize the building in which we are sitting. It is virtually inexhaustible, for its diminution in action in of the order of one ten-millionth of a gram per 24 hours."

Despite their patience, the members of the commission allowed a few incredulous "ohs" and "ahs" to escape.

For the first time, Sir Athel smiled. "If you care to put at my disposal a large block of some mineral, such as sandstone, or a marble object, I shall permit myself to demonstrate to you—without any danger to anyone, of course—one of the effects of the matter of which my motor is composed."

There was a moment's hesitation; the offer was tempting. Everyone, young or old, loves experiments; they always have a theatrical element. In the middle of the green table there happened to be an enormous marble inkwell weighing at least three kilos, whose specialty was never containing ink.

"Let's get it over with," said Monsieur Alavoine. "Exercise your power"—the word was pronounced with a strong inflection of irony—"on that block of marble…"

Sir Athel moved closer to it. "The object has no artistic value—that's good. You'll have nothing to regret."

He rummaged in his waistcoat pocket and took out an object that resembled, and might have been mistaken for, a gold propelling-pencil. It was slender and elegant. He held it up so that the entire commission could see it clearly.

"This is a little thing, gentlemen," he said. "The force enclosed in this little tube is, however, such that the most powerful adjectives cannot describe it." And, as he seemed to read evident signs of anxiety on the faces of his audience, he added: "Don't be afraid, gentlemen. The operation will be accomplished without any appreciable noise or troubling manifestation."

In truth, they were all holding their breath, and those who kept their faces straight were nevertheless feeling a constriction in their breasts. The Prefect's eyes were gleaming with curiosity; as for the Minister, whose duty was to be impassive, he contented himself with lowering his eyelids slightly.

Sir Athel reached across the table, drew the inkwell to the edge, and then, leaning over it as attentively as a surgeon seeking the exact place to deploy his scalpel, he touched the piece of marble with the point of his propelling-pencil.

There was a slight—very slight—crack, like a breaking watch-spring, and, instead of the inkwell, nothing remained on the table but a little heap of dust, scarcely big enough to fill an egg-cup.

Exclamations burst forth. Everyone got up and gathered around this residue. They were no longer able to doubt; they had seen, with their own eyes…

"I believe," said Sir Athel, "that one of your compa-triots, Dr. Le Bon,[18] calls this the dissociation of matter."

"Extraordinary!"

"Stupefying!"

"Astounding!"

"And with that little tube…"

Hands reached out towards the object that Sir Athel was holding between his thumb and forefinger, like the stem of a flower. He simply gave the shaft a slight twist and put the tube back in his pocket. "Let's not risk any accident," he said. "The object requires very delicate handling, and its use requires a rather long apprentice-ship. I've spent ten years making myself master of this force, gentlemen…"

"Of what is this substance composed?"

"How did you obtain it?"

"All questions that we will get back to later," Sir Athel replied.

"But, at the very least, what do you call it?"

"I have named it vrilium."

"Vrilium?" repeated the members of the audience, searching for an etymology they could not find, for it was not Greek.

"A purely fantastic name, gentlemen. Perhaps, though, you've read a very remarkable book by one of

---

[18] Gustave Le Bon (1841-1931) is now best known as a social psychologist, notable for his analysis of crowd behavior, but he also conducted a long series of laboratory experiments with "black light"—invisible radiations—which led him to con-clude (correctly, as it eventually turned out) that all matter is decaying, at a greater or lesser rate. His definitive work on *L'Evolution de la matière* (1905; tr. as *The Evolution of Mat-ter*) was, however, regarded as somewhat *avant garde* at the time.

my most celebrated compatriots: *The Coming Race*, by Sir Edward Bulwer-Lytton.[19] That novel—utopian, if you will, although I see it as an anticipation of the future—concerns a people whom science has armed with a force so powerful and irresistible, but simultaneously so easily manipulable, that it is at everyone's disposal, men, women and children alike. There is no obstacle that it cannot overcome, no resistance that it cannot break, to the extent that its effects neutralize one another; under the threat of mutual destruction and reciprocal annihilation, no one can attack his neighbor...

"By means of the development of this force, virtue, patience and goodwill reign on Earth—but only, mark this well, because that force is not in the hands of the few, but at the disposal of everyone, the weakest and the strongest alike. It re-establishes equality, and therefore liberty.

"Bulwer called this force *vril*, from I derived the name I've given to the substance I discovered: vrilium. As for the substance itself, a few words will suffice to enable to you understand its nature. It is analogous to the gallium that was recently discovered by your great compatriot Lecoq de Boisbaudran, and especially to the radium of your immortal Curie.[20] It takes its rank at the

---

[19] Lermina gives Bulwer-Lytton's forename, wrongly, as Henry, perhaps having confused him with the actor Henry Lytton or the diplomat Henry Lytton Bulwer (who was the novelist's older brother).

[20] Paul-Emile Lecoq de Boisbaudran discovered gallium in 1875. Radium was discovered by Marie Curie, née Sklodowska, although Lermina seems to be crediting the discovery to her husband, Pierre, who had died four years before the publication of the story, since he gives "Madame Curie" a separate credit later in the paragraph.

head of the so-called rare earths, whose names I can re-cite from memory: yttrium, palladium, osmium, ruthenium, vanadium and, finally, polonium, recently discovered by Madame Curie. Assisted by the works of my predecessors, Sir William Ramsay, Lord Rayleigh and Norman Lockyer, and of Messieurs Berthelot, Becquerel, Le Bon and many others,[21] I have myself discovered vrilium, of which I have attempted an initial utilization by adapting it to aviation.

"The motor of my apparatus is, therefore, vrilium, which emanates its own force, as radium emanates light and heat, but in such proportions that, adapted to an appropriate mechanism, it can produce rotations of 20,000 cycles per minute.

"The little apparatus that I took out of my pocket is equipped with an imperceptible drill-bit made of diamond; that is why it can disintegrate, under the rotation imparted to it by vrilium, the hardest of blocks in one second—on condition, of course, that one applies it to what Hindu science calls the center of *laya*—which is to say, to the point within any concrete mass at which all

---

[21] Sir William Ramsay (whose forename is misrendered by Lermina as Arthur) discovered argon in 1895 and went on to isolate the other noble gases. His discovery of argon was prompted by a puzzling result in atmospheric analysis obtained by John Wiliam Strutt, the third Baron Rayleigh (misrendered by Lermina as Raleigh), while helium had earlier been identified in the solar spectrum by the astronomer Norman Lockyer, one of the most important pioneers of spectroscopic research. Three generations of Becquerels made significant contributions to French physics, but Lermina's reference is presumably to the youngest, Henri, who was one of the discoverers of radioactivity.

the molecules support and sustain one another.[22] I shall reserve my explanation of that for later.

"But I have said too much, gentlemen, and am fearful of abusing your patience. If you would care to trust me, I should devote myself without further delay to the operations necessary to neutralize the effects of my vriliogire, and deliver your beautiful city from the anxiety that I have unwittingly caused it."

There was an approving acclamation. The young Englishman had overcome the mistrust and unacknowledged jealousy of scientific officialdom. Later, of course, when they had collected themselves, the commission's members would treat all these affirmations as fantasies, if not lies; in the face of the little heap of marble dust, however, they felt nonplussed, and could not hide their enthusiasm.

The Minister and the Prefect took possession of Sir Athel and discussed with him the measures that needed to be taken in preparation for the operation, which would take place the following morning at 10 a.m. The only anxiety that Sir Athel voiced was that the vrilium with which the buried apparatus was equipped was capable of producing enormous sparks that might terrify the neighborhood. It was important to prevent any panic.

Sir Athel promised to answer for everything—"at least to the extent," he added, "that human foresight permits." Furthermore, he supposed that any danger there might be would be to himself alone. When the Minister protested, promising to take all the necessary pre-

---

[22] *Laya* is usually defined in terms of yogic mysticism, in which it refers to the concentration of attention on internal energy flow, but it is also used in music as an Eastern equivalent of the Western concept of tempo.

cautions and offering to postpone the operation in order to give him more time to get everything ready, he simply said: "Monsieur le Ministre, the humblest chemist risks his life 20 times a day in his laboratory." And he concluded, with a smile, "And the statistics prove that it is one of the vocations whose practitioners survive to the most advanced age."

They agreed to meet on the following day, at 9:30 a.m., on the waste ground of the Rue des Carrières-d'Amériques. A cordon of troops would hold the public back at a sufficient distance. Sir Athel intended to act alone; he would not allow anyone to accompany him but the superior authority, the Prefect of Police...

"And the reporter from the *Nouvelliste!*" put in a masculine voice that was none other than Labergère's.

"I am unable to refuse you anything," Sir Athel replied, courteously.

"Very well! And me too?" hazarded Bobby. "If I hadn't made such a fuss about Coxward, would the newspapers have taken any notice of him? Was it not the insults heaped upon me that gave the warning? Sir Athel, you would not be so ungrateful as to reject me..."

"You shall be with us, my dear Mr. Bobby," said the Englishman.

The last salutations were exchanged. Sir Athel asked to be taken to the Carlton, where Labergère would come to seek him out the following morning. When they had shaken hands on the threshold of the Hôtel Beauvau, Labergère, left alone with Bobby, took him by the arm in a familiar fashion. "You, my dear Bobby, will come with me to the *Nouvelliste*. It's necessary that you be seen— you'll be photographed and your face will be on tomorrow's front page. We'll write my article together, and afterwards, we'll have a bite to eat at the Américain.

Truffles, champagne and pretty girls, eh, my brave Bobby! Tee hee!"

Bobby allowed himself to be drawn away.

All these individuals thought they were approaching a denouement. How could they possibly guess the horrible betrayal that destiny had in store for them?

PART THREE:
PARIS BEFORE THE CREATION OF MAN

I. A Catastrophe that is merely a beginning

The following day, at the appointed hour, everyone reached the rendezvous dead on time—not to mention the 100,000 Parisians who, enticed by Labergère's sparkling articles, had come to the Buttes-Chaumont and the neighboring streets in the hope of seeing the inventor of vrilium and witnessing the interesting operation that had been promised.

Moreover, with the versatility that is characteristic of our national spirit, on the mere assurance of a newspaper article, all anxiety had already disappeared. No one regarded the journey to the depths of Belleville as anything but a pleasure trip. It is true that Labergère, while faithfully transcribing the explanation given by Sir Athel, had, one might say, put an optimistic slant on the affair, in such a way that the operation that would be attempted was presented as child's play for the inventor of genius—and no one dreamed of reproaching him for it, for it was extremely useful to modify the mentality of Parisians, so prompt to panic, in the direction of calm.

The entire crowd, however—which included representatives of all social classes—displayed a certain amount of disappointment when it ran up against a deployment of troops, which relegated it to a distance of some 500 meters from the place of interest. There were a few scuffles, inasmuch as numerous people loftily claimed to be entitled by their positions to defy the or-

der—senators, députés and pass-holders, who were pro-
testing very loudly—but the regulation was pitilessly
enforced. No one got through.

That same morning, two incidents had occurred that
had made no small contribution to reawakening Monsieur Lépine's anxieties.

Firstly, there was a miserable drunkard who, during
the night, had found a means of getting into the enclosure—an imprudence that had cost him dear, for, having
obviously got too near the apparatus, he had been found
lying inert a few paces away, as if dead. He had been
urgently transported to the nearby hospital, but, despite
all the care lavished upon him, he remained deep in a
coma that gave reason to fear for his life.

"Well," said Monsieur Lépine to Sir Athel, "does
your vrilium have the potential to resurrect the dead?"

"Not at all," replied Sir Athel, with a smile, "but I
certainly believe that while a spark of life remain in a
organic body, however tiny, vrilium might galvanize it
and restore it to full vigor. I have, therefore, tried it out
on animals that that appeared to have been frozen to
death, having been encased in blocks of ice, and gave no
sign of life. The vrilium reanimated them and the animals were resuscitated without even giving any sign of
distress."

"You're decidedly a magician…"

"Don't forget that people once foisted that name on
the alchemists who were, as your Monsieur Berthelot
has demonstrated, merely precursors, whose only error
was to be ahead of their time…"

The second fact that had attracted the Prefect's attention had a certain gravity. One of the senior officials
of the Prefecture of the Seine, Monsieur Gérards, the
author of some interesting studies of subterranean Paris,

had come to find him early that morning and, placing diagrams in front of him, had demonstrated to him that the bedrock on which the terrain of the Rue des Carrières-d'Amériques rested had been recognized, in the wake of explorations that unfortunately remained incomplete, as presenting very particular characteristics of instability. Proof of that had already been provided by previous collapses, rather frequent in the area. There was considerable danger that the proposed operations might lead to new ones.

"We must admit," Monsieur Gérards had added, "That we know nothing at all about the subjacent rocks. On the basis of a few personal observations, though, I believe that I can deduce from the evidence of the discovery of certain fossil bones, that they rest on ancient strata, quaternary or perhaps even tertiary." The geologist concluded: "I am inclined to suppose that this part of Paris was disturbed, thousands of years ago, by a cataclysm of a volcanic nature, or something similar, and that its definitive settlement has not yet been completed—which gives rise to the possibility of dangerous collapses."

Monsieur Lépine, alarmed by these communications, had felt bound to transmit them to Sir Athel. For the first time, the English scientist had seemed slightly troubled, but he had recovered his composure very rapidly. "They're only hypotheses," he had said. "Every man who acts knows that he must expect the unexpected. You have seen yourself, Monsieur le Préfet, that the presence of the apparatus presents a continual danger. I don't want to have to reproach myself with any more human deaths. As unworthy of sympathy as poor Coxward was, the frightful accident to which he fell victim will leave me perpetually remorseful. I must do everything possible to avoid a recurrence of any similar catastrophe—and besides, I repeat, I am the only one at any risk. I shall answer for everything..." And he added, with a vague gesture: "Except the unimaginable..."

"Go on, then, Monsieur," the Prefect said to him, in a grave tone. "May the outcome fulfill all your hopes. Permit me to shake your hand as that of a brave man, worthy of all our esteem."

Labergère and Bobby, thanks to the personal authorization that had been given to them, were the only ones able to get into the enclosure. Sir Athel took Labergère to one side and said to him: "Monsieur, I have been completely satisfied with your conduct, and I thank you for the confidence that you shave shown in me. Despite my private certainty of success, I must take account of all possibilities. However well-prepared he might be, a man is always subject to the caprices of chances. In case any accident should happen to me, would you be good enough to take charge of a letter that I have written and addressed to its intended recipient, my fiancée, Mademoiselle Mary Redmore?"

"That is a service that one does not refuse," Labergère replied, "but I am quite sure that I shall not have to render it to you, firstly because we shall emerge safe and sound from the adventure, and secondly because, if any misfortune overtakes you, I shall partake of it in large measure, being absolutely determined to stick with you."

"I can't agree to that!" cried Sir Athel, sharply. "I have the right to risk my own life, but not those of others... I thank you for coming here this morning, but now I must ask you to withdraw."

"Not in this life. I'm here and I'm staying... and who knows? Perhaps a reliable man of good will might be a useful companion to you. One often has need of someone less knowledgeable than oneself. Anyway say what you will, I'm not budging—although I think you ought to send our friend Bobby away. Not being accustomed to Parisian night-life, he must be a trifle hung over—eh, Bobby?"

"I'm here," said the detective, drawing nearer, "and I fully expect that you will want to make use of my services."

"My dear Bobby, you're handsome and valiant, and you bear England's great glory on your shoulders—but you'll have the goodness to hop it."

"Hop it?" said the Englishman, staring at Labergère in bewilderment.

"That means be off, make yourself scarce—in a word: go away."

"Me, go away!" cried Bobby, striking a pose and extending his fists like a boxer. "Sir Athel, I have your word! I have the right to stay here and bear witness to everything that happens. The promise has been made, and, to ensure that it is kept, I shall not hesitate, if necessary, to fetch the British Ambassador..."

"Now, now, my dear Bobby, don't get upset!" said Labergère, who was treating him with increasing familiarity—for he quite liked the man—"it's just that it would be very annoying to have to tell Mrs, Bobby that you've been killed..."

"I'm as solid as the two of you, and if anyone's to be killed, we'll be killed together. I've redeemed the reputation of His Majesty's police, and I shall not fail in my duty..."

Sir Athel shrugged his shoulders. "As you wish," she said. "After all, who knows whether we might not be able to help one another? To work, now, lest people should think that I'm hesitating."

Let us briefly remind ourselves of the situation. Almost in the middle of the waste ground there was a basin-shaped excavation, half-full of sand and stones, with the famous vriliogire protruding from the middle of it, two-thirds buried, with its metallic roof uppermost, in the form of a German helmet, its spike being stripped of its propeller.

The vriliogire was tetragonal, the walls being comprised of metal lattices, one of which was equipped with a door. There was no handle or projection that might be gripped in order to open it. The closed door being maintained in its frame by the stones and sand that weighed upon it, it seemed impossible that it could be extracted from the vice-like grip without the aid of sturdy machinery such as cranes and jacks.

Even so, Sir Athel approached it, armed with tools that appeared to be made of copper, which permitted him to touch the apparatus from a distance. Over his hands and forearms he had put long gloves made of a supple and shiny metallic fabric, reminiscent of the chain-mail armbands worn by knights of old.

Slightly pale, but giving unequivocal signs in his expression of unbreakable resolution, Sir Athel went down into the declivity of the crater, placing his feet on the parts that offered the firmest resistance, while gesturing to his friends to leave him plenty of space. Then, with one of his rods, shaped exactly like an archbishop's crozier, he began lightly touching the colonnettes supporting the roof.

Crackling sounds were heard and short-lived sparks sprang forth. It was just as if an accumulator were discharging in contact with a good conductor of electricity, but the sparks were strangely colored, blackish with red-brown tints. At each discharge, there was a partial detachment of the roof from its supports. The metal cap came jerkily adrift, leaving an increasingly large gap between the two edges.

"Monsieur Labergère," Sir Athel then said, "would you be so kind as to pass me the S-shaped instrument at the side of the box? Don't be afraid—it's harmless." It happened, though, that the object was closer to Bobby. Eager to prove his willingness, Bobby leapt forward, seized the tool and, leaning over the edge of the crater, held it out to Sir Athel... but, having not taken any precaution to brace his feet on the moving sand, he slipped, and tumbled down to the bottom of the crater, rolling like a ball. He ended up between Sir Athel's legs. The latter, losing his balance, was thrown against the apparatus, which he struck, without intending to, with the full force of the rod that he was holding in his hand.

Labergère had hurled himself forward to catch Bobby and, bracing himself on his legs, has seized him by the feet of his trousers, trying to drag him backwards.

What happened then?

The effect was like a thunderbolt. The impact of the vrilium rod on the apparatus evidently caused it to rise up, tearing its self free on the ground and rotating. Then, at the top of the helmet, which was not entirely detached from its support, there was a dazzling flash, accompanied by fiery sparks almost a meter long—veritable blades of fire slicing through the air as they darted upwards into the sky.

Then there was a loud cracking sound—and all of a sudden, the ground collapsed within a perimeter more than ten meters across. Clouds of sand and stone rose up, falling back with an ominous sound. It was as if an abyss had opened up...

And into that frightful confusion, everything disappeared and was swallowed up: the apparatus, and the three men.

A gulf was suddenly hollowed out, into which the ground collapsed entirely: all the sand and all the stones in the vicinity. And when the Prefect, the Minister and the policemen came running, drawn by the noise of the catastrophe, they saw nothing but a chaos of stone and soil, more than ten meters deep, which had closed on top of the unfortunates...

There was a clamor of despairing cries.

The unfortunate Sir Athel Random had paid with his life for the heroic effort he had made to save Paris—and with him had perished his two courageous acolytes, Bobby, the detective, and Labergère, the reporter. A painful tragedy!

II. The Next Day's Anguish

The effect of this catastrophe on Paris was enormous. A hail of curses was launched against the government, which was deemed guilty of not surrounding the operation with any of the precautions indicated by the most elementary prudence.

Despite all denials, the rumor took form that the administration had refused to carry out the work of shoring-up and support demanded by the unfortunate Sir Athel, for reasons of economy.

This is veritable murder! cried the *Reporter. Has such carelessness ever been seen? What was the Highways Authority doing during all this time? Why were skilled engineers not summoned? How is it that no one hesitates to mobilize firemen for the most trivial incident on the pubic highway, but this time, when circumstances required a large-scale operation, for which it was evident that no single man could take responsibility, criminal negligence was displayed...*

Then it was the Prefecture of the Seine that came under fire. Were the substrata of Paris unknown, then? What use were the map and diagrams published at enormous expense, to the taxpayers' cost? Were we reduced once again to becoming the laughing-stock of Europe?

The *Nouvelliste* appeared, doubly framed with black lines, for, although Labergère had been on its editorial staff—his biography took up three columns on the front page!—was not Bobby also one of its own, by virtue to the zeal with which the newspaper had defended him against the unspeakable attacks of a brutal and mendacious press?

In fact, did not everyone bear a part of the responsibility, including the Minister who had authorized—with such facility!—the bold experiment of a man whose competence was only affirmed by himself, and the so-called scientists who had welcomed the most fantastic affirmations with culpable blitheness and permitted a man to risk his life without having submitted them to any preliminary proof? Oh, they had believed in the all-powerfulness of vrilium! These freethinkers had had faith! This time, it really was the bankruptcy of science; it was obvious that the unfortunate Random had been nothing but a madman who, by some sleight of hand, had been able to put one over on them. The pretended disintegration of the block of marble had been nothing but a trick of prestidigitation by which everyone had allowed themselves to be taken in, even the Prefect of Police, who was no fool.

The disaster had its repercussions in the Chambre des Députés: the leader of the extreme left had, so to speak, pounced on the cabinet, enveloping all the services in the same reprobation, including the Ministries of War, Marine and Public Works.

What could be expected of the members of a government that could not even defend the soil of a neighborhood of Paris? Today it was a fragment of the 19th arrondissement that had disappeared into the abyss; tomorrow it might be the entirety of France! (Loud applause from the extreme left and the benches of the right; the orator, returning to his place, is warmly congratulated.)

It required all the versatility and all the unction, seasoned with irony, of the leader of the cabinet to stave off the attack. Reproducing the celebrated metaphor of the block of stone, he showed himself to be upstanding, robust and devoid of cracks, in order to sustain the superb edifice of our country. "What good," he cried, "are bitter words addressed to us? What good are these unjustified attacks, to which we can only oppose the impassivity of clear and self-confident consciences? Will it be words that save the unfortunates who have been swallowed up? If we let these portfolios, of which certain people are so covetous, escape from our hands, will the earth then open up to disgorge its victims? We accept full responsibility, without hesitation, with stout hearts, because we are ready to assume others—which is to say, all the measures so far taken and yet to be taken for the difficult task of saving three men, three martyrs to Science" (Acclamations from the benches of the left and the centre. The orator, returning to his place, is warmly congratulated.)

A vote of confidence was proposed and passed with a majority of 293.

In the meantime, work went on.

The entire cohort of Parisian engineers had been mobilized: well-diggers, sewer-workers, masons and canal-diggers had been summoned to the site—for, although no one held out any hope of saving the buried men, it was vitally necessary, in order to satisfy public opinion, to give all possible evidence of good intentions.

This is what the waste ground looked like now. There was a hole—a large hole, an immense hole—about a dozen meters deep, with a perimeter of earth and gravel, almost vertical and seemingly well-balanced rather than unstable. At the bottom of the hole, there was a heap of debris, devoid of form and consistency, which seemed to subsiding further with every passing minute.

Buried under that mass, the unfortunates could not even have suffered. They must have been crushed immediately and instantaneously—and that was a veritable blessing!

Was there any chance at all of saving them from their fate, which had probably been sealed from the very beginning? Not one of the engineers was able to hazard an affirmative response. Moreover, given the nature of the terrain, it was certain that any attempted endeavor would only precipitate new collapses, thus increasing the mass of material beneath which the victims were no longer even suffering.

It was decided that the impossible would be attempted.

Solid stays would be established to contain the walls of the pit; then a sort of dredger would be installed, with which the greatest possible amount of sand and gravel could be raised. As for the duration of the work, how could any one anticipate it? It was hardly probable that the labor of displacement could be begun within forty-eight hours.

Although not satisfactory to anyone, these measures were the only ones that could be put in hand. No one there had any illusions, but attempts were made to rouse them in others.

Public grief manifested itself with its habitual intensity; the weather was fine, the terraces of the cafés were overflowing, and the theaters were full every evening. People would gladly have mounted fêtes, balls and galas for the benefit of the victims, but since they were dead...

The *Reporter* had a stroke of genius, with which to diminish the sad victory of the *Nouvelliste*. One of its reporters was dispatched to London with instructions to inform Mr. Bobby's widow and to bring her back to Paris. That was done, and the unfortunate woman—in veritable despair at the death of her husband, the brave detective—was paraded on the boulevards in a carriage over which floated a black flag with the following inscription, in letters of gold:

To the Martyr's widow, from the Reporter.

At the same time, a subscription was opened in its columns, in order to shelter Madame Bobby from need. The newspaper put itself down for 1000 francs.

Meanwhile, the *Nouvelliste*, which did not intend to allow itself to be overtaken, appealed to all journalists and intellectuals for a monument to be raised to the memory of Labergère, the hero of reportage, whose execution would be entrusted to the great Rodin. A statue reminiscent of Michelangelo's Moses was envisaged, the electrical horns of which would symbolize the nature of the accident in which he had perished.

It was only with Sir Athel Random that no one was preoccupied; after all, he was the true author of the catastrophe. Already, John Coxward had been the first victim of his supposed inventions, and now his pseudoscientific fantasies had caused the death of three more people. Only Emile Gautier, the scientific journalist,[23] raised a voice in his favor and published the theory of

---

[23] Emile Gautier did indeed work as a scientific journalist, but Lermina and his readers would have been much more familiar with his reputation as an anarchist firebrand. His most famous work was *Le Darwinisme social* (1880), which railed against economists who wanted to co-opt Darwinian theory as a support for laissez-faire capitalism, arguing—correctly—that Darwin's account of *The Descent of Man* paid far more attention to the roles of social co-operation (or mutual aid) and efficient parental care as key factors determining the success of the human species.

rare earths and vrilium in a well-documented article, which argued that the future would rehabilitate Sir Athel, the victim of an accident for which he was not responsible and was entirely beyond his control, due solely to the negligence of Parisian officialdom—followed by a furious assault on the senior officials of the Prefecture of the Seine.

Twenty-four hours had already gone by when the arrival in Paris was heralded of Miss Mary Redmore, the fiancée—already, alas, a widow—of Sir Athel Random. The unfortunate young woman, who bore a profound affection for Sir Athel, had wanted to pay homage to her inconsolable grief on the frightful tomb in which no vestige remained to remind her of the man she had loved. She was accompanied by her father, the energetic Mr. Redmore, who, having firmly taken the side of his daughter and refusing to admit that the French were not responsible for the horrible catastrophe, immediately made contact with our most eminent lawyers. He had decided to bring an action against the City of Paris and to claim therefrom, in the name of Sir Athel's family—whose power of attorney had been entrusted to him—damages that he estimated at 20,000 pounds sterling (which is to say, 500,000 francs).

A *complainte* was hawked on the boulevards:[24]

---

[24] A *complainte* was a satirical song fitted to the words of a traditional tune, closely akin to English "broadside ballads;" I have managed to conserve the rhyme-scheme, if not the scansion, of Lermina's doggerel without stretching the meaning too much (although substituting "an axe to grind" for "armed with a mere rod" might be reckoned a liberty too far). Fualdes was a magistrate murdered in Rodez in 1817 whose trial caused a great sensation and gave rise to one of the most famous 19th century *complaintes*.

Frenchmen, hear the tale
Beyond credibility's pale,
Of an Englishman whom
Fate sent to his doom.

To leave Blériot behind
With a mere axe to grind
The poor man essayed,
With vrilium's aid

To fly through space
And see the sun face-to-face;
But he fell into a hole
Where he saw nothing at all!

The publisher of this ode, sung to the tune of *Fualdes*, made a rapid fortune.

Perhaps it is time now, though, to explain what had become of the three protagonists of this tragedy…

III. Under Paris

Any man of calm judgment, resistant to the suggestions of a fantastic imagination, can have no doubt that, if a news-vendor's kiosk and three men were to be caught up in the collapse of hundreds of cubic meters of various materials, the probability militating in favor of their being crushed would not leave one chance in a thousand of their salvation.

Study the various facts reported in the newspapers, however, and you will be surprised by the role played in the most frightful instances by that force which we call—without understanding it—chance.

Without the need for any miracle, without any of the known and verified laws of nature being violated, a roofer falling from the sixth floor, rebounds from a balcony, and ends up sprawled in a truck full of manure, which makes a soft and flavorsome bed for him.

Of two automobilists traveling in the same car, imperiled by the same brake-failure, smashing into the same obstacle, sheltered by the same protective shell, one is killed stone dead, while the other escapes with a few temporary internal injuries, whose only result is to serve as justification for claiming compensation from that celebrated Party Responsible who is the anonymous author of all our ills.

In the grip of a tempest, nine vessels out of ten succeed in running before the wind and attaining calm water; the tenth—the sturdiest, the newest, the best-captained—disappears, snatched by the sea, and only one of its passengers survives: a cripple who has never sailed before and is, needless to say, ignorant of the most elementary principles of swimming.

There is a piece of orange-peel on my sidewalk; since this morning, 100 people have sauntered, jogged or raced past without even being aware of it. I go out, I see the orange-peel, and send it into the gutter with a single swift kick, whereupon I fall down and break my leg.

Life and death are at the mercy of thousands of circumstances—some of them visible, which we think we can avoid; others invisible and risky, which settle our account without our ever being aware that there was a calculation to make. There is nothing less implausible than the truth, nothing truer than the implausible. That is why, strange and stupefying as the course of this narrative might seem, the reader's incredulity is merely proof of inexperience. As Arago[25] has said, the word "impossible" does not exist, except in pure mathematics... and repetition!

That is why it would be evidence of a tiresome narrowness of mind to be astonished when we discover, at a depths that we have not yet had the time to evaluate numerically:

Sir Athel Random, sitting with his head in his hands, profoundly thoughtful...

Sitting? On what, pray?

Quite simply on the floor of his kiosk, his public urinal, or whatever name one cares to give it.

---

[25] Like many great scientists of his era, Dominique-François Arago (1786-1853) combined that vocation with that of statesman, and it was presumably in the latter capacity, either serving in the post-Revolutionary government of 1848 or contemplating the unfortunate advent of the Second Empire, that he proclaimed repetition to be impossible.

Are his bones broken? Is he, at the very least, stunned? Not at all; he is very calm, quite sound and in possession of all his faculties—merely a trifle astonished, first at finding himself inside his aviation apparatus, secondly at not hearing any noise, and thirdly at having experienced the sensation of a descent rather than a fall, without any violent shock.

Naturally, the darkness is profound, and it is only by touch that Sir Athel has recognized the floor and the walls. As yet, he has only dared to act with extreme precaution; he knows only too well, by experience, what perils an abrupt gesture might present in a locale furnished on every side with machinery as delicate as it is dangerous. He has, therefore, taken the wisest course, which is to make as little movement as possible and to reflect, as clearly and coolly as circumstances permit.

Sir Athel, as you will have divined, had a precise and methodical mind; he was addressing matters in strict order.

The situation of finding himself many meters underground, enclosed in an explosive box, was not, at first glance, one of those one would gladly choose to occupy one's leisure time. On the other hand, though, there was a real satisfaction in feeling his heart beating, bringing his muscles into play and observing the activity of his brain—in a word, in finding himself, after such an alarm, still very much alive.

Sir Athel engaged in a monologue—mutely, of course.

"I remember quite well," he said to himself, "that I was on the brink of success. In a few minutes, solely by the force of vrilium, suitably adapted—I would have slowly lifted up the vriliogire. My aim was, as soon as I had freed the door, to reach inside, with suitable precautions, in order to get to the central isolator, thus to neutralize the effect of the vrilium, which would have become temporarily inert. Then it would have been feasible to salvage the apparatus by ordinary means. A few solid ropes and strong arms would have completed the work.

"So what has happened? I remember that I had already discharged some parts of the condensers... a few moments more and I would have reached my goal... except that I needed—my memory is very reliable—one of the rods I had prepared, which, because of its curvature, which would have permitted me to get inside. I therefore reached for the upper catch of the door, part of which folded back and let my hand in, which finished the work...

"I was wrong, I now admit, to ask someone else—Monsieur Labergère, if I'm not mistaken—to obtain the required tool. That was when a heavy body bumped into me, causing my vrilium rod to collide with a part of the wall..."

He furnished himself with a few explanations, whose result was that somehow—he did not know exactly how—the door had been able to open and close behind him, while the charges of vrilium contained in the rods, suddenly liberated, had caused a collapse and the fall of the apparatus. Science includes numerous facts whose causes are unknown; the present phenomenon aggregated them into a unity, that was all.

What was evident was that, by virtue of the sudden shocks, certain control-switches had been released that had effected the neutralization of the vrilium—for, at the present moment, it certainly seemed that the apparatus was, so to speak, dead, producing neither force, nor heat, nor light: a question to be urgently addressed, if he should ever have the leisure to do so.

"All this," Sir Athel thought, "gives me very little information as to the means by which I might get out of the worse-than-precarious position in which I find myself."

Suddenly, he experienced a frisson. A thought—momentarily set aside—leapt to mind. He was not the only victim of this catastrophe—he had had two companions: Labergère and Bobby, the reporter of genius and the utterly British detective! Had the two unfortunates perished, whether by being blasted apart by the vrilian discharges that has caused and accompanied the collapse, or—which was more horrible still—being crushed by the debris?

Sir Athel was essentially good-hearted. His scientific research had no other object than to augment, if possible, the sum of well-being at humankind's disposal. What did his own life matter? He had made a sacrifice of it long ago. But had he the right to dispose of someone else's? In this instance, his responsibility was entire and undeniable. Why, knowing the perils of the operation, knowing that he alone could overcome them—how, rather—had he been weak enough to authorize those two men to accompany him?

In the case of Coxward, he had been able to allege in his defense that it was the boxer's own imprudence that had caused the accident; Sir Athel had been a witness to it, without actually participating in it. In this instance though, he could not address the slightest reproach to those two men, who had only followed him for his own sake. He should have put them off, pitilessly rejecting their request—it had been his duty as an honest man.

And Sir Athel asked himself, blushing, whether he had not been obedient to a ridiculous instinct of vanity in

141

accepting them as close-rage witnesses of what he thought would be a victory. He told himself that he had, after all, expiated his crime—for what hope had he of escaping from the gulf that had swallowed him up? Well, if he died, it would be no more than the punishment he deserved.

Beneath the weight of these painful thoughts, Sir Athel felt himself weakening. All his energy abandoned him. Whether it was lack of air, or simply the effect of moral tension, his nerves were overstretched, his brain became clouded, and a veil extended before his eyes. He experienced the frightful sensation of premature burial, and his hands, shaken by a convulsive spasm, clutched at his bosom in a desperate gesture.

That involuntary gesture saved him.

Beneath his fingers, he felt hard objects that were very familiar to him: little flat boxes, similar to chocolate-boxes, in which he had enclosed parcels of vrilium!

Vrilium! He was in possession of that miraculous product, that universal motor, that irresistible panacea—and he was allowing himself to become discouraged! What good would it have done him to make himself master of one of the most powerful secrets of nature, if that discovery could not bring him salvation in the most desperate circumstances?

And after all, since he was not dead himself, why should his two companions have necessarily succumbed?

Merely for having touched one of the boxes enclosing the vrilium, Sir Athel was already revived. No, no, he would not let himself go; he would fight; he would be victorious! And he seemed to see, in a vague half-light, the sweet face of Mary Redmore encouraging him.

"I'm in the vriliogire," he said to himself. "But where is the apparatus? That's what I need to find out, and for that I need light. The vrilium will provide it for me.

There was another danger, which was that of making a false move that would act upon one of the machinery's controls and unleash another discharge—for Sir Athel, who ha not envisaged using his aircraft before the first of April, had freely made use of it to store the samples of vrilium that he produced in his laboratory.

With infinite precaution, he took from his waistcoat pocket the same propelling-pencil that had earlier used to disintegrate the marble inkwell. He felt the instrument, delicately twisted a ferrule designed to modify the effects to be obtained, then pressed a switch. There was a slight click and a tongue of fire sprang forth, similar to an acetylene flame.

A dazzling light flooded the cabin, arranged like that of a telephone exchange; little boxes were installed on all the walls, equipped with handles or buttons, the whole assembly forming, so to speak, a sort of keyboard whose contacts activated various parts of the mechanism. A sheaf of wires linked the system to a sphere of exceedingly small dimension fixed on a metal stalk that traversed the cabin from top to bottom, and which, as we already know, controlled the two propellers at the vertical extremities of the apparatus.

At the first glance, Sir Athel understood what had happened. In the brutal impact caused by its fall, one of the interior switches had been released, and the motor had set the propeller-shaft working with an enormous rapidity. At its upper end, the propeller that had been broken no longer existed, but the inferior part was still intact; turning with vertiginous velocity, it had dug itself

143

into the soil, serving as a sort of corkscrew—or, rather, an Archimedean screw—and it had hollowed out a cavity into which the entire apparatus had descended, as if into a sheath where it had carved out a path, although impeded by friction.

That explained how the descent, instead of presenting the character of a fall in which everything was smashed, had been almost a glide.

But what had stopped it?

Having lit a lamp attached to the side wall, Athel, free in his movements and entirely master of himself, sought the answer. The charge of vrilium that activated the motor and the various parts of the mechanism was almost exhausted, but was still sufficient to produce very real effects. It was evident that a powerful object had opposed itself to the continuation of the movement, and Sir Athel soon established the cause.

After having perforated various layers of soil, sand and loose gravel that had not put up a relative resistance to his progress, the inferior propeller had found itself suddenly arrested. The enormous drill with which it was furnished at its centre had run into matter so hard that it had been unable to penetrate it; its rotational movement had been stopped and the apparatus had therefore been immobilized by the obstacle.

Sir Athel knew, however, that no know substance could resist the force of vrilium; the arrest must therefore be the result of an exceptional cause that he would lose no time in discovering. By dint of an accident, due to the rupture of one of the metal switches, the communication between the drive-shaft and the motor had been interrupted, but it would be easy to repair.

In sum, thanks to an incredible freak of chance—but one which proved the excellent quality of the materials employed in the construction of the armature, the vriliogire was essentially intact, and Athel did not doubt that he could easily restore it to working order.

This raised the most serious question, however. Would he be able to effect a new displacement? In which direction should he steer? In a nutshell, where was he, and at what depth?

The English scientist had the clear impression that he had lost consciousness—but for how long? Was he ten, twenty, thirty or a hundred meters below the surface? Had the descent taken place in a straight line or at an angle? All these questions inevitably remained unanswered.

Athel looked at his watch; the hands indicated 1 p.m.—which is to say that, since the moment he had begun the operation, at 10 a.m., three hours had elapsed. Where was the proof that it was three hours rather that 15? That could be verified mechanically. Carefully, he turned the winding-mechanism. The number of turns he had to make demonstrated to him that it was certainly 1 p.m. But for how long had he remained inert and unconscious? The terms of the problem were not getting any simpler.

Finally, what was surrounding the vriliogire? In what sort of matter was it encased and embedded? How could he find out?

To give himself strength, Athel opened a little bottle of Berthelot pills. Everyone knows that our great chemist had offered the hypothesis that the day would come when human nourishment by organic substances would be replaced by the chemical elements composing them, so effectively that alimentation would be assured by the condensation of the very essence of things—the elements of nitrogen, carbon, phosphorus, etc., comprising meat, vegetables, milk and so on—into the form of tablets or pills, whose very small volume would serve for the reparation of strength. Sir Athel had studied the problem for a long time and had partly resolved it. In a box a decimeter square, he was in possession of sufficient provisions to assure his alimentation for months on end. Fearing further physical weakness, therefore, he took two pills rich in nitrogen and added, in order to clear his head, a cup of coffee in pill form.

He felt revived and alert, experiencing the sensation that he was too much alive to die. He knew, moreover, that in the last resort he would have one supreme resource remained: a subcutaneous injection of vrilium, which, so long as the organs were intact, would render the necessary vitality to the whole being.

Self-confidence is the first condition of success.

In the very small space in which Athel was able to move, he examined all the various mechanisms of his apparatus one by one, and cut off all the contacts that might develop the action of the vrilium. He left nothing to chance; like a general inspecting all he parts of his battlefield, he decided what to do. It was then that, raising his eyes for the first time to the ceiling of his kiosk, he noticed that the upper part was elevated. Had he not, in fact, been in the process of detaching the Prussian helmet that crowned it? During the fall, the cover—for want of a better term—had tipped back, and through the gap thus made it was possible to see outside.

He stood on a stool and, thanks to his height, reached the top and was able to stick his head through the gap. The darkness was absolute, but he felt a certain warmth on his face. He got the impression that there was certain space extending therefrom. He took out the famous propelling-pencil, adaptable to any purpose, extended his arm and generated a bright white light.

He exclaimed in surprise. The vriliogire was not solidly encased, as he had thought at first. There was free space above him and in front of one of the walls—the one with the door, which he had not so far judged it prudent to open, for fear of flooding the interior with loose matter. It seemed to him that what was surrounding him was hard stone, or even rock.

He hesitated no longer; he unlatched the door and leaned out over the threshold, advancing the miniature torch into the darkness, which flooded it with light.

Athel had a cavern before him: a spacious grotto framed by enormous blocks of stone heaped up on one another, giving the impression of unbreakable solidity. He could not see the ground distinctly; prudently looking down before crossing the threshold, he perceived that there was a gap between the vriliogire and the floor of the cavern, more than a meter wide.

He lowered the light-jet, and it seemed to him that there was a deep abyss, in which his gaze could not distinguish anything. Beyond that interval was the floor of the cavern, which seemed to him to comprise a thin vault, like a crust of cement covering a space hollowed out below. That sort of carapace was, however, of solid appearance. Deciding to commit himself, Athel tensed himself, jumped across the gap and found himself standing, safe and sound, beneath the high ceiling of the cavern.

The air there was thick and heavy, almost suffocating, with a nauseating odor of mold—but such details seemed unimportant; Athel experienced a sensation of liberation. Had he not felt the unacknowledged dread that he would remain trapped, buried alive in the vriliogire, transformed into a coffin, to suffer a slow and horrible death of asphyxia while immobilized? Had any tourist confronted with vast spacious landscapes, the sky and clumps of trees ever experienced a more intense joy than that of our worthy scientist, enveloped on every side by a stone dome, with a bottomless pit at his feet? A new proof of the relativity of human enjoyments!

Sir Athel, carried away by his enthusiasm, cried: "Long live life! Long live science!"

"Who's that squawking up there?" replied a voice, which seemed to emerge from the depths of the Earth.

IV. All or Nothing

So little did Sir Athel expect to hear a human voice reply to his own that he remained momentarily speechless, as if choking. Recovering almost immediately, however, he cupped his hands in front of his mouth to form a megaphone and shouted with all the force of his lungs; "Who was that?"

Indistinct and seemingly distant, the voice replied: "Me, Eusèbe de Labergère, news-reporter at the *Nouvelliste.*"

"And I'm Sir Athel Random!"

"*Nom de Dieu!*"—pardon the expression, but we swear that it is accurate[26]—"You can be proud of being a jolly good fellow and of having got us into a pretty pickle!"

"Where are you?"

"I haven't a clue. Here or somewhere else, somewhere or nowhere, 200 or 300 feet underground."

"Are you hurt?"

"I don't know—but I'm utterly exhausted, unable to move my arms or my legs. Oh, what I'd give to be tucking into a special at the Café de Boubouroche!"

"Don't despair! We'll get out of this. It's already a great deal not to be dead. Come on, listen to me!" He moved the flame around him. "Can you see a light—a glimmer?"

---

[26] This avowal seems a trifle unnecessary, especially since what Lermina's text actually says is "N. de D." (unless, of courser, I have misinterpreted it and the letters actually stand for more violent curse than *Nom de Dieu*).

"I can't see anything. I'm too dazed."

"Good! Keep calm and wait!"

Labergère groaned a few more words that were inaudible. Athel, who had recovered all his logical faculties, told himself that the cave in which he found himself must obviously be connected to some other pocket or cavern, presumably the one of which its floor formed the ceiling. Armed with his lamp, therefore, began exploring the cavern carefully, gradually drawing nearer to the vriliogire, which occupied one of its extremities.

He had already made the tour twice, surprised not to find any opening by means of which Labergère had been precipitated into the basement—if that expression might be applicable at such a depth. Suddenly, he stopped in front of a black mass which he had already brushed as he passed it by, and which had given him the impression that it was a block of stone of a slightly deeper hue than the others. This time, however, as her deliberately kicked it, he had a surprise. It did not have the rigidity of stone; it was soft an elastic.

He leaned over, excitedly, and felt it with his open hand. "But it's a heap of rags," he murmured. "Unless…" He felt again—more vigorously, this time. There was flesh beneath the fabric. It was an organic body! He tried, vainly, to ascertain the form and nature of the object by the light of the lamp. He could only see a sort of rotundity, over which something like a sheath of black cloth was extended.

Suddenly, he released a cry. It was a human body, so tightly wedged in a frame of rock that it seemed impossible to extract it therefrom.

Was it alive or dead? It did not move—not a twitch or a tremor. Placing his hand flat on the cloth, however, Athel ascertained that the animal warmth had not disappeared. He knelt down, placed his ear to the projecting part, and listened attentively. There was respiration! There was life!

The cloth was that of a coat: an English coat—which led Athel Random to a conclusion, and a name sprang to his lips: "Bobby!" And when he shouted it out he felt a slight movement in the back in question. Somewhere, therefore, beneath that back, there was a head, with ears.

Athel, however, considered the matter anxiously. It certainly seemed simple enough to grab a fistful of the cloth covering the back and lift it up, drawing it out along with the rest of the body, but the stone formed such a narrowly-adapted border around it that it seemed impossible that the rest actually would follow the impulse. Fortunately, Sir Athel was not a man to give up easily. With considerable effort, he succeeded in introducing his hands between the stone border and the body, and with his legs spread, pulling with all his strength, he succeeded in parting the jaws of the vice that was compressing the unfortunate man's thorax.

There was a further anxiety then. He feared that the body, disengaged from the constraint that held it, might fall into the empty space that extended below him. It was necessary for Sir Athel to summon up all his above-average strength so that, supporting the body with one hand, he could use the other to right it.

Finally, the body swung around and the shoulders and head emerged. One last tug, and Bobby—for Bobby it was—emerged from the hole in which he had been so awkwardly wedged. But in what a state, alas! Livid, eyes closed, with a scratch on the forehead where droplets of blood were forming. Sir Athel felt for a pulse and sounded Bobby's chest. Nothing was broken. It was a miracle. Bobby had merely been rendered unconscious following a fall. Was not the vrilium at hand? The scientist's wallet was a veritable instrument-case, a surgical arsenal.

The little syringe made its appearance and, having laid Bobby's calf bare, Sir Athel gave him a tiny injection. Then, while waiting for it to take effect, he went in the direction from which he had heard Labergère's voice. Curiously, it was impossible to find another fissure in the stone floor. Had the entire conversation been conducted through the orifice in which the unfortunate Bobby had been wedged, then?

That was the case; he had immediate proof of it, for he reporter, growing impatient down below, started shouting: "Hey, up there! Do you intend to leave me rotting in these catacombs?" This time the voice, which had previously been muffled by Bobby's body—which had formed a stopper—sounded clear and vibrant. That also explained how the vrilium light had not been able to reach Labergère; he could see it now, above him.

"Listen to me," Athel shouted to him. "We can't pretend that we aren't in a situation that's more than critical. First, know that Bobby is alive, here, next to me, and that he'll be perfectly sound again in a few minutes…"

"Super!" exclaimed Labergère, in a child-like manner. "I'd have missed him."

"So the three of us will be able to combine our efforts to get out of here. It's a matter of staying calm and summoning up all our ingenuity. Are you beginning to shake off your exhaustion?"

"Yes, yes… if I could see more clearly, I'd be fine—but in the darkness of a cave with which one isn't familiar, you know, one can't get very far…"

"I'll light it up for you as brightly as possible, and you can answer my questions."

"Let's go!"

Sir Athel lay down on the ground and passed his light tube through the hole exposed by Bobby's extraction.

"Perfect!" cried Labergère. "Gas on every floor! That's the ticket!"

"Can you stand up and see where you are?"

"I'm on my feet. The place isn't very cheerful. A cave or grotto—whatever you want to call it—but enormous."

"How high is the ceiling, in your estimation?"

"Hmm! My eyes aren't too good at present... between five and six meters."

"Can you see any means of hoisting yourself up to the opening where the light is?"

"None! Not the slightest sign of a ladder. The walls seem to be all of a piece, without any rough patches to use as footholds or handholds."

"So you can't get up here?"

"It's quite impossible. It would need at least three men to form a human ladder."

"A question for consideration! I'll have to leave you in darkness for a moment—I have to see to Bobby."

"Pray do so—I have nothing but patience."

Sir Athel had heard Bobby stirring behind him. He turned round. Bobby was now sitting up on the ground. His eyes were wide open; he seemed utterly bewildered. He was making incoherent gestures, as if he were addressing a mute monologue to an invisible person. Evidently, the terrible shock he had experienced had deranged his brain slightly. When Sir Athel approached him, he recoiled in fear.

The younger Englishman talked to him slowly and softly, trying to impress on Bobby's mind the conviction that he was saved—an affirmation, alas, of whose absolute truth he was gravely in doubt himself.

As Athel continued to reassure him, though, Bobby gradually resumed his normal expression. Finally, he recognized his interlocutor and cried: "My God! Hurrah for England! Long live His Majesty the King and Emperor!" This effusion of loyalism succeeded in restoring his aplomb. "Well," he said, "we're alive! Ah, Mrs. Bobby will be glad! I'll send her a telegram immediately."

"Hmm!" said Sir Athel. "Take note, my dear Mr. Bobby, that we have to get out of here first."

Bobby looked around with a rather haggard gaze. "Right! Where are we?"

"Several hundred feet underground, to put it bluntly."

"Ouch!" said the detective. "That's a lot. We're doomed, then?"

"As long as the blood is circulating in our veins," Sir Athel replied, "as long as our heads are level and our muscles elastic, we must never despair. Have you any serious injuries?"

"None."

"You head's clear?"

"Very nearly."

"Well, I, Sir Athel Random, tell you that we must not admit defeat until we've tried everything to get us out of this. Come on, Bobby—you're an English citizen. You and I must do honor to our country. Don't forget that there's a Frenchman underneath us who will judge us."

"A Frenchman? Who's that?"

"Your friend Labergère."

"Is that so? So he's no more dead than we are!"

"Lean over that hole and talk to him."

"Hey, Monsieur Labergère, how do you do?"[27]

"Quite well, much obliged," replied the reporter, with a hearty laugh.

"Where are you?"

"I'll tell you when I know. For the moment, I'd like Sir Athel to tell us whether he has any idea how to save our skins."

"Listen to me, both of you," said the Englishman. "We've been precipitated into a sort of gulf—whose depth, unfortunately, we can't determine. By some miracle, the vriliogire withstood the explosion and hollowed out a path for us into a sort of shaft, to the bottom of which we slid. As you were above it, perhaps sustained by the roof, you've arrived at the place where, in one of the walls of the well, it was stopped by continuous rock. You, Monsieur Labergère, rolled into the pocket where Mr. Bobby and I ended up, but there was a hole in the inferior wall and you fell through it; the surprising thing is that you didn't break any bones. Monsieur Bobby wasn't positioned as conveniently, and was interrupted by the contours of the orifice, where he was mounted like a diamond in a gold ring. I've got him out of it; I'd like to do more. Let's reason it out. There's no humanly feasible means of going back up the shaft—which must, in any case, have been blocked. We don't have any means at our disposal for such an ascent, and even the vrilium can't give us any useful assistance.

"Conclusion: it's necessary for us to find another exit.

---

[27] This question and its reply are rendered in English in the original.

155

"We're protected against certain eventualities: against darkness; against hunger and against material objects that the vrilium can overturn. We'll carve out a path and, with the aid of science, perhaps we'll succeed in getting back to the surface..."

"Ah, Paris!" Labergère lamented, comically. "The boulevards... and a quarter-liter of beer, well drawn!"

"Finally, since you, Labergère, can't come to us, we'll have to come down to you, and it's from where you are that we'll begin our exploration. Mr. Bobby, have you any objection to raise against the plan?"

"None!" proclaimed Bobby, sticking out his chest. "With the vrilium, I'll go all the way to the end of the world!"

"Unfortunately, for the moment, so far as we're concerned, the world isn't very spacious and the end isn't far away. Let's get going. Mr. Bobby, don't budge. I'll go back into the vriliogire, a poor wreck that I must force myself to abandon. I'll get various objects that we might need. Hold the light-stick at arms length, Monsieur Bobby, and let me do what I have to do..."

With a lithe bound, Sir Athel went back into the cabin. Five minutes later, he came out again, armed with a little box and a coil of rope as thick as a little finger. "Now, my dear Mr. Bobby, I'll have the honor of attaching this around your armpits and lowering you down to your fiend Monsieur Labergère. You don't have any objection?"

"From now on, I consider myself on military service, and you as my commanding officer."

"Very good. Let's go!" In a few moments, Bobby was securely moored beneath his arms. With the best will in the world, holding the box that had been entrusted to him in his arms, he let himself slide into the hole in question, which was large enough for a body to pass through vertically, and the descent began.

Five meters! Labergère had calculated correctly. The affair proceeded without difficulty.

"I have Bobby in my arms!" shouted Labergère. "My heart is palpitating. But what about you? How the Devil will you get down to us?"

"Like this!" said Sir Athel, who, suspending himself from the edge of the ceiling, let himself fall, lithely and skillfully, and landed on his feet.

He immediately re-lit the lamp that had gone out momentarily. "Each of you take a Berthelot pill, quickly," he said. "We'll need all our strength."

"It's not that bad," said Labergère, chewing the chemical aliment, "but it's not as good as a beefsteak…"

"We're in no position to play the gourmet. The box, Mr. Bobby!"

He opened it and took out two rods, which he gave to his companions after having activated the luminous flow. "Let's look around," he said.

Marching in single file, with Sir Athel in the lead, they set about exploring the enormous hollow pocket in which they were imprisoned.

Suddenly, Sir Athel released a cry of joy. "There's a way out…" Which meant that he had just discovered a cleft, high up and narrow, that seemed to have been sliced through the rock by a hatchet-blow.

"We're saved!" said Bobby, who was in an optimistic mood.

"Provided," Sir Athel corrected him, "that the tunnel, which seems very narrow to me, leads somewhere."

"Anywhere's better than here!"

"Very true," said Labergère, approvingly. "And remember that above us, there are good Parisians strolling, hurrying, chatting... perhaps there's a brasserie directly overhead! Why, where the Devil has our Englishman gone?"

In fact, Sir Athel had just introduced himself resolutely into the cleft and had disappeared. "Wait there a minute!" he shouted. "No point in risking all three of us in this preliminary exploration."

There was a long silence; then the voice resumed: "Come on, both of you. Be careful—there's a rather steep descent."

"A descent!" sighed the reporter. "We were scarcely hoping to descend, as old Corneille said. Who knows, my dear Bobby—perhaps, in the end, we'll come out at the Antipodes, on some unknown Pacific island... that wouldn't bother me, but it's a long way—and I've got a meeting in two hours in the Rue Taitbout!" He slid rapidly into the tunnel, whose sheer walls scarcely permitted his broad shoulders to spread out.

Bobby, ever-obedient, followed directly behind.

"Well," said the reporter, "what do you think of our situation, Monsieur du Vrilium?"

Sir Athel, bracing himself with his feet, shone the light of his torch at the top of the side-wall. "Do you know anything about geology?" he asked Labergère.

"Hmm! I have some vague knowledge of it, as everyone has. A good journalist has to be good at everything, whether it's maintaining a foothold at a conference at the Sorbonne on the revolutions of the globe..."

"Good! You'll understand me—that's all that's necessary. I confess that I'm profoundly astonished. Although I knew no more than you about the depth we've attained, I never imagined how the sediments would be compounded. The rocks surrounding us belong to the last period of the Tertiary Era—the one we call the Miocene, just at the beginning of the Pliocene. It's in that epoch that the rocks on which Paris now stands were elevated.

"In that case," said Labergère, lighting a cigarette—the last he had in reserve, alas—"it was before 1830."[28]

"It must have been hundreds of thousands of years..."

"The stone's well-preserved—it isn't showing its age."

"And yet what quakes and deformations the ground was subjected to in that epoch!" exclaimed Sir Athel. "Powerful phenomena of which we can scarcely form any idea, continually modifying the climatic conditions, which passed with amazing suddenness from excessive heat to glacial cold... solar radiation of which tropical heat can hardly give an idea, succeeded almost instantaneously by downpours of snow and rain, which furious desiccating winds froze into glaciers. It was a time of volcanic eruptions in Auvergne and the microlithic rocks..."

"Excuse me for interrupting, my dear Monsieur," the reporter interrupted, softly, "but could you leave the explanations for later. Time's getting on, and"—he checked his watch—"it'll soon be time for aperitifs."

"You're right!" said Sir Athel, laughing. "When the scientific demon gets a grip on you, you forget everything else..."

"Can this science with the forbidding names at least indicate a means of egress to us?"

---

[28] The ironic reference is to the year of the July Revolution that put a final end to the Bourbon dynasty and the *Ancien régime*.

"None at all, alas! The upheavals that occurred in that period, however, were so enormous that they permit all sorts of hypotheses. Who knows whether, at the moment when we least expect it, we might find a way out…"

"Unless we don't find one! That's perfectly understood. At any rate, I'm taking notes for the finest item of reportage I've ever penned. I have my title: *Journey Through the Miocene*! But I confess to you that I'd rather be in a position to assert my authorial rights."

They resumed their march; the fissure suddenly widened, then the ground became increasingly difficult, with projections and hollows that tripped them up.

Suddenly, a triple exclamation, combining surprise and disappointment, escaped all three throats. In front of them was a wall, completely blocking the way. It was high, slick, sealed as perfectly as if it had been made of cement, without a single fissure or crack. The long tunnel through which they had been walking for such a long time was cut off.

Labergère let out an oath as energetic as it was impolite. Even brave Bobby, despite the correctness of his manner and language, released an equivalent in his own tongue. Only Sir Athel remained mute, as if choked—but large drops of sweat were moistening his forehead.

This time, it was the end: desperation, death….

If they retraced their steps, they would find themselves in the cavern they had quit more than two hours ago, from which they already knew that no escape was possible. They were surrounded, buried, imprisoned….

"We're f-----," said Labergère, laconically.

"Goodbye, Mrs. Bobby," murmured the detective, dolorously.

"And it's all my doing!" said Sir Athel. "May death come soon to deliver me from immortal remorse!"

"Come on, old chap," said Labergère, in a conciliatory tone, "don't be so hard on yourself. It's true that our beautiful career is over, and I know that my death is a true catastrophe for the entire world—but the world will get over it. It only remains for us to take our leave; it annoys me, because I've always dreamed of dying beautifully, and it's ugly and dirty to kick the bucket in a cave—even a Pliocene one! If only one could offer oneself a nice meal with champagne, coffee and assorted liqueurs... cherry brandy or Fernet Branca!"

Bobby's voice rose up, as tearful as a child's: "Personally, I don't want to die. Come on, Sir Athel, try something. You're a scientist. You have the vrilium."

At that word, Sir Athel raised his head. Yes, Bobby was right. With that enormous force at his disposal, had he the right not to employ it, even imprudently or madly? Since all seemed lost, had the moment not come to risk everything? "Listen, friends," he said, in a resolute tone. "Mr. Bobby's right—I have the vrilium. Thanks to the apparatus I placed in this box here, I can attempt to pierce or knock down the wall that is barring our way and beyond which—who knows?—we might find salvation."

"Perfect," said Labergère. "Let's go..."

"You know full well what we're risking. Perhaps that wall is part of the foundation on which the vault overhead rests. Deprived of that support, it could collapse—then we'd be crushed, killed instantaneously..."

"Well, we'll die, that's all. If we stay here twiddling our thumbs, it's no less certain that we'll croak, and perhaps very nastily. We might fall out, start fighting... even eating one another."

"Ugh!" said Bobby.

"But yes, my lad. When you've gone out of your mind, you'll be quite capable of wanting to gnaw on my arm—so, Monsieur Random, you have my full authorization... let your jolly vrilium drill into it, cut it, slice it, demolish it... whatever happens, it will settle things— and tell yourself, before you begin, that I, Labergère, don't hold anything at all against you. It isn't your fault that that imbecile Coxward crashed in your aircraft, and I acknowledge that you've risked everything to repair the damage he caused and save our brave Parisians from the most intense fright they've ever experienced. You've risked your neck; it turned out badly. Bobby and I are here as amateurs; that's our business. So, here's my hand; put yours there, and let's shake hands as friends who'd obviously rather be clinking glasses of export vermouth on the terrace of the Café Cardinal—or the Véron, for preference—but who are, at least, taking the thing philosophically, like the brave fellows we are, only regretting that we don't have any longer..."

Labergère, who was not sentimental, had delivered this little tirade in a slightly hoarse voice, which, coming from the heart, caught in his throat.

Sir Athel took the hand that was extended to him.

"Well, me too," said Bobby, advancing his own. "I don't hold anything against you either. It annoys me, that's all."

The three men shook hands vigorously.

"The oath of the Horatii... over the clock!"[29] sniggered the incorrigible Labergère.

---

[29] The reference is presumably to the positioning of Louis David's painting of the *Serment des Horaces* in the Louvre rather than to the original oath sworn by the three Roman

Sir Athel did not say a word. Pale, but very calm and perfectly composed, he knelt down, opened the box that Bobby had placed on the ground and took out the various instruments, which he arranged carefully. Then he stood up. He was radiant; despite the frightful risk that he and his friends were running, his passion for science had gripped him again—for he was about to undertake one of the most interesting experiments that had ever been conducted with vrilium.

"Stand a few meters behind me," he said. "Fragments of stone could be blasted away, which might hurt you... let's minimize the risk as far as we can..."

Then, taking up a sort of drill whose bit was sheathed at the tip of a strong metal rod, in which a small sphere evidently containing vrilium was lodged, he applied it to the wall. He flipped a switch; a spark sprang forth; a grinding sound was heard, like a rotatory movement of enormous velocity. The drill disintegrated the gypsum rock and a whirlwind of fine dust rose up and fell back.

"Victory!" cried Sir Athel. "The wall's no more than 30 inches thick. I'm going clean through it." He withdrew his drill, which left a large hole. Then, patiently, he resumed the operation to one side. Burglars proceed in this fashion when they want to detach the armored door of a strong-box.

In a few minutes, he had formed a frame, leaving no more than a little gap between the holes. Sir Athel then modified his apparatus, substituting for the drill a sort of jack-hammer, and another switch clicked. This time, the

---

brothers, in which no *pendule* [clock] could possibly have played a role.

sparks were larger, crackling like revolver-shots—and the stone panel cracked, broke, fell...

An opening was contrived, a meter square—large enough to permit the passage of a man.

The tunnel walls had not shifted at all.

Seizing the torch, Sir Athel leaned through the opening and cried: "Friends! A prodigy! A cave of diamonds!"

V. A Menagerie such as has scarcely ever been seen

Of diamonds, no—but of ice! Dazzling facets, whirling stars, worlds aflame. In the radiance sent forth by the movement of the three vrilian torches, fireworks burst with moving fulgurations, fiery colors that reduced crystals to dust...

Intoxicated by the life recovered in this apotheosis of enchantment, they shook their torches madly, whose flashes, similar to those of lycopodium,[30] provoked meteoric ripostes, launched auroras, gyrations of radiance, sometimes dying away into a dark background like infinite space, sometimes soaring through the void like melting lead bullets.

Sir Athel had been the first to leap enthusiastically through the open exit, which let out on to a platform, the summit of a vast pillar from which the grotto it overlooked seemed to extend the richness of its reflections and cometary tails to infinity. The other two followed him. Dazzled, they stared with dilated pupils, like children, enjoying the intoxication of that beauty in that kaleidoscope of splendor, having forgotten everything—all their fatigue and the fear of death that had passed through their minds—enveloping themselves in that magnificence, which penetrated them, reigniting their will to live!

Sir Athel recovered his composure first. Dragging himself out of the physical daze to which he had been

---

[30] Lycopodium powder consists of extremely fine plant-seeds, which—like fine particles of flour or any other organic substance—can form an explosive mixture with air.

subject, he sought to take account of the dimensions of the cavern, its origin and its orientation.

There was no doubt in his mind that this glacial excavation dated from a time so distant that science had not yet been able to calculate it. It was the work of one of those telluric upheavals that had accompanied and determined the formation of our ground. The grotto was immense; seeking to direct the light of his torch, he perceived nothing above him but eccentrically-formed peaks: needles with sharp tips, square towers formed like those of the Middle Ages, platforms and balusters suspended from above in defiance of all the law of statics…

Down below were mounds, hill and pointed blocks whose tips darted forth as if launching themselves to meet the stalactites hanging down from above—and also profound, dark, almost pitch-black hollows. Down there, at the limit of vision, an enormous dark patch stained the whiteness of the glacial snows, and there was another on the summit of one of the peaks, hiding its crest, which reminded him of a gigantic bat.

Then he perceived that the cold was intense, especially by comparison with the oppressive temperatures in which they had been immersed for such a long time—and, turning towards the opening that had granted him passage, he felt a warm draught coming therefrom, flowing briskly into the grotto. Taking a little thermometer from his kit, he observed that the ambient temperature was six degrees below zero—a temperature that did not pose any danger to the human body.

He addressed his companions. "Well, my friends, what do you think of this spectacle?"

"Unequalled!"

"Beautiful!"

"Magnificent!"

"Splendid!"

The excessive adjectival exclamations stumbled over one another.

"As a stage-set," said Labergère, "it puts the Châtelet in the shade! All it lacks is dancers in tights!"

"What a décor for a Christmas fantasy!" added Bobby.

"You like it, then," Athel went on. "Me too—but if you think about it, we ought to curb our enthusiasm. For one thing, it's cold..."

"That's true. My fingers are numb."

"And it would be as well to take stock somewhat."

"I shan't refuse... as to that, where are we?"

"On the summit of a peak of rock and ice," Athel replied. "And I should add, to draw you out of the dream and bring you back to reality, that—saving further examination—we're hardly any further forward than we were before. We know how we got in here, but we have absolutely no idea how to get out."

"Damn!" said Labergère. "I wasn't thinking about that any longer. One can't ever get a moment's rest, even a hundred feet underground... it doesn't matter; I had ten minutes of enjoyment! Now, O thou who art the god of wisdom, tell us what's what..."

"First, have we all our tools? The box?"

"Under my arm," said Bobby. "I'm just following orders..."

"That's good. The vrilium will be useful to us; it can still help us. First, we have to get down..."

"From our perch," said Labergère. "But that doesn't seem very easy to me."

"It's child's play. I can see ledges that will serve as footholds, and in case of interruption, the vrilium will cut out the steps of a stairway for us. But look around you, Monsieur Labergère, and tell me what idea you've formed of the grotto."

"I can see that it's enormous—a veritable cathedral—but what's that down there, between two peaks of ice? Something colossal, totally black... rounded in form, and shiny..."

"I can see it too. Entirely motionless, isn't it?"

"Absolutely—but it's not the only one. They might be enormous bocks of black stone... basalt or granite? Perhaps something like moraines, the rocks carried by melting ice that one finds at the edges of glaciers..."

"That's possible," said Sir Athel, evasively. "I'll examine that one."

"We'll go together."

"I'll go alone, if you'll permit me."

Sir Athel's peremptory, almost authoritarian tone astonished Labergère slightly, but he was beginning to respect him profoundly and did not reply.

"Let's get our strength back first," Sir Athel said, his tone becoming natural again. "We need sleep, and it's necessary for us to find a corner where we won't be too cold."

"We can go back in there," Bobby put in, pointing to the opening by means of which they had penetrated the grotto.

"I think that might be impossible," Athel replied.

"Why?"

"Look for yourself. The needle on which we're standing is covered by a layer of hardened snow. Examine it closely, and you'll see that the current of warm air coming from the opening has already begun to melt the frozen section directly ahead of it. It won't be hard enough to support us... it will give way beneath our feet and we'll slide into the void."

"That's true, damn it!" said Labergère. "But then, perhaps we can clear the place with vrilium—which seems to be good for anything—and install our bedroom here, profiting from the relative warmth."

"Let's try!" said Sir Athel.

The vrilium flame worked its marvels again. The ice and snow were removed from a circle four meters across; then the rock was dried out, and the men lay down, without worrying overmuch about the future.

Labergère and Bobby, exhausted, slipped into a profound sleep, but Sir Athel kept watch. He knew full well that they were in no immediate danger on the platform that isolated them, but a vague, obscure idea was haunting him, inspiring a fear of new complications, even more terrible than those they had overcome....

He waited patiently. Labergère was snoring, Bobby breathing heavily. They were deeply asleep—he was free to act. With infinite precaution, he slid towards the descending slope of the platform. Having put a metallic headband around his head, to which he had fixed a vrilian lamp, he began to make his way down.

Accustomed, like all Englishmen, to physical exercise and various games of agility and skill, and being exceptionally robust, Sir Athel made marvelous use of the slightest cracks in the rock and the ice. Soon, he reached a sort of ledge that allowed him to get a few moments' rest. He took deep breaths of the fresh air, which gave his lungs new strength. Although he could not pretend that he had his friends had got out of the frightful pass to which fatality had brought them, he had never felt such freedom of spirit or more active courage. He had accepted the struggle; he was certain that he would not weaken.

He resumed his descent. Now he was beginning to see into the depths of the cavern, composed of confused strata that overlapped one another, as if the waves of a river had suddenly been fixed in an abrupt freeze, which had stopped their movements while they were still in-complete.

A large open space extended at the foot of the crag, forming a sort of dark-hued mound, like the stains he had perceived from above with Labergère. A crown of ice surrounded the base of the entire area, however, daz-zlingly white, making the black mass lying beneath it stand out even more. Sir Athel finally set foot on that gallery; he had accomplished the hardest part of his task. Now, more than ever, he felt gripped by a curiosity so intense that his heart was beating as if to break out of his chest.

With a prudence redoubled by the dread of com-promising the success of his self-appointed investiga-tion, the young Englishman made a tour of the entire crown of ice, projecting the light as far as was possible. He perceived other black stains, of smaller dimensions than those already remarked.

He felt something crack beneath his feet; he de-tached his lamp, bent down and looked; he had just walked over an object that he had partially crushed. Picking it up, he uttered an exclamation of surprise.

Well-versed in paleontological science, he had just recognized the bones of a wing that he immediately identified as belonging to a pterodactyl, an extinct ani-mal whose skull had suggested to the great anatomist Richard Owen the thought that no vertebrate organ had ever been constructed with more economy of materials, in order to combine lightness with strength.

Then, as if the discovery had corroborated a certain idea that he had not dared admit to himself, in his modesty as a scientist, he crossed the islet of ice resolutely and marched towards the enormous black patch that had attracted his attention. He recognized very quickly that it was neither a block of basalt nor a mass of granite, but the entire corpse of a gigantic animal: a mammoth, long extinct and known to us primarily by virtue of skeletons found in the depths of paleozoic strata.

Yes, it was definitely that gigantic, ponderous mass, one of nature's rough drafts, of which the elephant in the descendant, reduced in size by a third. With a passionate fever, Sir Athel saw before his very eyes a reproduction of a prodigy already observed in Siberia: the absolute conservation by the cold, in its entirety, of a colossal animal, with its hide and flesh. He hoisted himself up on to the monster's shoulder in order to study that enormous head at closer range, with its two curved tusks. With his hands he felt the cold-stiffened hair. He went down to the immense feet that seemed to be carved out of a block of marble.

He no longer had any thought, now, for the danger that he and his companions were running. He was living a scientist's dream, touching those limbs which no human strength would have been able to lift—what a triumph for a seeker! What a victorious response to the adversaries of evolution!

Seized by a kind of madness, Sir Athel climbed up the mammoth's corpse to look more closely at the other black patches, which—there as no longer any doubt—were preanthropic animals, anterior to the appearance of man. When an initial inspection had confirmed his hypothesis, he came back down and began running through the cavern...

Here he found intact, in its age-old immobility, a megatherium with its massive hind-quarters and its forward-projecting paws, armed with claws like sabers, which seized its prey and tore it apart.

Further away, lying on its side as if asleep, was a mastodon, a gigantic proboscidean, a giant mammal of primitive times, six meters tall and eight meters long, not counting the trunk.

There, doubtless taken by surprise and immobilized by the cold, was a megaceros, the ancestor of our red deer, with enormous horns spreading out like a fan, cutting through the air at a height of four meters. That one, leaning over on its front legs, which were flexed towards the ground, seemed ready to resume a leap interrupted by the cataclysm.

He almost fell, his feet tripping over the scales of a monstrous crocodile more than two meters long, crouching on its belly with its mouth agape, as if for combat.

Finally came the two masterpieces of the collection—the only term that could characterize the astonishing aggregation of monsters. One was a brontosaurus, the giant of the dinosaurs, with a length of more than fifteen meters and a weight of more than fifteen tons, which was lying full length, its long neck raising its minuscule head into the air. The other—the black patch that Labergère had noticed while standing on the wall of the block of rock and ice—was a dinornis, a giant bird, the prototype of our ostriches, which measured more than three meters from head to foot. The latter animal was still upright adjacent to the mass that supported it, astonishingly well-preserved, with its long, stiff feathers still shiny.

What terrestrial upheaval could have determined this stupefying phenomenon? Evidently, a surge of cold had descended upon the regions, so terrible—so devastating, one might say—that a group of animals had attempted to flee before it, all rivalries and hatreds forgotten in the course of that terrible flight. By virtue of the sudden afflux of snow and ice, they had been blocked into this cavern, where the cold had overtaken them, instantaneously freezing their blood and marrow. Then the abysm had closed over them, burying them in that glacial and eternally-preserving temperature...

Millennia had passed, and these formidable specimens of the first efforts of creative nature must have remained eternally unknown—and it had been necessary, for their rest to be troubled, that John Coxward the boxer, having stolen a watch, had jumped over Sir Athel Random's wall in order to escape his pursuers, and had taken refuge, drunk and panic-stricken, in the vriliogire!

What tricks destiny plays!

In his long journey through the grotto, Sir Athel had become exhausted, but he could not abandon his companions—who, not finding him next to them when they woke up, might become scared and commit some imprudence...

The courageous Englishman, his strength renewed by the joy of his discovery, climbed back up to the platform where he had left Labergère and Bobby by means of the muscular force of his arm and back. He found them calm and motionless, snoring and breathing noisily. Letting himself slump to the ground, he fell into a deep sleep.

Alas, his sleep would not have been so peaceful, if he had been able to foresee the frightful catastrophe that was about to unleashed on Paris!

VI. Collapse

Bobby was the first to wake up. While still half-asleep, he saw himself at the seaside, in a little cottage in the village of Inverstead, near Hastings—a delightful house, with four rooms and a basement, which Mrs. Bobby had inherited from an uncle and in which they dreamed of spending their old age.

Suddenly, he shivered: something had just fallen on his eyelid. He shook it off; it was followed by the impression of a pinch on the nose. This time, he sneezed, then snorted and opened his eyes. His vrilian staff was stuck in the ground a short distance away; he saw nothing unusual, but received another tap on the nose. Something strange was evidently happening. He lifted his hand to his face and found that it was damp. Then, descending to his collar, he established the disturbing truth: his coat, waistcoat and shirt were literally soaked. It was raining!

He leapt to his feet, which splashed in a puddle of water.

"Hey, gentlemen!" he cried. "Wake up! We're being flooded."

At the sound of his voice Labergère and Athel abruptly woke up—and they both exclaimed in surprise as they experienced the same sensation of humidity.

"A downpour!" said Labergère. "It reminds me of Ivry!"

Sir Athel was in no mood for jokes, though. Very quickly, he had perceived that the rain of droplets was coming from the melting of stalactites hanging from the vault. At the same time, pricking up his ears, he thought he could hear the soft and persistent sound of running streams. He was also in no doubt that the rock on which they had taken refuge had lost the greater part of its vestment of snow and ice—and that, in consequence, the projections and cracks of which he had made use in his nocturnal expedition were disappearing.

"It's a thaw," he said. "The hole that we made in the sealed wall of the cavern has given passage to a current of warm air…"

"Good" said Labergère. "One can get out one's summer jacket…"

But Athel leaned towards him excitedly. "Don't laugh," he said, in a low voice. "Perhaps it's a disaster—which is to say, the final catastrophe. Who knows whether these enormous lumps of rock, retained by the ice that serves the function of cement, might collapse on top of us?"

"Damn it! Here's the silliness starting again… I have to get out of here."

"We have to try one more time… but let's not hide the fact that the situation is more critical than ever…" He suddenly interrupted himself and, his mastery of himself notwithstanding, his physiognomy expressed an anguish so profound that Labergère, in spite of his insouciance, started anxiously.

"Eh? What's the matter?"

Athel went to the extreme edge of the rock. "Listen!" he said. "Tell me, you two, whether my ears are ringing, whether I'm going mad, or whether there really…"

"I can hear something," Bobby said, in as quavering voice. "It's as if something were moving out there…"

"That's true!" cried Labergère. "There's a stir down there. Look! Doesn't it seem to you that those enormous black patches we noticed when we arrived are moving, little by little?"

They had lit their torches and were leaning forward, turning up the flames so that the light would carry into the depths—and in the masses of granite and basalt, there was a sort of oscillation.

"Those stones must be alive!" said Labergère, in a strangled voice. "What's happening?"

"What's happening," cried Sir Athel, despairingly, "is that we're witnessing at this moment the most astonishing phenomenon that has ever occurred since the first formation of the Earth. What's happening is that down there, below us and around us, is that colossal monsters swallowed up in the glacial period—which is to say, since an epoch whose distance we cannot calculate—are now suddenly awakening, resuscitated from their age-long sleep, under the influence of the rise in temperature that we have brought about in our imprudence and stupidity: mine most of all!

"That's what's happening? No human intelligence could have foreseen it!"

Bobby, struck by a sudden idea, remembered words that he had heard in school. "They're antediluvian animals!" he cried.

"Neither more nor less, old chap," said the reporter, trying to recover his Parisian spirit of mockery. "Something like the generous Mr. Carnegie's diplodocus,[31]

---

[31] The American philanthropist Andrew Carnegie financed several dinosaur-hunting expeditions. When a near-complete specimen of a diplodocus was discovered in 1899—the species had been named *Diplodocus carnegii* after him—he had 11 casts made of it and donated them to numerous museums around the world, including the Jardin des Plantes in Paris.

which, if we're still alive tomorrow, we can all go to see at the Jardin des Plantes... if that catches you with its horns, I bet you it'll do you some damage!"

In the depths of the cavern, the movements increased. There was something like the rustling of heavy fabric, then dull thuds like heavy timbers standing themselves up and bracing themselves with some difficulty, upon the ground.

There was a frightful crack: a mass detached itself from the vault and fell with a frightful racket, smashing into icebergs, rebounding on to the rocks, amid hoarse trumpetings of fear and pain, never before heard by any human ear.

The thaw proceeded with lightning rapidity; around the spur on which the three friends stood, huddled together, paralyzed by the horror of the spectacle vaguely glimpsed in the tenebrous depths, there was no longer anything but collapsing, disintegrating blocks of ice, dragging enormous blocks of stone down as they fell, which rebounded....

"The vrilium! The vrilium!" cried Bobby.

Ah yes, the vrilium! Powerful as it was, could it contest that colossal and tumultuous release of natural forces? Could it lift up a mountain?

Meanwhile, in the midst of this atrocious disorder, animals stood up, whose enormous spines shrugged off lumps of rock, which slid from their thick skin and broke at their feet. Loud voices replied; feet stamped on the ground. Had these escapees of the Tertiary Era not already witnessed identical upheavals, when water, earth and fire had delivered themselves to the unimaginable conflict of disturbed elements? They represented brute force, blind instinct and the omnipotence of preservation, the persistence of life in fabulous longevity, the cohesion of primal energies in which the future of worlds was seething.

Men! Ah, what were they in the face of these aggregations of muscles and tendons, these Leviathans that fable had scarcely dared to describe!

In vain, Labergère and Bobby, who were nothing less than terrified, tried to calm their nerves; in vain, Sir Athel, bewildered, made appeal to the intelligence by which thinking beings had vanquished brute strength...

They felt diminished, shrunken, weakened to the point of no longer having any idea of resistance. They were no longer speaking, hardly able to think; in their weakened brains, everything lost its shape, its form; ideas wandered without becoming fixed; the sensation of memory, comparison and judgment atrophied.

The water was still falling, clattering now like stormy rain; the vrilium torches were extinguished, and nothing any longer persisted but the fantastic noises produced by that fauna suddenly evoked by a prodigious palingenesis...

And while they were thus transfixed, hypnotized by the mystery, stifled by the unknown, the final catastrophe was accomplished. In the tumult of thunderous noise, the entire grotto came apart and caved in. The quivering rocks fell; the needles of ice cut through the air like steel blades.

Everything collapsed, disintegrating, in a frightful dismemberment. The monsters howled, clamored and roared—and, as if the incredible still wished to challenge the possible, a part of the vault broke away and enormous fissures opened up...

And the light of the Sun burst though, in a triumphant flood.

VII. The Invasion of Paris

It was a Sunday at the end of April, one of those fine days that are the heralds of the month of May. It was 8 a.m.; the idle city was getting up late. Before departing for somewhere in the countryside, people were lying languidly in bed, making up for having to rise early during the week.

In the populous neighborhoods of the Buttes-Chaumont, the Rues Secrétan, Bolivar and Botzaris, the housewives go easy on the workers who have toiled all week; they get up first and, having made sure that the babies are sound asleep and will not wake their fathers, they slip outside for the morning provisions, running to the shops, attentive to the quality of the vegetables and the quality of the meat, preoccupied with not making too big a hole in the Saturday wages. They are cheerful and alert, vivacious and loquacious, indulging in rapid conversations at the street-corners with other hurrying women, especially impatient to escape to some corner of the suburbs where one can drink in the fresh air—and other things—while the children laugh and sing on papa's shoulders.

The weather had been poor for the previous fortnight; on this beautiful sunny morning there was a resurrection of light. Faces and hearts blossomed. It was good to be alive!

One of these groups of brave Parisians had paused at the corner of the Rue Pradier and the Square Boucher-de-Perthes; the gossip was well under way—without malice, so much does well-being soften character. Suddenly, the greengrocer, who was standing on his doorstep slicing up a pat of butter, stopped up in bewilderment. Holding his knife at full stretch, he released a horrible scream, turned round, threw himself through his doorway and kicked the door shut.

The women turned round, and yelps of terror sprang from every throat.

And enormous black shape was blocking the far side of the square: a demonic apparition that put an enormous ink-stain upon the blue horizon.

And suddenly, without a single word being exchanged, the women fled, shoving one another, elbowing one another, legs slicing, their dry throats uttering bewildered cries for help. They reached the Rue Bolivar; there they bumped into other groups that were calm, and raised the alarm.

There was a frightful monster behind them!

"The Devil!" howled one old woman, making the sign of the cross.

"The Devil!" others laughed.

Were they mad, then? Two policemen were just passing by, placidly. They threw themselves upon them, hands clutching at their capes. Indulgently, they listened, asked questions. There, in the square...

Also believing that they were dealing with madwomen—but how did they come to be so numerous; there must be something there?—they set off to take a look.

Besides, as proof that something abnormal was happening, all the windows in the Rue Laugier were open and frightened faces appeared in their frames, arms beating their air in convulsions of horror, mouths wide open and shouting...

And at the precise moment when the two officers reached the corner of the square, brushing the house whose second floor was level with its back, the mammoth appeared, heavy and solemn, its monstrous head with its flat, wide forehead swaying from side to side, scoring the pavement with its curved tusks, its eyes hardly visible beneath the vast rags of its ears. It was coming forward without haste, monumental, putting down the four power-hammers that were feet one by one, breaking the ground.

The two representatives of the law remained nailed to the spot, devoid of any arrogance, their eyes popping out of their heads. The younger, in a surge of courage, gripped his service revolver in his fist and fired at a range of four meters.

The bullet ricocheted and shattered a shop-window.

The other, calmer, simply said: "Let's go warn the post!" And, lest anyone forget that he was in authority, he shouted at the crowd of women, terrified but even more curious, who were obstructing the corner of the Rue Bolivar: "Move on! Go back home and don't do anything whatsoever before Monsieur le Commissaire has arrived!"

The mammoth walked on, its hindquarters swaying, swishing its hairy tail, which beat the air like a gigantic brush.

When the policemen shouted, the women fled, drawing away the curiosity-seekers who were gradually accumulating, all gripped by panic. Some ran towards the Rue Manin or tried to climb over the gate of the park, others launched themselves at top speed in the direction of the Rue de Crimée. The latter did not get far though, for at the corner of the Rue du Plateau a terrifying silhouette appeared: the megatherium, a giant armadillo four meters in height, with bizarre jaws and a drooping lip. Strongly supported by its hind legs, the latter advanced in bounds, its exceedingly short fore-limbs high above the round, armed with mighty claws. Its face was horrible, diabolical, the pre-eminent eyes rolling, alternating black and white in a frightful fashion.

Before this new apparition the crowd stopped and turned round, and the gallop resumed in the opposite direction, towards the heart of Paris—and the two monsters followed them at a distance, seemingly not in any hurry, at walking pace.

At that moment, the summoned policemen arrived at a run, sabers in hand, ready for any combat—as if it were a matter of a strike—and with them came the Commissaire, a short fat man full of dignity, who had put on his sash in order to be more imposing. But their two colleagues—from before the deluge—were now running along the Rue Botzaris and, as if the labyrinths of the neighborhood had no secrets from them, went into the Rue de l'Atlas heading towards the Boulevard de la Villette.

The Commissaire, correct and very pale, stepped back so as not to get in anyone's way, without knowing what to do. The authority, however, put on a brave face.

Suddenly, from all the streets in the vicinity of the Square Boucher-de-Perthes—and was that not, in truth, a discreet homage to the first man to reveal the importance of the quaternary period of man on Earth?[32]—other

---

[32] The Square Boucher-de-Perthes is named after the amateur geologist and anthropologist Jacques Boucher de Crèvecoeur de Perthes (1788-1860), who devoted much of his free time to the investigation of "antediluvian man." His discovery of flint tools in the Somme valley gave rise to his conviction, popularized in *Antiquités Celtiques et Antédiluviennes* (1847) that human beings had existed in the early Quaternary period no-

monsters, other giants and other colossi surged forth: hipparions, ancestors of our horses, twice the size; a mastodon, a shapeless mass, a veritable block of flesh four meters in length, from which four menacing tusks sprouted like blades; brontosaurs; triceratops; and others that science had not catalogued, roughly-hewn sketches of giant rhinoceroses, enveloped in their carapaces as if in armor, with three tapering and sharpened horns of the summits of their skulls, their giant hindquarters undulating, thighs sheathed in leather, shoulders from which sprouted bones reminiscent of the piston-rods of transatlantic steamers; reptiles marching on their hind legs in the manner of kangaroos...

Above these moving mounds something oscillated: a little mass of bones forming a head, attached to the end of a thin neck two meters long, as if it were a military standard to rally the nightmare troop; it was an iguanodon, measuring more than five meters, balanced on its tripod—two hind limbs and an endless tail—while its anterior limbs were ridiculously short and armed with redoubtable spurs. It seemed to be hurrying towards some eagerly-anticipated combat, cleaving a passage through the hindquarters that pressed upon it like a wall.

Meanwhile, after having tried to take off 20 times over, awkwardly hindered in the employment of its wings devoid of feathers or scales, a monstrous pterodactyl with a wingspan on ten meters finally climbed up

---

wadays known as the Pleistocene. Highly controversial at the time, the conclusion eventually proved to be correct. Boucher also wrote an early scientific romance, "Mazular," included in his *Nouvelles* (1832), to which Lermina might also be paying homage.

to the top of a house and heavily launched itself over Paris like a gigantic airplane.

It was an invasion of prodigious ancestors, escaped from their tombs!

The herd poured out towards the exterior boulevards, following the slope of the ground. At the corner of the Rue de l'Atlas, the mammoth had bumped into an advertising hoarding that it had flattened. In the Boulevard de la Villette, the mastodon had entered into conflict with the omnibus offices, which had oscillated and then collapsed. As a tram arrived at top speed, the brontosaur whose flank it had brushed made an abrupt movement that threw the heavy carriage off its rails, spilling travelers. The trolley broke and fell upon the ancestor, discharging a thousand volts into it; that made it angry, and, quickening its pace, it set off towards the Faubourg du Temple.

Uncomprehending people fled, howling. It was universal panic, in all its horror. A maddened street-urchin cried: "Look at the dirty beasts! They have hair on their feet!"

Prior to this inundation of flesh and bone, which no obstacle could possibly halt, there was an irrational flight, a whirlwind of fear.

The iguanodon, more active than the rest, went by at top speed, overtaking the herd; occasionally, it paused and put its head through one of the open second-story windows, doubtless peering out of simple curiosity, and terrified ululations went up from the startled household. Unmoved, it continued on its way, as if it knew where it was going—and as it rested briefly in the Place de la République, nose-to-nose with the monumental effigy of Marianne, those members of the crowd who had the courage to look saw some sort of rag wrapped around its neck: something resembling a human being.

The iguanodon departed. The others appeared at the junction of the Belleville funicular railway. There was a hesitation, or a collision, the way ahead being too narrow for the movement of those astonishing hips, which tried to turn back and jostled one another, banging into both sides of the street, ripping up a shop here, a public urinal there, which disintegrated noisily. It would not have taken much for them to flatten the barracks.

Feeling hemmed in enraged them and, wrenching themselves from the grip of their mutual pressure, they scattered, some towards the Boulevard Saint-Martin, others towards the Bastille. Others, having followed the iguanodon, went into the Rue Turbigo or the Rue du Temple... and still the crowds fled in panic, horses drawing suddenly-emptied omnibuses at high speed, coach-drivers spilling from their seats, tram-drivers releasing their controls. Iron shutters were hastily lowered over the shop-fronts. There was an indescribably disorder, dominated by bestial growling,[33] the clamors of men, the high-pitched yelps of female voices... and the news of the invasion exploded through Paris, messages sent by telephones, telegraph and pneumatic tube carrying the incredible information—which seemed, at first, to be a colossal hoax.

Troops were mobilized; the Republican guard was sent forth. The Municipal Councilors were attempting to run away from the Hôtel de Ville, but all the exits were blocked; some sort of ornithorhyncus had blocked the

---

[33] The word I have translated here as "bestial" is *thérion*, derived from the Greek, which is usually used in specific reference to *the* Beast (of *Revelation*) rather than any mere animal.

Metro station in the Place de la République, and the ex-asperated travelers were flocking back through the tunnels to get their money back!

On that particular morning, Monsieur Lépine had been called out to the suburbs on urgent business. Monsieur Davaine, the head of the Sûreté, Monsieur Larmion, the chief of the municipal police and Monsieur Ostriot, the secretary general, were awaiting the orders of the Minister of the Interior. Opinions clashed and contradicted one another.

Finally, the Prefect arrived and went into his office, whose windows, wide open to admit the first breezes of spring, overlooked the quay. Not knowing anything, having come from the Left Bank, he did not understand why all these officials were gathered there, shivering.

"What's going on?" he demanded, in his curt, authoritative voice.

They all tried to reply at once, and the explanations, in consequence, lacked clarity.

"What?" he asked. "A menagerie has escaped? Lions, bears, tigers?"

"Worse than that! Monstrous, unknown animals, which are devastating Paris, massacring the population…"

The telephone rang. Monsieur Lépine pounced on it. "Hello? Monsieur le Ministre de l'Intérieur! … Information? … I'm making inquiries … What, on the boulevards? … A serpent 20 meters long passing through the Panoramas? … Right, I'm on my way … Shouldn't we warn Monsieur le Ministre de la Guerre urgently? … The Governor of Paris! … Yes, yes, Monsieur le Ministre, I'll take care of everything! … Immediately!"

He replaced the receiver, then turned to his staff.

"The less one understands," he said, "the more necessary it is to expend energy. There must, as usual, have been a crazy exaggeration. Monsters! Are there any such things as monsters?"

A clamor went up: "There! There! Behind you, Monsieur le Préfet!"

Monsieur Lépine had his back to the open window. He felt something settle on his shoulder, brushing his ear. He turned round precipitately—and his nose bumped into that of the iguanodon.

The horrible beast had reached the Boulevard du Palais via the Rue du Temple and the Boulevard Sébastopol, had paused—without any obvious reason—in front of the Prefecture of Police, and, finding an open window at head height, had stuck its neck into it. It was moving its head, which terminated in a horny beak, back and forth in the prefectorial office.

"What's that!" cried the Prefect, hurling himself backwards.

"It's the invasion of monsters!" replied the head of the Sûreté, who knew everything.

The creature, however, was not menacing. Dazedly, it executed its stupid and pointless oscillatory motion. And it had no weapons to defend itself!

The Prefect ran to the door and saw a policeman, who was taking a nap in the corridor, in complete ignorance of the catastrophe. "Brigadier!" he cried. "Come quickly!"

The other woke up with a start and leapt to his feet.

"Draw your saber," commanded Monsieur Lépine, "and cut that for me!"

That was the iguanodon's neck.

The Brigadier twirled his weapon, thrust with a sure hand—and cut nothing! The blade rebounded from the epidermal layer and leapt into the air.

At the same instant, something came clambering over the balcony—something that might have been a human being, which had hoisted itself up the beast's neck.

The something rolled on to the carpet with a dull thud. Yes, it was definitely a man, but so disheveled, distressed and devastated that it longer looked like one. While the head continued oscillating monotonously, almost touching the ceiling, the unfortunate was lifted up and set on his feet. Someone held his head up, and Monsieur Lépine cried: "But I know this man! It's the English detective, Bobby!"

They tried everything to reanimate him. They forced brandy down his throat. It was not his national whisky, but it was restorative even so. Suddenly, Mr. Bobby stood up straight, recognized the Prefect, set himself within arm's reach, and said: "My God! It's an awful business!"

"What business?"

"I don't know anything about it—a hole, holes, ice, rocks, black forms that move... and then the collapse... a neck that passed over me, which I clung on to, and which carried me off!"

"Explain yourself! What's happened?"

It seemed that the iguanodon looked at Bobby, and confirmed his story with a nod of its head. Then the neck disappeared through the window like a hosepipe dragged backwards.

Bobby released a long sigh. It was the end of the nightmare, at least for the moment. And he explained more clearly...

Incredible and inexplicable the adventure was no less real.

Monsieur Lépine took up his hat and addressed his staff: "Follow me, gentlemen! Let us do our duty!"

Amazing things were happening in the great city.

A triceratops had stopped in front of the Porte-Saint-Denis and, having tried to go in and found it too narrow, had moved back. In the fashion of an ancient battering-ram, it ran at the stones, horns forward, smashing Louis XIV's glorious stones into smithereens.

The mammoth, more calmly, filling the entire street, jogged past the Gymnase and paused briefly in front of the Maison Rouge. It seemed tired now; its tread became heavy and, having arrived in front of Brabant, it folded its limbs and lay down, blocking the entrance to the Faubourg Montmartre.

A brontosaur, which measured 20 meters in length, had exerted all its strength to get into the Passage des Panoramas, but it had been stopped half way by the narrowness of the arcade and remained there, its head in the gallery of the Variétés—on the artistes' side—while its tail garlanded the terrace of the Café Véron.

A megatherium had stood up on the steps of the Opéra, like an orator intending to address the people, and then had leaned against the doors, like a vigilant warden ready to welcome the subscribers.

The pterodactyl, whose flight was ponderous, had perched on one of the cornices of the Madeleine, perhaps to catch its breath. Its agitated tail hung down, caressing the rear side of the statue of Jules Simon.[34]

---

[34] Jules Simon was a spiritualist philosopher and statesman, who served as minister of public information in the "govern-

Already, three hours had passed. It was noon.

Finally, the authorities, convinced of the reality of the peril, had taken measures. Through the deserted avenues came the artillery, galloping horses with sleek hindquarters drawing cannons and machine-guns. If they had to bombard half of Paris, the action would be prompt and energetic.

The entire population of the Right Bank had shut itself up in the houses, breathless, having even lost he will to flee.

In battle formation, the troops advanced prudently, loaded weapons at the ready. The shells slept in the cannons, impatient to awake; the batteries were lining up in the Boulevards, while Monsieur Lépine marched at the head of a contingent of policemen in the vanguard…

And then something happened that was no less strange than what had gone before.

As they advanced further, the defenders saw the monsters totter, stumble on their monstrous limbs, then fall. One of them filled the Olympia with its enormous mass. Another, the one at the Opéra, dragged itself to Carpeaux's group and, having raised its head to savor the line of dancers, let itself fall back…[35]

---

ment of national defence" installed in September 1870, immediately after the catastrophic French defeat at Sedan, which attempted to organize resistance during the siege of Paris; it was dissolved when Adolphe Thiers became the notional head of government in February 1871; the Communist uprising took place shortly thereafter. The pterodactyl's caress thus carries a considerable symbolic burden, of particular significance to Lermina, who had obviously not forgotten his terrible experiences of that period.

[35] Jean-Baptiste Carpeaux was a sculptor whose work *La Danse* still stands in the Opéra's Palais Garnier; it was com-

The gigantic flyer on the Madeleine seemed to flatten itself against the stones, then slipped, and its flaccid mass, as if emptied out, fell down, engulfing the stalls of the flower-market.

The enormous saurian at the Variétés, squeezed on to the paving-stones of the passage, was subject to a fluctuation along its dorsal spine, which diminished with every passing second.

The iguanodon from the Prefecture dragged itself to the parapet, which it attempted to climb over, turned upon itself, and fell into the Seine—where it crushed a barge whose occupants had just enough time to jump into the water.

And the same phenomenon was reproduced on all sides...

These unfrozen denizens of the Quaternary had only been reanimated by a false, temporary life. They bore, even so, the burden of their antiquity and their decrepitude—and, one by one, under the pressure of the ambient air, beneath the spring sunshine, ill-adapted for life in an atmosphere hundreds of thousands of years younger than the one than they had previously breathed, they were dying, being too old in a world that was too new.

By 1 p.m., Paris was saved.

Delightedly, Monsieur Perrier, the director of the Museum, examined the cadavers of the ancestors and spoke joyfully of having new galleries constructed for the reconstitution of these witnesses to Paleozoic times.

Forgetting its plans for strolling in the countryside, the entire population of Paris gathered around the

---

missioned by Napoléon III and was controversial when first revealed by virtue of the alleged obscenity of its nude figures. Again, the dying monster is making a statement of sorts.

enormous corpses, at which they laughed because they were inanimate—and the terraces of the cafés and bars filled up. Card-players shuffled their decks on the marble table-tops....

But what became of the actors in this frightful drama?

Sir Athel Random, alas, never came back. Into what abyss had he disappeared? Under what mass of rock was he buried? And yet, who knows? Men deader than him have been resuscitated...

Poor Mary Redmore! This time, all hope was lost... and she returned, weeping beneath her long mourning-veils, to London. Mr. Redmore still had it in mind to sue the City of Paris for millions in compensation, but wise advice deflected him from this project, to the great regret of the men of law who would have been enriched thereby.

Sir Athel had taken the secret of vrilium with him! And the wreckage of the vriliogire was buried in the bowels of the planet!

But what of Labergère? How had he escaped the pandemonium of rock and ice? When he reappeared that evening in the offices of the *Nouvelliste* to dictate an account of his subterranean excursion, he said that he had found himself, without knowing how, in one of the tunnels of the North-South Metro line—incomplete, of course. On emerging therefrom, he had gone to take the glass of beer he had been coveting for such a long time, and then had come back to reclaim his place in the broad daylight of journalism.

A banquet was organized in honor of Bobby, who made a speech thereat somewhat reminiscent of one of Theodore Roosevelt's, to which the much-fêted Mrs. Bobby listened in tears.

And thus ended the most fantastic, the most astonishing and also the most heart-rending adventure of the first half of the 20th century. There are still plenty of people who claim that it never happened.

THE ELIXIR OF LIFE

Foreword

Can human life be prolonged? This is a question that, sooner or later, secretly or otherwise, presents itself to the investigative mind of the scientist, whether he is an alchemist or a professor of the Collège of France.

The spiritualist school, which considers life as something immaterial, complete and existing independently, furnishes audacious and solid research evidence, but the cold positivist argumentation of the Ecole de Médecine de Paris came along to destroy these beautiful dreams in the name of pure experimentation, making life no more than the more or less perfect result of chemical actions accomplished according to laws operating within the intimacy of tissues.

The struggle between these two opposed tendencies is curious to observe. Bichat,[36] sensitive to the effective power of life, defined it as "that which resists death"—a poor definition in philosophical terms, but excellent for the physician who, sooner or later, will establish the cur-

---

[36] Marie-François-Xavier Bichat (1771-1802) was a significant pioneer of scientific physiology, but found the burden of past assumptions about the essentially "spiritual" nature of life difficult to shake off.

ative force of that mysterious power. Claude Bernard[37] claims to know what it is and, inverting Bichat's spiritualist definition, had made the study of life the constant preoccupation of his research. Superlative results regarding the particular functions of various organs have been acquired by this approach, but the goal to be attained seems to draw increasingly further away, and Bichat's celebrated adversary declared himself defeated in one of his last works.[38] I quote from memory: "life is what makes the egg of a chicken and the egg of a nightingale, which are similarly constituted chemically, produce a chicken on the one hand, and a nightingale on the other."

Without wishing to dwell too long on this question, which is overly entangled with "first causes," let us posit the existence in human beings of a force that incessantly renews elements that are used up and conserved the form of the body. The experiments of Flourens,[39] feeding madder to animals, have proved, in fact, that the most durable and most resistant cells of the human body, bone cells, take a maximum of *one month* to renew them-

---

[37] Claude Bernard (1813-1878) was one of the most accomplished French physiologists of the 19th century, renowned for his work on the nervous system.

[38] Papus gives a reference here to "Claude Bernard, *Science expérimentale.*" The book, which was a definitive attempt to revolutionize medicine by the introduction of the scientific method to its research and practice, is actually entitled *Introduction à l'étude de la médecine expérimentale*; it was published in 1865.

[39] The physiologist Pierre-Jean-Marie Flourens (1794-1867). Lermina must have known his son, Gustave, who was one of the leaders of the Paris Commune, and died during the insurrection in 1871.

selves. The result of this, as Maldan[40] has remarked, is that a person that we see after an interval of three or four months is no longer the same, materially speaking, as the one we saw before. The physiognomy has not changed, though, nor has the general form of the body; there must, therefore, be some kind of force within the person that conserves acquired forms independently of the incessant renewal of the cells.

Where, then, is this force to be found?

In human beings it is carried everywhere by a little cellular element, the blood corpuscle, which restores the force to organs that have need of it and which then goes in quest of a new provision of the force for itself before returning. This is called circulation. If corpuscles are prevented from reaching an organ, the organ soon dies, which indicates to us that the blood corpuscle is the seat of the force, which is nothing other than life.

One primary, rather coarse, means of restoring life to someone who lacks it is, therefore, to infuse him directly with a certain quantity of living blood corpuscles. This is called transfusion, and it is the method of rejuvenation used by certain rich Orientals.[41] But the force in

---

[40] Papus gives a reference to "Maldan, *Matière et force*, Dentu, 1882." I have been not been able to obtain any more detailed identification about the author.

[41] The suggestion that rich Orientals used blood transfusion as a method of rejuvenation is, of course, a myth. Christopher Wren, the English architect, had carried out a pioneering series of experiments in animal blood transfusion in 1657 and a series of injections of lamb's blood into human patients was carried out in Paris a few years later by the natural philosopher Jean-Baptiste Denis (1625-1704). Although three of Denis' patients reported that it the treatment had been beneficial, the fourth died and Denis was subsequently sued by his widow.

human beings is not only fixed in this perpetually-circulating element; nature has lodged a little of it throughout a series of reservoirs in which the force is condensed, subject to tension, accumulated in order to be released later in response to need. These reservoirs are nervous ganglions, often gathered into a plexus, and their ensemble constitutes the mysterious system of organic life represented by the sympathetic nervous system. All around the heart, all along the vertebral column and inside the abdomen are found *reserve centers of vital force*; all the organs that operate without being subject to the action of our will do so under the influence of these centers.

Now, a fact long known to the Hindus and Orientals is that life thus stored in reserve can *emerge from the human body* and act at a distance. A man who possesses the secret of that action can, therefore, cease to draw upon on the blood that ought to revivify him—a procedure worthy, at most, of the ignorant—and have recourse to the vital reserves, invisibly attracting to himself the force that he requires. To those who doubt the action of life outside the human body, I shall cite the delicate and rigorous experiments of William Crookes [42] of the Royal

---

Blood transfusions were then outlawed in France until the 1800s, although experimentation was revived in England in the 1790s by Erasmus Darwin. In 1890 such experiments were still highly likely to do more harm than good; no headway was made on the issue of compatibility until Karl Landsteiner categorized the A/B/O blood groups in 1909.

[42] Papus gives a reference to "William Crookes, *Force Psychique*." William Crookes (1832-1919) was the most famous physicist caught up by the vogue for spiritualist trickery. In 1870 and 1871 he published two papers on "Experiments on the Psychic Force," which were rapidly translated into French.

Society of London on Psychic Force and its action at a distance—action verified by mechanical measuring devices.

Have we, then, you might ask, fallen back into the domain of Animal Magnetism and Spiritism? Call it what you will; it is unimportant. It is a matter of actual, indisputable facts, which the Académies will admit in a few decades.

Since I have strayed into the terrain of occult science, why should I not extrapolate the hypotheses to their conclusion in telling you the origin of human life, according to the occultists.

You will accept, I suppose, that life is held in reserve in the ganglions of the sympathetic nervous system. Where does it come from before being condensed there? From blood corpuscles, either directly or via the intermediary of the cerebellum, if one believes the admirable but unfortunately little-known work of Dr. Luys.[43] Where does a blood corpuscle obtain the force that it carries everywhere, under the influence of the oxidation of hemoglobin? From the air that bathes and vivifies all the living beings on Earth, either directly or in solution.

Setting its chemical composition aside, where does the air come from? An occultist of high repute, Char-

---

The wide reportage given to a demonstration of the supposed abilities of mediums that he staged for the Royal Society caused something of a sensation in France.

[43] Papus inserts a reference to "Dr. Luys, *Le Système nerveux*. Paris, 1865." The reference is to Jules-Bernard Luys (1829-1897), a significant pioneer of physiological psychology; the actual title of the book cited is *Recherches sur le système cérébro-spinal, sa structure, ses functions et ses maladies.*

del,[44] shows that the terrestrial atmosphere results from the action of the Sun on our Earth; the Air is a modality of the solar Force. The primary origin of Life is, therefore, the Sun; by a series of successive transformations, it is eventually lodged in a nervous ganglion in the form of human life. When I burn wood, do you think I am doing anything other that extracting the sunlight that the wood had condensed when the plant was alive? The same is true for life in all its modalities.

A third means, even more mysterious than the preceding ones, therefore consists of secretly going in search of the vivificatory elements in the Sun itself—but then we are dealing with Magic, a word that rings false in the ears of contemporary scientists and literary men take the responsibility for trying to make them understand it better than we do ourselves.

In fact, authentic centers of research exist in our own day in which Magic is studied in all its branches: The *Groupe independent d'études ésotériques*, which publishes the journal *L'Initiation,*[45] treats these ques-

---

[44] Papus inserts a reference to "Chardel, *Esquisse de la Nature humaine*, 1840." The reference is to Casimir Chardel (1777-1847); the full title of the work cited is *Esquisse de la Nature humaine expliquée par le magnétisme animal*, and its original publication was in 1826

[45] Papus gives the address of this organization as "58, rue St.-André-des-Arts, Paris," but modestly refrains from mentioning that it is his own. In the same spirit, he does not mention that all the researchers he cites were either his friends and collaborators or contributors to his journal. "F.-Ch. Barlet" was the pseudonym of Albert Faucheux, a disciple of Guaita who subsequently became very interested in astrology. Little is known about Lejay or "Polti et Gary" save their signatures; the latter

tions, and numerous researchers—Stanislaus de Guaita, F.-Ch. Barlet, Julien Lajay, Polti et Gary, Augustin Chaboseau—apply the Occult Science to our various contemporary sciences. The list of Mage-Littérateurs grows every day, representing every school, from the ultramontanist Catholic Joséphin Péladan, the initiator of the movement, to the charming poet Gilbert-Augustin Thierry, passing through the Catholic socialist Paul Adam and the poets Alber Jhouney, Victor-Emile Michelet, Paul Marrot and L. Mauchel.[46]

Here, therefore, is a new school rising over the horizon, a school simultaneously scientific, artistic and social, and in the name of all its partisans I thank Jules Lermina for having lent his talent as a writer to the exposition of the thesis that life can be mysteriously infused from one being to another: the redoubtable secret of the Elixir of Life of the ancient alchemists and Oriental initiates.

But can one become immortal?

---

collaborators had published a book on "the theory of temperaments" in 1889.

[46] As with the previous list, all of these were writers who were personally know to Papus or, at least, contributed to his journal. Thierry was perhaps the most notable, attracting warm praise from Anatole France, although Paul Adam—whose relevant work only forms a tiny minority of his huge output—was the most successful. "Alber Jhouney"—the signature used by Albert Jouney—had made a considerable impact in 1887 with *Le royaume de Dieu* but his career proved meteoric. Mauchel was presumably only known to Papus by his signature, which appeared on an article on "Balzac occultiste" that Papus reprinted in the special issue of *La Plume* he was invited to edit in 1892.

Ask Doctors Brown-Séquard and Variot,[47] or await Jules Lermina's next novella.

Papus

---

[47] Charles-Edouard Brown-Séquard (Papus has "Brown Se-quart") succeeded Claude Bernard as professor of experimental medicine at the Collège de France in 1878. In the 1880s, when he was in his seventies, he began to promote the hypothesis that human rejuvenation might be achieved by the transplantation of animal testicles—a practice enthusiastically taken up by his colleague Serge Voronoff, who made the practice notorious (many of the transplanted "monkey glands" were rejected, and some infected their hosts with syphilis). A physician who signed his academic papers G. Variot was the first person to carry out an experimental trial of Brown-Séquard's thesis at the Hôtel-Dieu in 1889; that news must have been hot off the presses when Papus penned this preface. Brown-Séquard had worked extensively in America (with Alexis Carrel, the tissue-culture pioneer) and in London; while resident in London he was a near neighbor of Robert Louis Stevenson, who used him as a model for Dr. Jekyll (and thus, tacitly, Mr. Hyde).

I

It was scarcely three months after I had presented my thesis and finally obtained the title of doctor that had been the ambition of my youth. With what joy I had written to my worthy father, with what emotion I had opened the letter bring me, along with his warm congratulations, the 500-franc bill that would permit my installation in Paris.

A physician in Paris! At the age of 27! It is necessary to have experienced these illusions to understand their full force, to reveal all their savor. I was esteemed by my professors. I had passed my examinations with exceptional success; I had, during those years of study, made a few fast friends; was it not inevitable that the future should seem radiant?

It is true that my resources were slender; I knew that my father, a small farmer in the Sarthe valley, was making a considerable sacrifice in sending me a small sum of money, and that I could no longer count ion anyone but myself—but I had faith in myself, in my passion for work and in *science*, which is indulgent to those who love it sincerely.

I therefore set resolutely to work, taking the *agrégation* as my next objective,[48] which I had decided to pursue while starting in practice. I was strong, I was sober; in sum, I fund myself in excellent condition, and I had best admit that I have now arrived at, and gone beyond, the goal that I had set myself.

---

[48] *Agrégation* is the French qualification entitling someone to teach in a *lycée* [secondary school] or *collège*.

It would be disingenuous on my part to insist on the hardship of my early days, which I sometimes rather miss: those days of youth when bread dipped in a glass of water seems so good. In sum, I was, at the outset, comfortably lodged, thanks to easy-going suppliers— which some angrily call creditors, but were in truth my financial backers, since it is necessary, on pain of death, for a man who has no capital to obtain a few advances. I was properly furnished, comfortably dressed and, if I economized somewhat on nourishment without anyone being aware of it, I maintained a smart appearance and a healthy physiognomy.

I cannot say that clients flocked to my door; however, I religiously followed the prescriptions I had written at the time, in my conscience and on the copper plaque nailed above the building's coaching-entrance: *Medical Practitioner, consultations between two and five p.m.*—a healthy dose, as is evident.

I was only occasionally disturbed in my work, and I would have been able, if I had wished, sometimes to neglect the confinement to quarters that I had fixed, but I respected the word I had given, and in any case, imagine if a client had come while I was absent! I hardly ever went out before 6 p.m. and, after a rapid and frugal meal, hurried home, always fearful of missing the opportunity that would inevitably present itself eventually.

Needless, to say, I also looked after everyone in the building for free.

One evening in September, I had lit my lamp early and I was studying assiduously, dreaming of the day when I would be able to proclaim my ideas and theories from the height of a professorial chair, when I was snatched from my reverie by a loud ring of the doorbell. Leaping out of my chair, I hastened to the door and opened it, holding a lantern aloft in order to examine the visitor's face.

It was a lady dressed in black, but whose external appearance did not present any of the romantic characteristics that one might suppose. She was about forty, and plump, with rather coarse features. She was weeping. I hurriedly introduced her into my "consulting room" and, a trifle loquaciously, I put myself at her disposal.

I soon perceived, however, that he poor creature was in such a state of agitation, and had, moreover, climbed up to my fourth-floor apartment in such haste, that it was impossible for her to utter a word. I had not been in practice long enough to be unsympathetic to human weakness, and I was just about to get her a glass of water—with sugar, if you please!—when she murmured: "Monsieur, I beg you... come, come quickly... my child..."

A sob cut the speech short—but had she any need to say any more? She had need of my services—and for a child!

I have always adored those little creatures, and it had been one of the most heart-rending things I had experienced to stand at the foot of a crib, powerless and ignorant, saying: "Oh! Meningitis! What an enemy!"

"I am under your orders!" I exclaimed, grabbing my hat. "Do you live far away?"

"No, no—the next house. Pardon me for coming here, but it's precisely because it was so close..."

It would have been unbecoming and futile to be wounded by that excuse. I affirmed once again that I was ready to follow her, and we went out.

Walking beside the woman in the street, I questioned her. What illness was her child suffering from? For how long?

"It's my daughter! She's dying, Monsieur! Six months ago, she was so healthy, so strong, so beautiful…"

"How old is she?"

"Ten. You see, Monsieur, I'm a widow. I live alone with my daughter. We don't see anyone except Monsieur Vincent…"

"Monsieur Vincent?"

Had the poor woman thought that she detected—mistakenly, to be sure—a certain suspicion in my tone? She immediately added: "Oh, he's an old man, Monsieur. Sixty, perhaps 70 years old… but so good, and he loves my Pauline so much!"

We had reached the house. We went up to the second floor and went in to an apartment that was neat and respectable. It was perfectly in order. From the dining-room, which served as a point of entry, we went into the bedroom. There, at the first glance, I saw the girl she had called Pauline lying on a little bed next to her mother's.

It is strange that sickness and death, contemplated in hospital during a period of internment, do not produce one hundredth of the effect that we feel at the bedside of our first patients. My heart had suddenly become constricted, and I felt myself grow pale.

The poor child was white, so white that she seemed no longer to have a single drop of blood in her veins. Beneath her blue-rimmed eyelids, her eyeballs seemed dull and grey, and her long, thin hands were extended on the bedclothes, where their pallor stood out even more.

"A candle!" I demanded, sharply. And I leaned over the bed, examining with profound attention the poor creature on whom Death had already set his finger, as evidence of an inevitable summons. It was anemia in its final phase. But what lesion could have caused that state?

Under interrogation, the mother repeated to me, in greater detail, that her daughter had always been sturdy, that she had been in perfect health six months before, and that everyone had admired the lively bloom of youth that was already evident in her little girl.

"And it can't be said," the poor woman continued, while weeping, "that there has been the slightest change in our life. We've been living here for three years. The apartment is airy, overlooking the gardens. I don't send Pauline to school; it's our neighbor, Monsieur Vincent, who gives her lessons, and he's too reasonable to have pushed her too hard."

In truth, I was almost afraid to touch the poor creature, whose sudden exhaustion alarmed me in its seeming inexplicability. I could not convince myself, however, that there was no means of saving her. Aided by her mother, I sounded her chest with minute care, and I established—with veritable amazement—that she there was no sign of any defect. The heart was sound, and I could not perceive the murmur characteristic of anemia there or in the neck. The lungs were equally sound and well-developed. Beneath that consumptive thinness, the vital framework was exceptional, with no symptoms of lymphatism.

The mother was not poor; with a little pension she had inherited from her husband, former member of the Paris guard, she had an annual income of two thousand francs. In addition, the old man she had mentioned, Monsieur Vincent, took his meals with her, and paid well.

Unfortunately, the young girl had not received any regular treatment. With a stubbornness based in an irrational mistrust, the mother had never called a doctor, contenting herself with anodyne remedies—water in which iron nails had been boiled, or some such. And now I was constrained to admit to myself that all my efforts to reanimate that organism, so strangle depleted, would not result in a prolongation of life, even for a few days.

I sat there, crushed and defeated, despairingly awaiting an inspiration that could not possibly arrive.

The mother watched me silently, doubtless reading the poignant thoughts that my face betrayed. I did not yet know how to hide my impotence beneath banal and consoling phraseology. There was no merit in that; a physician ought to act upon the brain as on any other organ.

At that moment, we hard the sound of footsteps in the next room.

"That's Monsieur Vincent," said the mother.

The door quietly came ajar—but at the same moment, I saw the little girl sit up and turn her head, her hands reaching out in the direction from which the almost imperceptible noise had come.

I supported the child and, to my great surprise, felt a supreme effort in that poor body, as if she wanted to escape from my arms. The door closed again, and the girl fell back, dead.

I let out an exclamation, simultaneously surprised and desperate. That excessively swift and painless death, that sudden extinction of the vital flame, amazed me, and I experience a sort of rage against my intelligence. For, in truth, I did not understand what had just happened before my eyes at all; it seemed to me that I was prey to a nightmare.

The mother, with a heart-rending scream, had hurled herself upon the poor motionless corpse. I moved away from the bed and mechanically, as if embarrassed by the futility of my presence, opened the door and went into the first room.

That was when I saw Monsieur Vincent for the first time.

Clear of complexion, he was wearing a grey, almost white, coat. He was of medium height, rather plump, but what struck me immediately was that it was impossible to estimate exactly how old he was. His hair was white and cut short, forming three distinct peaks on his forehead and his temples, but his face was so fresh and so rosy, and his eyes were shining so brightly, that I honestly asked myself whether I was looking at an old man or a young one whose hair—by virtue of a predisposition less rare is generally believed, with respect to the pigmentary tissue—had become discolored in his adolescence. And yet I remember full well that the dead girl's mother had spoken of Monsieur Vincent as a septuagenarian.

He was standing next to the window, looking sad—but not as much, it seemed to me, as I might have expected. He bowed politely and interrogated me with his gaze.

"She's dead," I told him.

A sudden contraction disturbed his face, and in that reflex movement I saw all his features become creased, displaying the thousand wrinkles that are a sure indication of old age. The appearance of freshness was entirely superficial. Moreover, doubtless by virtue of an afflux of blood to the heart, provoked by emotion, his complexion had suddenly taken on a yellowish, parchment-like tint; the skin had crumpled beneath his prominent cheekbones. Within the space a second, a death's-head had imprinted itself on his face—and without saying a word, seizing his hat with feverish haste, Monsieur Vincent ran to the exterior door as if possessed by a terror he could not master, opened it, and literally fled, with a vertiginous rapidity.

I thought that the abandonment of a friend at the supreme moment would be a new cause of despair for the poor mother, and I was all set to go back to her, in spite of the falseness of my situation, when I heard a knock on the door.

Thinking that Monsieur Vincent, gripped by remorse, had decided to come back, I opened it immediately. It was two neighbors in search of news of the little girl. When they were informed of the catastrophe, they shook their heads.

"It was bound to end this way," said one.

"What do you mean?" I asked, sharply.

The woman was about to reply when the mother, having heard the sound of familiar voices, came out of the bedroom and threw herself into her neighbor's arms, sobbing.

My role was finished; I bowed and went out, experiencing a sentiment of inexpressible relief at leaving that house in which my sensibility had been put to such a stern proof. Even so, I went down the stairs slowly, oppressed by an anguish whose nature I could not precisely define. It seemed to me that I was leaving an inexplicable mystery behind.

Just as I was passing in front of the concierge's lodge, he stopped me.

"Well, Monsieur Physician?" he said, inviting a response.

"I was called too late," I hastened to reply.

The man looked at me with astonishment, as if he could not comprehend. I gave him a few rapid explanations. He swore violently; them brandishing his fist at an invisible enemy, he groaned: "Oh, the bandit! When I think, Monsieur, that she was a colossus of heath, so pink and fresh!"

"How long has she been ill?"

"Six months, Monsieur—six months exactly."

"Who were you calling a bandit just now?"

"Him! That old tocasson[49] who had nothing but skin on his bones, and who came to nourish himself via the mother at the daughter's expense! Oh, he's certainly profited!"

"What?" I cried. "Do you think she's died of starvation?"

"Well, of what else, then?"

"Come here, husband, and don't get mixed up in other people's business!" shouted a female voice from the depths of the lodge. "It's the doctor's business to find out the truth!"

"At the end of the day, that's true!" said the concierge, breaking off the conversation unceremoniously.

---

[49] There is no English equivalent of this *argot* term that can convey the full complexity of its meaning. It was sometimes used to refer to a worthless horse, but Lermina—who co-authored a dictionary of *argot* and was sensitive to its subtler inflections—is using it here because it was primarily applied, with similar contempt, to old women who are trying to look younger than they are. "Mutton dressed as lamb" is the most similar expression that English can offer.

II

I went back home, feverish and almost angry. The first time that someone had made an appeal to what it pleased me to call my science, I had bumped into a desperate case; brutally, death had barred my way, and I seemed to hear the words of supreme despair murmuring in my ear: "You won't go very far!"

I was not only suffering from that egotistic sentiment of humiliation, though; the anguish I had felt a little while before had increased. To drag myself out of it, I tried to organize my thoughts, to gather together the facts I had observed and to obtain therefrom a response to the doubts that were irritating me.

The child's condition did not correspond with any known observations. I opened my books one by one, but could find nothing that satisfied me anywhere. The sick girl had not presented any of the classical symptoms, and that as exactly what troubled me most: the absence of symptoms seemed more certain with every passing moment. Was it necessary to believe, in accordance with the concierge's insinuation, in ill-treatment, in starvation? In addition to the mother's appearance, though, the profound and unfeigned affection that she had for her daughter giving the absolute lie to any such supposition, the physical state of the patient provided formal contra-indications to that hypothesis.

During the short time in which I had been able to examine her with my stethoscope, I had been particularly surprised by the healthy state of the vital organs. There had evidently been a loss of vitality, slow or rapid, but it had not been brought about by any of the accidents that ordinarily leave easily-detectable lesions in an organism. But why had the two neighbors seemed to find something that was inexplicable to me so easily understandable? Why had the concierge seemed, in his rapid interjections to be accusing the strange person I knew as Monsieur Vincent—who, it is true, had made a poor impression on me at first, but whom no indication permitted me to suspect. And where would such suspicions have led me? So horrible can certain hypotheses be that I stopped myself, and once again, combining my observations, acquired the conviction that there could be no possible basis for them.

Then again, I repeat, there are faces that do not lie, and that of the mother radiated the most perfect honesty. She loved her daughter, had never left her. No, no, it was futile to follow a trail that everything demonstrated to be false and slanderous.

In the end, that examination of reason and conscience exasperated me to the point that it was impossible for me to remain alone any longer. I needed to hear human voices, to exchange ideas, to refresh my brain in the flow of current banalities.

I went out.

When I went into the circle of light projected by the gas-lamps in the brasserie, from which emerged the moving silhouettes of young people, there was a clamor of greetings. Since I completed my thesis, they had not seen me three times—and amicable gibes rained down upon me as hands that drew me forwards, forcing me to sit down in front of a pile of saucers, the obituary obelisk of vanished tankards. I could not resist; the noise and exuberance restored my serenity.

It was necessary for me to explain my perpetual reclusiveness, to justify my ingratitude to my old friends, to confess my ambitions and my hopes, but above all to clink glasses, again and again, while absorbing the horrible alcoholic dilution that people decorate in our great country with the name of beer, and whose principle virtue—particularly appreciated by its vendors—is to condemn the unwary to a raging thirst, the mother of repetition.

Under that brain-inflaming influence, until the moment my stomach began to ache, my ideas became clearer. I resumed the active perception of facts and, at the same time, felt an invisible desire to recount the strange adventure in which I had been involved that night. Naturally, I was not long in succumbing to it, and I narrated the incident in a single breath.

As it concerned a child—the eternal problem that excites the most skeptical—they listed to me attentively, and no one jeered when I confessed the dolorous emotion that my ignorance had caused me to experience.

"Listen," said Gaston Dussault, a young doctor whose great merit we all recognized. "I don't claim to be able to give you the key to the puzzle that you've put in front of us. My observation will be of a more general character, and—alas!—scarcely encouraging in nature. There are two phases in a physician's life. The first—his youth—comprises ardent curiosity, a desire to conquer evil, a devotion that no one can discourage. That's also the time of unrelenting hard work, 25 hours of reading or writing a day, burning one's eyes on the wicks of smoky and malodorous candles. Now, while we're swotting away like that, life goes on, actively, rushing around and outside of us. We stuff our ears so as not to hear the noise that humankind is making, the vast illness suffered by the lungs, the heart, the brain. We demand of others that science should do everything, that the past be heaped up in weighty and pricy volumes, and we don't have time to learn the secret of life and death in the only book that's always open, with schematic illustrations that are always new, sincere and conclusive—and that book is here…"

With a circular gesture, he indicated the boulevard. The gas projected its white bands, though which the tide of strollers rolled ever on.

"There's the great manual of internal and external pathology," he continued. "There's physiology in action. What do we see of all that—we, the young, riveted to the hospital or the dissecting-room? And this is a volume, a chapter, a paragraph in the vast medical encyclopedia that is society entire." He paused, then cried out in a tone whose sincerity struck us forcibly: "Ah, to have the time—which is to say, the money of everyday life—and to consecrate it entirely to reading the human library, that universal dictionary in which every man is a page, to spell it out, to transcribe it, to annotate it… and after that, to practice medicine! What am I saying? After that, medicine would be practiced—for then one will have autopsied, not cadavers but living beings, brains, breasts and hearts. Ten years of observations accomplished with the supreme courage that we put into shuffling the cinders of erudition, and the true flame would spring forth!"

"But after the forced labor to which we are all condemned," I cried, "less than half our lives remain…"

"To become the second man who is in every doctor," he went on, "the discouraged, the skeptical, the ignorant, the banal and routine practitioner who aims for the *Croix d'honneur* and the Académie. When we escape from our books, we're blind, and no longer see human beings…"

At that moment, I let out an exclamation and put my hand on his arm. "Look," I said.

He followed the direction of my pointing finger.

"Who's that?" he asked

"That's the old man I was talking about just now—Monsieur Vincent."

Indeed, lit by the harsh light of frosted glass, the old man was moving forward slowly and painfully, and I shivered in contemplating the incredible change that had come over him, in scarcely an hour, since I had last seen him.

He seemed to me to be pale, thin, stooped and worn out. At each step he dragged along the asphalt he looked around, turning his shaky neck, whose vertebrae I imagined I could hear cracking.

"Hey!" cried one of our neighbors. "That's old Thévenin. He's not dead, then?"

"So it is," Gaston went on, having looked at him more attentively. "I didn't recognize him at first."

"Who's Monsieur Thévenin?" I asked, impatiently.

Without answering me directly, Gaston continued, as if talking to himself: "I met him a few months ago. He was alert and rejuvenated..."

"Since I believed myself, on seeing him an hour ago, that I was facing a man still young... it's possible, after all, that grief has produced this metamorphosis..."

"Come on," said Gaston, touching me lightly on the shoulder. "I'll tell you what I know about him..."

Monsieur Vincent—I shall continue to give him that name, which really belonged to him; his name was Vincent Thévenin—had passed through the zone of illumination whose center we occupied. I got up hurriedly and followed my comrade.

Within a moment we had picked up the old man's trail again. He was going along the boulevard, lost in the cheerful and laughing crowd enjoying the luxuriant and vivifying summer evening. His narrow back seemed to belong to some macabre character.

"Talk," I said to me comrade. "Quickly, tell me what you know about that person, who interests me, frightens me and irritates me all at the same time."

"Let's follow him first," said Gaston. "I know his past; I'd like to know something of his present."

I was obliged to restrain my impatience. Adjusting our pace to that of Monsieur Thévenin, we disposed ourselves so as not to lose sight of him.

I noticed then that he stopped in front of every café, remaining on the threshold and seeping it with his gaze, doubtless searching for someone...perhaps a woman, Gaston suggested, laughing. Indeed, he paused preferentially in front of the establishments frequented by the young women of the quarter.

"I was only joking," Gaston added. "Besides the fact that Thévenin has always been chaste, he must be more than 100 years old...."

"A hundred!"

"I'm 35," my interlocutor went on, "and when I was 15, the person who told me Thévenin's story affirmed that he was already alive in 1789."

The old man had, however, resumed his course—or, rather, his silent glide, which gave him a fantastic character. The further he went, the more he seemed to be bowed down by an increasingly heavy weight. His apparent feebleness was accentuated. In truth, we were beginning to dread that he might get to the point of evaporating into the air and disappearing entirely.

Having reached the extremity of the boulevard, he stopped, as if hesitating over which direction to take. It was getting late, though, and the strollers were becoming scarce. Because we were very close to him, almost close enough to touch him, we saw him sketch out a gesture that had both anger and discouragement in it, and he set off into a side-street.

We did not lose track of him, and soon saw him cross the street and march straight to a coaching entrance, in front of which a fat woman—evidently a concierge—was imbibing the fresh evening air, dandling a plump and sturdy boy of six or seven on her knees.

Scarcely had the lad caught sight of Thévenin when he leapt down from his mother's lap and ran towards him. He hurtled into the old man so hard that we feared for a moment that the latter would be knocked over. Quite the contrary, though; with a strength that astonished us, Thévenin seized the boy in his arms, lifted him off the ground and embraced him for a long time.

"Poor man," I murmured, sympathetically. "He's thinking about the dead girl."

The fat woman called her boy back, however, remonstrating with him and shouting: "Let the gentlemen go! Little imp! I beg your pardon, Monsieur Vincent..."

He replied by softly stroking the cheeks of the little boy, who had come back to hug him.

"Oh, I know you're the Papa Gâteau of all the little children," the woman went on, "and as soon as they see you in the distance, they run to you..."

The concierge stood aside to let Monsieur Vincent pass, but he did not go in. He seemed to hesitate. Then he said, timidly: "Wouldn't you like to entrust him to me? I'd teach him so many beautiful things!"

"Oh, with pleasure Monsieur Vincent. But you know that he stays in the country, with his grandmother. To borrow him for a week, I need to kick up an almighty fuss... and the air's so good out there!"

Monsieur Vincent did not insist. He embraced the child once again and disappeared into the long corridor. He seemed veritably rejuvenated.

Gaston drew closer. "Is that really the scientist Monsieur Vincent Thévenin who just went in?"

"Yes, Monsieur. Oh yes, a scientist, and such a brave man! A father to all the children, you know—and they know it well, the little rogues. They're under his feet all day long."

"He lives here?"

"For 10 years..."

"I knew him slightly at one time He seemed to be very old..."

"You'd never believe it! Why, six months ago, he was so worn out he could hardly draw breath. Suddenly, bang! It was like the wave of a magic wand. I don't know what he came up with to cure himself, but in less than a month he was as back on his feet, as right as rain—to the point where, if I'd been a widow..."

She laughed frankly, like a woman who could admit a certain licentiousness into her character without anyone holding it against her.

"How old do you think he is?" I put in.

"Oh, a dried-up husk. Ninety-five, at least!"

"That's the man," Gaston continued, when we were some distance away, having resumed our walk. "Highly-esteemed, highly-respected, loves children. What do you think?"

"Nothing—I'm waiting to hear his story."

"It's quite simple, in sum—I mean, for us, who don't admit the impossible as scientific fact. Monsieur Vincent de Bossaye de Thévenin is the last descendant of a great family, which emigrated during the French Revolution. His father was one of the hundred shareholders, at 2400 livres in the famous Mesmer, whom he followed to Switzerland—where, as you know, the celebrated thaumaturge was resident until his death in 1815. Monsieur de Bossaye senior came back to France with the Bourbons and died soon afterwards, leaving a son— the man in whom we're interested. Vincent followed the lessons of Carra and Saussure, qualified in medicine, and became an associate of the famous Deleuze, who was nicknamed the Hippocrates of animal magnetism under the Restoration.

"After that, he broke entirely with academic routine. For some years he was secretary of the Société Magnétique founded by the Marquis de Puységur, and he eventually became the secretary, the alter ego, of the Marquis de Mirville, the director of the Société d'Avignon and author of a very strange work on *Spirits and their Fluidic Manifestations*.[50]

---

[50] This list of celebrated Mesmerists runs through several of the principal names associated with the tradition; Jean-Louis Carra (1742-1793) was one of its earliest scientific investigators, whose *Examen physique de magnétisme animal* was published in 1785, but the date of his demise makes it unlikely that Vincent can actually have been his pupil. It is unclear whether the reference to "Saussure" is to the Swiss physicist Horace-Benedict de Saussure (1740-1799) or his son, the phytochemist Nicolas Théodore (1767-1845), but if the former is intended the same criticism applies. Chronology makes it far more likely that Vincent could have been an associate of Jean-Philippe-François Deleuze (1753-1853), who wrote an exten-

I interrupted Gaston excitedly, exclaiming: "In sum, this great scientist is a spirit... a madman!"

"Why get carried away like that?" Gaston went on, smiling. "The man who, 100 years ago, could have foreseen the electric lighting of railway stations would have seemed worthy of being shut up in a lunatic asylum. Science begins with a minimal fact and grows by hypotheses." He became more animated. "A madman! Do you think that Crookes, who discovered a new metal, thallium, and posed the irritating enigma of the radiometer, whose visible functioning still remains inexplicable, is a madman?[51] Well, study his latest research and tell me is you don't feel *something* becoming shaky within you that you thought quite solid.

"To get back to Monsieur Vincent, though. About 1825, that man—who combines the astonishing patience of a fakir with the active perseverance of a seeker—was the universally-acknowledged and respected leader of hat bizarre population of magnetizers and their patients, who were much more numerous than is believed, whose good faith was not under the least suspicion, and who

---

sive *Histoire critique du magnétisme* (1813-19). Armand-Marie-Joseph de Chastenet, Marquis de Puységur (1751-1825) founded the Société Harmonique des Amis Réunis before the Revolution of 1789; the descendant society of which Vincent was secretary is fictitious. Charles-Jules-Eudos de Catteville de Mirville (1802-1873) is a more likely employer; the work cited, *Pneumatologie, des esprits et leurs manifestations fluidiques*, was published in 1854.

[51] Crookes' radiometer, or "light mill," which he demonstrated in 1873, did indeed pose an intriguing puzzle, whose solution is still subject to some controversy. It consists of a set of vanes mounted on a spindle inside a partially-evacuated glass bulb; when exposed to light, the vanes rotate.

had the passions and courage of the apostolate. Alexandre Bertrand and Georget were his pupils—and yet Thévenin never allowed his name to be spoken. He did not get directly involved in the famous quarrel with the Académie, which, despite Husson's report, ended in an absolute refusal of the erudite company to take magnetism seriously. You know that that decision dates from 1837, on the initiative of Dr. Dubois d'Amiens? [52]

"Dr. Thévenin did not protest. On the contrary, he seemed to lose interest in the matter and broke with his adepts—but I know from a reliable source that he did not abandon his studies. The man from whom I obtained all these details, who was one of Thévenin's last pupils, told me, a few months before his death, that his master's science terrified him—that's the very word he used. And he added: 'Don't think that any sleight-of-hand is involved, or any charlatanism, let alone those cerebral *disequilibrations* that can explain everything in the interests of money or pride, if not folly. Monsieur Vincent is the

---

[52] The names cited in this paragraph refer to the clash of ideas that occurred when the controversy regarding animal magnetism came to a head in the late 1820s and 1830s. Fréderic Dubois d'Amiens (1799-1873) was the secretary of the Académie de Médecine de Paris who published the report that convinced the society to dismiss all such practices as quackery—a document whose partiality was stridently criticized by Dr. Husson of the Hôtel-Dieu, who had encouraged the practice of magnetic medicine within the hospital by Pierre Froissart, Jules Depotet de Sennevoy and a physician surnamed Georget. Alexandre-Jacques-François Bertrand (not to be confused with Alexandre Bertrand the archaeologist) was one of the most important academic analysts of the practice; he published *Du magnétisme en France et des jugements qu'en ont porté les sociétés savantes* in 1826.

coldest, the most strictly positivist man I've encountered in my entire life. He has never worked by trial and error, leaving it to chance to decide whether his observations are well- or ill-founded. He proceeds slowly from one point to the next, step by step, submitting each progress obtained to the most minute verification. Perhaps it's because of that very slowness that I have so much trouble following him; my imagination continually carries me away, drawing me on to false trails. He goes straight ahead, without deviating from the determined track by an iota.'

"You will understand how curious I was to obtain details. Science, indeed! But what science? To all the questions I asked him, my friend replied with a discretion equivalent to a refusal to divulge his master's secrets. However, this is what I was able to find out. Monsieur Vincent was not preoccupied with second sight or the prediction of the future. His studies were uniquely devoted to the physiological, or even physical, fact of a radiant force—the exact term more recently employed by Crookes—emanating from the human body, and whose action, attractive or penetrant, can be exercised at a distance without the aid of a material conductor. From there to hypnotism, and especially to suggestion, is only a single step.

"With the audacity of youth, I went to Monsieur Vincent's house and attempted to obtain his confession. A very singular man, in truth, who made an impression on me like no other I have ever experienced. While I spoke to him, under the authority of my friend's name—who was no longer alive by then—to offer myself as a sort of successor as his pupil, Monsieur Vincent stared at me. And, strangely enough, I felt an effect that was neither somnambulistic numbness not hypnotic fascina-

tion—but it seemed to me that an irresistible attracted
was being exercised upon me. Don't misunderstand me:
my body itself wasn't drawn towards him, but something
that emanated from the entire periphery of my body, as if
some impalpable, ethereal substance were being projected towards him through my pores. The effect didn't
last more than a few seconds, however, and then suddenly ceased.

    " 'How old are you?' he asked, abruptly.

    " 'Twenty-six,' I replied.

    " 'You work too hard,' he said. 'You're expending
yourself too quickly and too soon. Take care—be more
economical with yourself.'

    "I didn't quite understand, feeling young and vigor-
ous—with the reservation that, after the singular effect
I've just mentioned, I felt a sort of lassitude, as if I had
overstretched myself.

    "I tried to get back to the subject that had brought
me, but he interrupted me. 'Don't expect anything from
me,' he said, rather rudely. 'In the present state of knowledge—or rather, in the face of universal ignorance—it's
forbidden for me to communicate what I know to anyone.'

    " 'But why?' I asked. 'Why not help us, we young
folk, to fight against the stupid routines?'

    " 'Why?' he concluded, raising his head and fixing
me with his gleaming eyes. 'Because... because my
science is criminal!'

    "And then, without my having asked, he launched
into an amazingly eloquent speech, sketching a complete, encyclopedic picture of present-day science for
me. There was not a system, not a theory, nit a discovery
that he had not studied and verified. With a sarcastic
verve that sometimes became ferocious, he flagellated

the prejudices, timidities and laxities that arrested all researches on the threshold of real science. An unparalleled prophet, he predicted for me ten years ago, the modest progress that we have accomplished since then; he saw, positively, beyond our horizon, and without any charlatanism, by the force of deductions whose authority I appreciated myself. And when he had finished, he added, dismissing me with a gesture: 'I refuse you my science, which is criminal… yes, criminal—for it augments, increases a hundredfold, the terrible inequality that creates victors and vanquished in the struggle for existence!'

"Following that enigmatic speech, I had to leave— taking with me, I confess, an impression of terrified admiration. Yes, in a few minutes of conversation, that man had appeared to me as a sort of superhuman being, superb and sinister at the same time. Was it a nervous predisposition? It's possible. However, if I wanted to describe in a single phrase the strange concept that had leapt into my mind, suddenly and irrationally, like those phrases that sometimes obsess the memory without any appreciable cause, I would tell you—please don't laugh at me—that that man put me in mind of a savant vampire. What does that mean? Even today, I'd have difficulty explaining it clearly. Try if you want to—another time! It's late. Let's go home."

"One more thing," I said. "Did you see Monsieur Vincent again?"

"Yes, I've run into him several times—sometimes old, worn out, as he appeared to us this evening; sometimes, on the other hand, rejuvenated, lively, rosy-cheeked and robust."

"And you believe he's a centenarian?"

"Recall the dates I cited, and draw your own conclusions."

A moment later, we went our separate ways. Alone in my apartment, by the light of my lamp, I soon resumed my interrupted studies.

People often laugh at the rapidity with which children pass from one idea to another. One moment, all their attention is focused on something, when a fly takes off and their train of thought is suddenly modified, and they forget whatever held their interest so forcefully a second before. Is the difference between children and adults really so vast, after all? The importance of the facts that attract their attention is, in reality equivalent, and can similarly be measured by the varying intensity of their sensations. The movement of a cat leaves us indifferent, but a passing skirt tears us away from our present reflections and sometimes carries us far away from the road we were following.

Can I tell what circumstances prevented me from following the definite plan that I had formed of seeing Monsieur Vincent again and subjecting him to closer scrutiny? I would find it very difficult. New impressions, some trivial, some more serious, were superimposed on that one; from time to time, the memory of that strange individual crossed my mind, but in the fashion of a vague vision without precise contours.

Weeks, months and years went by, and brought about important changes in my situation. My father died, leaving me a tiny fortune amassed *sou* by *sou*, with the superb tenacity of the peasant who deprives himself of everything in order to ensure his child's future. The clientèle had arrived, and I had given up my professorial ambitions. Finally, I got married and, after a legal but brief interval, became the father of an adorable daughter.

Obviously, Monsieur Vincent and his criminal science were far from my thoughts. More and more years went by. Prosperity arrived; my studies of nervous diseases and my experiments with hysterics had caused something of a stir. My daughter grew more and more adorable and adored. I was happy, and yet I had a history, for the Académies welcomed my communications and the journals printed them. An epidemic of cholera brought me decisively into the light and won me a benevolent decoration from the government.

It was exactly 10 years since I had spent a few hours chatting on the sidewalk with my friend and mentor Gaston about the person in question—I had even forgotten his name—when chance, which rules all our lives, reminded me of him in circumstances even more bizarre than the first time.

One of my colleagues, Dr. F***, the director of a sanitarium, wrote me a note asking me to call on him when I had the time, with a view to examining one of his patients.

Finding myself overloaded with work at the time, I put off responding to his invitation for a few days. When a new, more urgent letter arrived, however, I hastened to see him. The case that he wanted to talk to me about was most interesting, and fell precisely within the purview of the specialist studies to which I had devoted myself. It was a matter of the very curious phenomenon of multiple personality and, for several hours, we dedicated ourselves to experiments over ever-increasing interest. Fearing that we might exhaust the patient completely, however, we fixed a further appointment for the following day.

We went into the garden in front of the magnificent establishment, known and admired throughout Europe, and my colleague slowly led me through it, telling me the results of his personal observations of the subject we had just been examining. Just as we reached the main gate and were exchanging a farewell handshake, a little boy ran out of a pathway fringed by laurels and privets, raced towards the doctor and threw himself into his arms.

The latter lifted him up and said: "My son, Monsieur—eight years old... and a fine fellow."

He was a handsome child with delicate features, but he seemed a little pale to me. I caressed him, thinking about my little daughter, so pink and lively, and I said: "Why were you running so fast? One would think that you were running for your life." It was a banal question, to which I attached no importance.

"Oh, just for fun," the scamp said. "To tease Monsieur Vincent."

"Monsieur Vincent!" I exclaimed. "What Monsieur Vincent?" The name had struck a chord in my memory like a clarion call.

With a certain irritation, the child replied: "Pardon! There's only one Monsieur Vincent... that's Papa Gâteau!"

Papa Gâteau! There had been a Monsieur Vincent with that nickname 10 years before!

"He's a very singular individual," my colleague put in.

"Would that be Vincent Thévenin?"

"The very same. Do you know him?"

"He's not dead, then?"

"Ah, you too!" said the doctor, laughing. "You thought he'd disappeared. Not at all. 110 to 115 years old, my dear chap. And they say that madness isn't a certificate of longevity!"

"And how long has he been in your establishment?"

"About four months—and he was admitted in very curious circumstances. I'll tell you about it tomorrow, for I have to get back to my daily duties now. It's 6 p.m..."

"6 p.m.! I'm late too. We'll discuss Monsieur Vincent tomorrow."

"As you wish, my dear colleague."

I threw myself into my carriage, closing the door behind me. I was in a singular state of agitation, bitten by an indescribable curiosity. Within a second, I had remembered everything: the little apartment in which I had been patiently waiting for clients who were to arrive; the poor mother running to me for help; the funereal bed on which the little girl was lying. I asked myself whether, faced with the same mortal problem, I would have been any more adept today than I had been then—and, in truth, I shivered, telling myself that I was no more able now than then to comprehend that catastrophe. I tried to salvage my pride by supposing that certain symptoms had escaped my diagnosis that I might now perceive at first glance, but I knew that I was lying to myself. No, I had found nothing, and were I summoned in identical circumstances today, I would still find nothing!

That blow to self-respect, and the sincere regret of the researcher, was then juxtaposed with the memory of Monsieur Vincent, that strange, almost fantastic creature who was alive, still alive, everlasting in spite of the abominable senility that had had disturbed Gaston and me so much as we followed him through the streets. By what miracle had he resisted the crushing weight of a century, to which a further 10 years had now been added?

I recalled the inexplicable words that Gaston had reported to me: "*My criminal science multiplies a hundredfold the terrible inequality that creates victors and vanquished in the struggle for existence.*" And also the words that my friend had let slip, like the expression of a reflex: "savant vampire." Those coupled words did not, in reality, present any meaning to my intelligence. But I repeated them mentally, like the terms of an insoluble problem, the expression of an algebraic unknown.

Until I returned to my study it was impossible for me to extract myself from this obsession. Fortunately, my work, the occupations of the evening and sleep, eventually rescued me from that abnormal state of mind. In the morning, the haunting had vanished and all that remained of the emotion was a curiosity that no longer seemed to be at all unhealthy.

At the appointed hour, I met up with Dr. F*** again. He seemed to me to be anxious. Interrogating him with an interest dictated by the sincere sympathy that he inspired in me, I learned that his son's health had been giving him cause for concern for some time. He cut short these confidences, however, gripped one again by the passion for research, and we went to the infirmary to see the patient we had examined the previous day. For several hours, we were absorbed in the study of amazing manifestations of catalepsy and hypnotism. Then we came back to the doctor's study in order to compare notes.

"Now," I said, permit me to remind you that you promised me yesterday to talk at greater length about your inmate, Monsieur Vincent."

"I haven't forgotten, and I'll do better than tell you from memory. I have the custom, on the admission of my patients, of writing down the interesting circumstances of our initial interview." The doctor got up, opened a box and took out a few sheets of paper, which he handed to me, saying: "Read that while I take care of a few things I need to do—I'll be back soon."

Left alone, this is what I read:

Today, April 15, 1888, at 6 p.m., I was handed the card of a visitor who was asking for an immediate interview. It bore the name of Vincent de Bossaye de Thévenin, of the Faculty of Medicine of Paris. I started in surprise. As an alienist, I have made a special study of the history of animal magnetism, and I recalled having encountered that name in an era that was already distant. It seemed to me that it must have been borne by a contemporary of my grandfather, or at least of my father. I gave instructions for the person who had proffered the card to be introduced immediately, and a moment later I saw an old man come in, showing unequivocal signs of decrepitude throughout his body, while singular vestiges of youth subsisted in his parchment-like face. His gait also testified to a certain vigor.

Monsieur Thévenin bowed; I returned the gesture and invited him to sit down, then asked him the reason for his visit. "I have come," he said, in a voice that had no senile tremor, "to ask you to admit me as a resident— paying, of course." He made the last remark hastily, as if relying in advance to a possible objection.

"Pardon me," I said, "but are you really Dr. Thévenin?"

"The former pupil of Mesmer, the friend of Puységur. That's me."

"You must be very old?"

"109 years."

"Don't take the objection I must make to you amiss, but don't you know that my establishment is specifically designed for mental patients?"

"I know that," he said. "My request is all the more justified. I'm mad."

Well-accustomed as I am to all kinds of eccentricity, this seemed to me to be a trifle excessive.

"You'll permit me to doubt that," I said. "You appear to me to be in full possession of your reason."

"You're mistaken," he said, with the same calmness. "I'm mad—and, I emphasize this point—one of the most dangerous madmen in existence."

"Very well. But since you're a physician, and one of the most knowledgeable, you've doubtless analyzed your condition, and can easily give me the reasons for your peremptory affirmation."

He fixed his eyes upon me with a strange penetration. I understood how, in his prime, the man had contrived to be one of the most fervent and convinced adepts of magnetism. He remained silent for a few minutes, surrendering himself quite placidly to my observation. Then I continued: "Accepting your hypothesis, you are doubtless experiencing, at this moment, what I would call a lucid interval?"

"That's an error."

"I believe that I have considerable experience, however, and I cannot discover in your features or your expression any characteristic symptom of mental alienation."

"The most dangerous kinds of madness," he said, "are those that the human eye cannot detect." And he added, in a scarcely-perceptible voice: "I have been mad for 50 years, and no one, even among the most knowledgeable, has suspected my condition."

"But in the final analysis," I cried, "of what does this madness consist? Do you have visions? Do you evoke the dead? Do you believe yourself to be Mohammed or Jesus Christ? Are you made of glass? Are you not yourself?"

"I am," he replied, curtly, "a man who cannot die—and, until today, has not wanted to."

"So, according to you, it's solely thanks to your will that you have lived 110 years?"

"That's correct."

"You possess an infallible means of prolonging human life?"

"Not the life of another, but my own."

"The Great Work!" I cried. "The philosopher's stone."

"Not alchemy, in the sense that you mean."

"And do you intend to tell me what this means is?"

I had observed by now that I was dealing with a particular kind of reasoned monomania, and I was attempting to press the subject forward on his own terrain.

"I can't tell you," he said, emotionlessly, "for two reasons..."

"Which are?"

"The first is that, by revealing my secret to you, I would be running a great risk, in the present condition of society, of being treated as one of the worst criminals..."

"Do you admit your own culpability?"

"No, in the context of the superior law of the struggle for existence. Yes, in the view of reigning prejudices..."

"Have you killed anyone?"

"Yes," he replied, without hesitation.

"Have your crimes been discovered?"

"No."

"Have they given rise to pursuits directed against the innocent?"

"No."

"Your victims, however...what became of them? Have you got rid of them?"

"No."

"But no one has perceived that they died a violent death?"

"No one."

The madness was becoming increasingly distinct. *"You mentioned two reasons that impose silence on you. What's the second?"*

"I keep silent," he went on, in an earnest tone, *"because one of two things would happen. Either, knowing my secret, you would be powerless to make use of it, or, having succeeded in using it, you would commit the same crimes that I have committed."*

"Some poisonous preparation, presumably," I said, smiling, *"which leaves no trace."*

"Don't try to find out—you won't succeed. Let's cut this short. I'm coming to you, as an alienist, and I'm saying: 'I'm mad, dangerously mad. Will you intern me?'"

"A voluntary admission would give you the right to a voluntary exit. I can only admit you on condition of having total authority over you. For that, it would be necessary for you to submit to an examination by two physicians, whose certification would be my guarantee. Do you accept that condition?"

"Yes—but in my turn, I have conditions to make."

"I'm listening."

"My objective, in entering your establishment, is to die. So long as I'm free, I'm certain of stating alive, not

234

having the courage to make no further use of my secret. Here, I cannot do that, and nature will take its course. I demand to be treated like your other inmates, with the sole difference that no one from outside should be admitted to see me."

"Don't you have relatives, friends?"

"I'm alone, quite alone. No one has any claim on me."

"I can assure you that your desire will be respected, unless you are summoned to appear before a superior authority."

"Oh, that's of no consequence to me. So, no one, except for you and the members of your staff, will be able to see me. On the other hand, I can assure you that no one will perceive my madness, and that I shall not be subject to any fit or fury, or any eccentric fantasy. Besides, if you observe the treaty that we are signing here faithfully, I shall be dead in three months."

"You realize that the surveillance exercised by the warders precludes any possibility of suicide?"

"Oh, they won't be able to do anything against me."

"You know, too, that before being interned in the place of your choice you will be searched, so minutely that it will be impossible for you to conserve any substance that might permit you to kill yourself?"

"They can't take my 110 years away," he said, smiling for the first time since the beginning of our conversation. "I know how much life remains within me... about 12 weeks."

All discussion being futile, I had only to accept my strange client, who fixed a very high price of admission himself, in exchange for which he demanded a very comfortable...

Here the doctor's manuscript ended. A note was written in the margin: *Building 2, no. 17.*

I had read these lines with profound interest, and when I had finished, I experienced a sensation of disappointment. Monsieur Vincent remained no less enigmatic to me than before.

My colleague came back in. "Well?" he asked. "What do you think of the former mesmerist?"

"I don't really know what to say. It's hardly an ordinary madness. But I'm thinking that Monsieur Thévenin entered this establishment on April 15 and it's now September 10, and he's still alive—his infallible diagnosis was mistaken."

"Absolutely."

"How has he behaved since he's been your guest?"

"I've never encountered a more docile inmate, or a more agreeable business arrangement. He submitted with the best possible grace to the examination of two of my colleagues, who did not hesitate to confirm my diagnosis of monomania. He was, in fact, a rather banal example of rational rectitude on all points but one. Thus, his situation being regularized, I had no other objective than to make his final years—or his final months—as pleasant as possible. I installed him in a detached building with a rather spacious garden. Two nurses were specially attached to his service. He has assembled a scientific library of the most curious sort, and seems to be working. Only one detail confirms his mental derangement. For an entire fortnight, he spent several hours a day lying naked on the ground. He warned me in advance, adding that he was attempting an experiment. As it was June, in a relatively warm spell, I did not think I ought to oppose him. He soon desisted of his own accord.

"During the first month, I didn't notice any change in him. From mid-May on, however, symptoms of decrepitude began to manifest themselves, and when he made his first singular experiment in June, I thought that he had predicted the date of his death accurately in fixing it at three months. When the fit of nudity—excuse the expression—had passed, we resumed our ordinary relations. I confess that I had rarely encountered as much erudition and boldness in the observations of any of my colleagues. If that man did not have the double monomania of magnetism and what I call his pretended vital will, I would proclaim him one of the greatest savants of the day.

"At the beginning of July, I perceived that his strength was declining further and further, but without any diminution of the lucidity of his mind. I must admit that I felt sorry for that centenarian, alone, abandoned by everyone, spending his final days sitting in an armchair in search of revivifying sunlight. I discovered one day that he adored children, and I brought my little boy to see him. I can't describe the expression of joy that lit up his face. If I hadn't known him so well, I would almost have been afraid of the gleam that suddenly came into his eyes.

"As for my little Georges, his sympathy was unhesitating. He ran to the old man as if he had known him for years. There was a sudden friendship, as children often conceive. Since then, not a day has gone by when Georges hasn't spent several hours with him. The effect of that distraction on the centenarian has been such that, since then, he seems to have found a veritable new youth. Yes, it's as if a restorative blood were running through his veins. His thinness has disappeared, and I wouldn't be surprised if he has a new lease of life. He has an astonishing constitution."

"But didn't you tell me, when I arrived, that your son is giving you some cause for anxiety?"

"Oh, a little weakness—summer fatigue… and he's growing. I'm not worried. Two months ago, he was full of beans. That will come back."

For a few moments, I was gripped by a singular desire to see the singular individual that I had only seen before in rather bizarre circumstances. I said as much to my colleague, but he observed that the agreement he had made prevented its satisfaction. Was he not formally prohibited from introducing into Monsieur Vincent's presence anyone not part of the establishment's personnel?

I had to give in. I did not insist, and I took my leave of my colleague, resolving to put the incoherent, almost crazy, ideas that were haunting me painfully completely out of my mind.

And yet, I had a sort of inexplicable fear within me, which was making my head spin. Like Pascal, I saw a gulf open in front of me—and in its utmost depths, I could see a sneering face, which had the features of Mesmer's pupil!

III

I had resumed my work and had once again put the aggravating memory of that individual out of my mind when, one morning early in November, I received a telegram that caused me an inexpressible emotion.

It was signed by Doctor F***, and read as follows:
My child is dying. I appeal to all my friends. Come.

I bounded out of my armchair. A few minutes later, I leapt into a carriage whose driver, enlivened by the promise of a large tip, whipped his horse vigorously.

I cannot say that the telegram surprised me. Hidden beneath the everyday preoccupations that I had made into a rampart against the visions of remembrance, there was a latent thought of which it seemed to me that the news was the explosion. Monsieur Vincent's silhouette, graven in the lobes of my brain, was inseparably linked with that of a child, the poor girl that I had seen long ago, dead before having died, and who had left me that impression—absolutely inadmissible from the viewpoint of true science—of having had the life, the animating force, drawn out of her. And here, once again, the appearance of that centenarian, stubbornly alive, was confused with that of a child, so vigorous, it seemed, six months earlier, but dying today!

I was not conscious of the length of the journey, so absorbed was I in my meditations, and when the carriage stopped, when the driver got down opened the door, and called, "We're here, sir!" I staggered out like a drunk, not knowing where I was or where I was going. It was by instinct, and instinct alone, that I set off along the long ash-lined driveway that led to the main building, after being admitted by the concierge.

When I arrived at the front steps, a male nurse who seemed to be on sentry duty greeted me. Without even asking my name he preceded me into the house and opened a door, introducing me into a drawing-room in which, at first glance, I recognized four of my colleagues, undoubtedly summoned as I had been by the telegram, who shook my hand silently.

After a brief silence that I did not venture to disturb, incapable as I was of stringing two words together, one of them spoke. They had examined the child. They had all established that the organs were sound and that they presented no natural characteristic that might give rise to fear of a fatal outcome. However, in spite of their common diagnosis, they could not pretend that the situation was not grave. The child was suffering from a kind of exhaustion—that word struck me—of the vital faculties, without there being any appreciable lesion to explain the degeneration.

At that moment the father came to join us. He was in a state of despair that was painful to see. Having lost a wife he adored two years before, he had transferred all his affection to the little creature that an unknown malady was about to take away from him. He saw me and came to me, wanting to talk to me—impeded by the sobs that filled his throat, however, he took my by the hand and drew me away.

A moment later, I was beside the bed; mute and chilled, I recognized with horror with same appearances that had left an ineffaceable distress in my mind ten years earlier. The child, seemingly drained of blood, was no longer moving. It was a total exhaustion, as if all his blood had run out of an invisible wound, and the illusion was so complete that I asked the poor father, in a stammer, whether there had not been any hemorrhage.

He replied in a low voice. The child had not suffered any accident; the depressive effect had developed slowly; then, all of a sudden, in the last few days, the acceleration of the malady had taken on a lightning rapidity. Even so, he had still been running around the garden the day before.

"Is Monsieur Vincent still alive?" I asked, suddenly, obedient to an impulse beyond my control. I could have sworn that another personality than mine had spoken through my mouth, so involuntary were the words.

The father did not seem surprised by my question.

"Yes, he's quite grief-stricken. He was so fond of my little Georges, who returned his affection in full, for he never wanted to leave him. It was necessary to carry him away to bring him here—and he still resisted in spite of his weakness. It was like an attraction from which he didn't want to remove himself. But what does Monsieur Vincent matter? Examine the child and tell me—oh, I beg you—how he might be saved…"

I did not have the courage to proffer the generous lie. Even if my colleague still preserved some hope, how could I doubt? And yet… an obscure idea sprang up within my mind.

We stayed together in this fashion, the father not daring to question me any further, dreading to hear words from my lips that would be a sentence of despair, me not daring to be drawn into the mysterious path along which I felt myself slipping irresistibly.

Suddenly, a voice like a feeble breath escaped the child's lips. "Monsieur Vincent!" he sighed.

"He still wants to see his friend, you see," said the father.

But I had already launched myself towards the widow—and paring the curtains, I saw the man pass by on a pathway, attended by two nurses, heading for the house. I released an exclamation. "On your life," I said, addressing the father, "don't leave your child for a second—and whatever I do, whatever anyone might tell you about me, say that I'm acting on your orders."

"But what do you mean?"

"Don't forget—on your orders."

And without explaining any further, for I saw that the child was trying to get up, I threw myself outside.

At the foot of the front steps, I saw Monsieur Vincent, about to climb up.

"I forbid you to take another step!" I said to him, seizing him violently by the arm.

"Who are you?" he said. "What do you want with me?" And, turning to the attendants, who had paused, he said: "I want to speak to your master."

"And I repeat that you shall not pass. I'm acting on the instructions of Dr. F*** himself, who orders that you be returned to your lodgings immediately." I gave the nurses my name; they did not think it appropriate to disobey me. Besides, I had passed my arm insistently beneath that of the old man, and I was dragging him away rapidly. He did not have the strength to resist me.

"You," I said to one of the attendants. "Go to your master and tell him that I'll come back in half an hour, and that I'm making a supreme effort to save his child."

We had arrived at the lodge. I made Monsieur Vincent go in, and the two of us found ourselves alone in a little garden, over which the trees extended a vault of autumnal foliage.

I was finally face to face with the man! I stared at him.

He was very pale, and in his white and puffy face his eyes were like two shiny black holes.

We remained thus for a few seconds, looking at one another like two enemies studying one another before a duel. I was prey to a certain anger, which was making me tremble, but which must have communicated an excessive glare to my gaze—for his eyes seemed to flee mine.

Suddenly, I reached out towards him, touched his shoulder, and said: "Monsieur Vincent de Bossaye de Thévenin, you are a murderer!"

He did not reply, but this time, in his turn, he looked me full in the face.

"Oh, don't try to fascinate me," I said, sneeringly. "I'm not a child, and you shan't kill me…"

He raised his head, in a challenging manner. "What do you want from me?" he asked. "I don't know you…"

"But I know you, Monsieur Vincent. Do you remember a poor mother who came in search of a physician ten years ago"—I cited the street and the date—"for her young daughter, who was dying? Do you remember the physician you met in the outer room? And that…"—I emphasized every word, slowly and distinctly—"…one minute earlier, on hearing your footstep, the poor little girl had made one last effort to go to you, and had fallen back dead in my arms…"

"Ah! That was you!" said Monsieur Vincent.

"Yes, it was me, who also saw a strange phenomenon: the almost instantaneous metamorphosis of a vigorous man with a fresh complexion and relatively robust appearance, into a pallid, worn out, exhausted old man."

"Go on."

"Do you remember, again, that on that same evening you attempted to persuade a good woman, the concierge of the house in which you lived, to entrust her child to you?"

"That's right. She refused."

"That was ten years ago... and I find you again here, still living—you, for whom death is lying in wait. Living... while over there a child is dying, without any internal injury, without any scientifically detectable illness. Do you understand now, Monsieur Vincent, why I prevented you from going into that house, into which you were introducing yourself in order to steal from those dying lips the last breath of a life, to which your own is attached?"

"Come in," said Monsieur Vincent, pointing to the door of the lodge. He spoke with perfect simplicity, without irritation. I obeyed him, and we went into a study whose walls were completely hidden by bookshelves. He invited me to suit down, and did so in his turn. "What are you suggesting?" he asked,

I had recovered my calmness; I knew that I would obtain nothing from the man by intimidation. I resumed with more composure: "I'm not suggesting—I know..."

"What?"

"You've devoted yourself since youth, for almost a century, to the practice of magnetism. What your means of action are, I don't know. Present-day science is in the process of discovering the laws of hypnotism and suggestion, but it has not yet obtained the results that you have researched and attained. I'll use your own words; your science, according to you, is criminal: it multiplies a hundredfold the terrible inequality that the struggle for existence creates between the victors and the vanquished. I'm basing my assertions on your own confession, which I have, and I tell you that you are a murderer! Dare you tell me that I am not on the track of the truth?"

Monsieur Vincent let his head fall into his hand, appeared to reflect for a few seconds, then sat up straight and said: "Why didn't I meet you sooner?"

"Are you regretting not having the opportunity to teach me your abominable science?"

"No science is abominable," he replied, gravely. "The scalpel in the surgeon's hands might be a murder weapon; the hypnotism and suggestion that you mentioned might be instruments of crime..."

"Your science, according to you, is nothing but criminal..."

"Don't say that. Between it and the use that I have made of it there is all the distance that separates good from evil, the remedy from the poison..."

"You admit that!"

"I admit it. I horrify myself, not so much because of the crimes I have committed than the cowardice that led me to commit them..."

"The cowardice that leads to you attack children!"

"No, that's not it. The cowardice of not wanting to die."

"Explain yourself—for it seems to me that I've been carried away by a nightmare."

"Yes, I want to talk. But I must demand that you swear on oath..."

"To do what?"

"You're a man of science. I'll reveal the supreme secret to you, but you must make a solemn promise never to use it yourself..."

"Do I need to swear to not being a criminal?"

"And never to reveal it to anyone..."

"I swear it."

"Listen to me, then. There are three distinct phases in a human being's life: one of radiance, from infancy to the final limits of adolescence; the second of consummation, which lasts until the end of middle age; then the third, which is old age terminating in death.

"Every living organism—especially the human, which is the most complete expression of life—exhales during the first period of excessive vitality. A child absorbs more vital fluid than it consumes, and radiates the excess from its entire being. In the second phase, a creature consumes as much as it absorbs; there's an equilibrium of force. In old age, that equilibrium is broken; the absorption is inferior to the consumption; the vital expense is superior to the acquisition—which results in enfeeblement, which results in death.

"Now, in the present state of science, it seems to you impossible—does it not?—that a man, an old man, might beak the laws of nature and, by the exercise of a particular skill, steal from a child, for example, the vital effluvia that are in excess; to attract to himself, by means of a sort of endosmosis, all the fluid of which only one part, the exterior, is at his immediate disposition. That is, however, the truth. Yes, I am a criminal; yes, I am an assassin, because for forty years I have contrived to rejuvenate myself perpetually, a new Aeson.[53]

"Yes, I've killed children, but not, as the ignorant might be able to believe, or Johann-Heinrich Cohausen foolishly invented in his *Hermippus redivivus*,[54] by ab-

---

[53] In Ovid's *Metamorphoses*, Aeson, the aged and estranged father of the hero Jason, is restored to youth by means of Medea's magic.
[54] Johnann-Henirich Cohausen (1665-1750)—Lermina gives the forenames as Jean-Henri—was a German physician well-

sorbing the air escaping from a child's lungs, or in the fashion of the legendary Vudoklacks,[55] by sucking their blood... no, by drawing into myself the excess of vital fluid that escapes from their entire organism...

"Ah, if only I had had the courage to stop at that! But I swear to you that there is no intoxication more profound, more addictive, more insanely pleasurable than that! When the warm and revivifying fluid penetrates the chilled limbs; when the assimilation takes place, penetrating the pores, insinuating itself into all the organs, it's unparalleled, entire absolute pleasure...it's the sensation of resurrection, if a cadaver were able to feel its own rebirth!

"And still I cried out to myself: 'Stop! But you must stop!' And still my entire being continued to drink these

---

known in his own country for his satirical sense of humor. *Hermippus redivivus* (1742) is a joke, which offers a tongue-in-cheek account of a method of human rejuvenation supposedly based on the work of the alchemist Jan van Helmont, which involves old men breathing in the exhalations of young girls, allegedly impregnated with vivifying "salts." Humor does not always translate well, however, and the hoax was not so obvious to all of the readers of the French and English versions of the text. The English translator did his best in the edition of 1744 but the demand that generated a second, expanded edition in 1749 was probably somewhat credulous. That text inspired both William Godwin's *St. Leon* (1799) and Percy Bysshe Shelley's *St. Irvyne* (1811), two of the most significant Gothic novels dealing with the theme of longevity.

[55] I have left this word in the idiosyncratic form that Lermina uses; he is presumably misquoting from memory a word that is spelled in various different ways in French references to Slavic vampire lore, and is usually rendered into English as *vorkalaka* or *vyrkalaka*.

effluvia... and I killed! And I murdered! And the only remorse I could feel was for a thirst unslaked!

"Through my fingers and my gaze—oh, the gaze especially!—that attraction exerted itself which gives the victim a sensation of self-abandonment, not painful but delightfully intoxicating..."

He talked. He went on an on, the old wretch, with an orgasmic voluptuousness in his voice and his eyes... and I did not interrupt him, perhaps because of fear. How can I know?

Sensing that I was spellbound by his horrible and sublime infamy, he told me everything: what passes had to be made by the hands, what direction it was necessary to give to the gaze—and I listened, burying that hideous information, which intoxicated me like some poisonous liquor, in the utmost depths of my soul.

"And now that I've told you everything," he finally cried, "It's necessary that I die. Take me to the child!"

"Horrid old man!" I cried. "Do you want me to serve as your accomplice?"

He leaned closer to my ear—and, in truth, it seemed to me that his voice was like some subtle liquor, which flowed into me...

"You, whom I have initiated," he said, "do you not understand that *our* science also gives us the power of restitution? I am only alive by virtue of what I have stolen from that child, and I have told you that I want to die."

And I obeyed. I could not do other than obey him.

We went up the front steps together; together we went into the house; together we went into the drawing room, where the four physicians were still talking in low voices, and from there into the bedroom where the child was dying...

The child, who had recognized the footfalls of Monsieur Vincent, sat up, his eyes turning to him, his arms reaching out to him...

That was the supreme moment, the atrocious instant that I remembered, and which had preceded—as a blow precedes pain—the death of the little girl.

The physicians were behind us. The father was standing up, uncomprehending but hoping—as the desperate do—for a miracle.

I saw the child's body quiver, hesitate between two movements: to surge forward or to recoil.

Monsieur Vincent looked at him with dilated pupils, and he advanced slowly, his hands seemingly inert but active... as I, who knew everything, could see.

The child lay back gently. Monsieur Vincent was still approaching. Finally, he placed his hand on the little invalid's forehead. And suddenly I saw—oh, I cannot doubt it!—a rosy tint extend across the boy's face, clarify his lips, at the same time as gleam lit up in the depths of his dull eyes. And I understood full well, myself... and myself alone. The man was *reinjecting* into the child the life he had stolen.

"Your child is saved," said the old man, in a voice that was no more than a whisper. Then, turning to the physicians and standing up straight, he said: "Messieurs, you will bear witness to the fact that Doctor Bossaye de Thévenin, the last surviving pupil of Mesmer, has resurrected a corpse..."

So saying, he shuddered, and would have fallen down if I had not caught him.

"Carry me back to the lodge," he whispered to me.

I lifted him in my arms. The body was no longer heavy.

I deposited him on his bed. There, obedient to his ultimate wish, I remained beside him, and he talked to me at length—at great length—in a voice that grew ever weaker. He confided to me things that no mortal ear had ever heard, and which made me shiver. Those things I know, and can never forget—and I am afraid of old age, which will come, and which can render one criminal.

The child lived.

Monsieur Vincent died the following day.

One of my colleagues ran into me a few days later and said: "Did you see that old charlatan? How he tried to claim the honor for a natural reaction?"

As for me, I know—and I am afraid of my science.